The Hormone Factory

the
HORMONE
FACTORY

Saskia Goldschmidt

Translated from the Dutch by Hester Velmans

 OTHER PRESS
NEW YORK

Translation copyright © 2014 by Hester Velmans
Production Editor: Yvonne E. Cárdenas
Text Designer: Julie Fry

This book was set in Kabel and Foundry Serif.

10 9 8 7 6 5 4 3 2 1

Library of Congress Cataloging-in-Publication Data
Goldschmidt, Saskia, 1954–
    [Hormoonfabriek. English]
    The hormone factory : a novel / Saskia Goldschmidt ;
translated from the Dutch by Hester Velmans.
    pages cm
    "Originally published in Dutch as De hormoonfabriek by
Uitgeverij Cossee in 2012"—Title page verso.
    ISBN 978-1-59051-649-2 (pbk.)—ISBN 978-1-59051-650-8 (e-book)
    I. Velmans, Hester. II. Title.
    PT5882.17.O65H6713 2014
    839.313'7—dc23
                                            2013045254

Do not go gentle into that good night,
Old age should burn and rave at close of day;
Rage, rage against the dying of the light.

—Dylan Thomas

1...

Day by day I seem to be sinking more deeply into the gloom that has characterized so much of my time on earth. I know them well, the days when it feels as if you're stuck ankle-deep in filthy, glutinous sludge and even the slightest movement demands just too much effort. The hours you lie in bed motionless because you're locked in a cocoon of wretchedness. It's from that supine position that you survey the world. The sun that rises and shines, as if its light could possibly make any difference. Mizie entering the room with her mirthless smile. The hustle and bustle of people in the street, as if their comings and goings made the world even one jot better or worse. Yes, for years I operated under the same delusions. Ah, how I believed that I mattered, that with my abilities, my determination, my intelligence, I would make the world a better place! And I have left my mark, that's true. But whether it's helped the world—who the devil knows? Out of the frying pan and into the fire, that's all it ever amounts to, for every damn one of us.

Way back when, even in the darkest days of my depression, I always knew I'd eventually emerge from my cocoon, that I'd reconnect with the world and dive back into the fray. And I didn't do it half-assed; I was one of the winners. Ever since

Darwin, we've known that it's either eat or be eaten. I always was a contender. But in the final analysis, all that striving has left me with just a single insight, and that is that none of it matters. Whether you're the winner or loser, perpetrator or victim, it doesn't make a damn bit of difference.

I have now come to accept that this time I won't escape. This is the end, the godforsaken final chapter. And how I long to turn my back on this madhouse, to breathe my last! I'm done for, finished, and high time too!

• • •

But death is a heartless thing; first it goes for the tender morsels. The reckless kid leaping on his motorbike only to crash headlong into an eighteen-wheeler, the fat sow in her fully automatic Volkswagen stalling in the middle of a railroad crossing, the young mother blissfully giving birth only to realize once the labor is over what a risky business it is to pop such a frail little bundle out into the world. In the prime of life, that's when death likes to get them.

But a tough old geezer on his deathbed like me it prefers to ignore. Endlessly putting off the time of departure.

I am still complete master of my mental faculties, which, like some cruel joke, make me exquisitely aware of each and every physical debility. Damn this body, slave to so many uncontrollable urges! The bodily functions are packing it in one by one, like lab rats being used to test something that leaves them belly-up in their cages gasping for air. The pain keeps getting worse and the reprieve of sleep grows ever more elusive.

2...

Ezra has been arrested, the silly fool. Mizie has tried to hide it from me, but the young thing assisting her with my mortifying care left her newspaper behind. Front-page news. Well, that's par for the course. A total lack of self-control, right at the most critical juncture in his life. That boy never did know where to stop. In his passions, his ambitions, his drive, and his physical needs. Always hungry for more. Whether it's food, attention, power, or sex, he never can have enough. The fear of being overlooked, of missing out, was in him from the moment his mother gave birth to him. The fate of being the youngest in the family. Having to fight for attention right from the start.

The greed with which that child latched on to his mother's breast—it was something I'd never seen in any of the others. He drained her from the word go. He was so rough with her, the little monkey, so determined to suck his mother dry to the last drop that she howled in pain. His toothless mouth clamped on her nipple and refused to let go, no matter how loud she screamed. A little monster, he was, our youngest. Rivka, who had always taken pleasure in nursing her brood, gave up on him soon enough. He devoured her very peace of mind, that boy, he just sapped too much of her energy and lifeblood. One day I came home unexpectedly, catching her unawares. There she sat, gripping the bottle, a struggling Ezra in her lap. The boy, all red in the face from howling, kept trying to grab her breast, safely tucked away inside her copious bra and black lace blouse. A flushed Rivka had Ezra in a stranglehold and was attempting to force the flaccid rubber nipple into his mouth; he immediately spat it out again in disgust. He always did have good taste, my youngest. When she saw me she began to cry.

"Mordechai, this child, this cuckoo in the nest—I've tried, but I can't. I breast-fed all four of the little girls with love. But this devil child—I can't take it anymore, *you* deal with him!"

She hurled the bottle across the room, thrust the screeching infant into my arms, and fled the room in tears. I had come home to change before leaving for London for an important meeting to secure our foreign interests. It was February 1939, and this was promising to be a mammoth session, one that would almost certainly end with a lavish dinner to celebrate a successful outcome. For when I negotiate, I keep at it until I've struck a great deal; I won't stop until it's done.

I carried the boy to the office—we lived next door to the factory—and ordered Agnes, my willing, discreet, and smooth-tongued secretary, to fetch Alie Mosterd. I knew she was suckling another little tyke. She worked in packaging and her family was always struggling to make ends meet, so a little extra income was bound to come in handy. It was soon settled. Alie would nurse the boy for five guilders per month plus a weekly food parcel, including all the necessary vitamins and minerals. Not to mention free supplements for her entire family. Five guilders was an enormous sum; in those days a liter of horse piss cost me only four-fifty. But hey, you can't feed a baby on horse piss, and problems are for the solving. If anyone deserved a little extra, it was Alie. A sweet gal, healthy too; didn't smoke, didn't drink, always punctual, had started working here as a young girl. She'd begun to look a bit run-down, however. Her husband worked in our warehouse and was reliable, a simple but decent fellow. With her, Ezra would be in good hands. We arranged that she'd come and give the boy five feedings a day. That would take the pressure off Rivka. I had our little girls to think of too, after all. They didn't need a mother suffering from nervous exhaustion, and I didn't need a wife who wouldn't stop blubbering. We'd see if it was still necessary in a few months' time, once the boy was ready for solid food. I asked Agnes to please inform Rivka of the arrangement after she had calmed down a bit. Then I changed my clothes in a hurry and got to the airport just in time to catch my plane to London. Getting things done pronto, that's always been my forte.

3...

Speed is my middle name, unlike my twin brother, Aaron, who was always slowness incarnate. He was stuck in first gear all his life, whereas I was always stepping on the gas, shifting from neutral to sixth in the blink of an eye. Getting ahead, that's what life's all about. Aaron just didn't have it in him. Whether it was school, or women, or self-preservation, he always seemed to be two steps behind. When we were kids, I'd take to my heels as soon as a gang of Catholic scum started coming after us, but Aaron would freeze like a petrified rabbit in the headlights. I can't tell you how many times I had to rescue him from the clutches of his Christian persecutors. Except for that last time, years later, when I failed to save him. Although I could have, if he hadn't been so goddamn stubborn. It was that fanatical rectitude of his, trumping every instinct for survival. I'm not one to let my conscience bother me; it was Aaron's moral principles that sent him toppling into the abyss. As if we weren't all animals—eat or be eaten. Not to speak ill of the dead, but Aaron was a loser his entire life.

• • •

I threw myself wholeheartedly into the competitive fray. Those were the days, the time when we were constantly coming up with one scientific breakthrough after another. It was an incredibly exciting struggle that never let up—to be the first, to crush the competition, to outsmart the best in the world day in, day out. And were we ever good at it!

Without tooting my own horn, I can safely say that in this nation of wusses, this swamp pit of small-minded burghers who look down their noses at dreamers, I was one of the first to realize that commerce needs science, and vice versa. To run a successful meatpacking operation is one thing: it takes skill and business savvy. But to get further ahead, you have to have guts; you have to use your head and dream big. My father plucked my brother and me from school and got us started in the meat business. He wouldn't let us go to university, and the thought of it still makes me fume. Shit, how I'd have loved to be allowed to study—I'd have chosen chemistry, naturally, which I consider the most fascinating of all subjects. There's nothing finer than knowing how to analyze and then purify some substance, to synthesize the compounds it consists of, and so to unravel nature's mysteries. To contribute to man's mastery over matter, that was my burning ambition as a young man. But it was out of the question. I had to join the firm.

"You are a De Paauw," said my father, "and De Paauws don't have time for egghead tomfoolery. You can't live off your brains; brains won't bring in a cent—unless you're making headcheese or sausage, of course. Butchering, meat production, that's what's in our blood, we've never done aught else, and oughtn't to aspire to anything more either. There's no other meatpacker in these parts that's got a more sterling reputation than ours."

And although I'm no pushover, I never was able to stand up to my father. I was afraid of him, as were most people. You should have seen Aaron—he'd start shaking whenever my father called for him. He'd begin to stutter, which is why he never earned my father's respect, which did eventually come to me. Bringing Aaron into the firm was a farce. My brother was such a softy that he tended to screw up every transaction. But he could not, would not, disappoint my father, so he stayed on, a stone around our necks, while never, not even for a single day, being happy there. Lived only for others his entire life, did what was expected of him, his loyalty aimed at all mankind. And right when he finally has a chance to start over—he gets trampled to death under the great scumbag's storm-trooper boots. No idea why my brother keeps popping up in my mind. Haven't thought much about him in years. Best that way too. Crying over spilled milk doesn't get you anywhere. What's done is done, there's nothing you can do about death's unpredictable ways.

• • •

While we were trainees in our father's business, I kept a low profile, ostensibly meek and subservient, like Aaron. Meanwhile I was eagerly taking in everything that went on, both within the firm and outside, for as I've often said, an inward-looking company will miss the boat. Navel-gazing has never been a productive tactic in business. To get somewhere you have to dare to break new ground, you have to dare to dream. And to stick your neck out; if you don't take any risks you're never going to get off the ground.

When my father passed away and at age twenty-seven I took over as head of the firm, with Aaron (heaven help us!) as my deputy, I immediately swung into action.

It was the early nineteen-twenties, and we were processing two thousand pigs and three-fifty head of cattle a day. We produced sausages, hams, and smoked meats, as well as bacon and gammon for the English market. Blood and bone meal went into fertilizer; we had a refinery for fats and oils and, last but not least, a soap factory. The hog bristles were used to manufacture brushes. We extracted value from every scrap of animal corpse, from head to hoof. Except for those dratted organs. There was nothing you could do with them. No one could give me a reason why every animal was stuffed to the gills with those weird gummy parts. What damn use were they? Darwin had taught me that everything on earth that's alive exists for a reason, or it would have become obsolete or extinct long ago. But in our predominantly Roman Catholic region, that sort of reasoning would not have gone down very well. "After all, the Good Lord never created anything for nothing," I'd occasionally proclaim, to justify my interest in discovering the hidden uses of organs.

My hunch was confirmed by a breakthrough then being made in the pharmaceutical field. Two Canadians—a physician and one of his students (I'm telling you, not even an experienced scientist; no, a mere medical student)—had succeeded in isolating a substance in the pancreas, insulin, which was found capable of combating diabetes, a disease commonly resulting in a fatal coma. This substance was extracted from the pancreas, which got dumped by the ton on our plant's refuse heap each and every day. What a game changer that was. When I heard about it, I walked outside and just stood there staring at the colossal mountain of offal in our factory yard. Who'd have thought that stinking pile contained unsuspected riches, like the copper ore trapped in rock deep in the earth's crust, or the gold in the mud of a riverbed? My instinct was telling me that there, within that putrid waste, a hidden treasure lay buried, a golden tomorrow. All we had to do was plumb the secrets of the animal organs, and beat the world's many other treasure hunters to it. There, standing at the foot of that mountain of slime, I cursed my father's shortsightedness. If only he hadn't prevented me from learning to ferret out the secrets of those bloody body parts myself!

We had no time to lose, and I, Mordechai de Paauw, Motke to my friends, was determined to win the race. It was my destiny, I was sure of it.

But I had to find someone, a researcher, an ambitious, dedicated man of science, someone prepared to go into partnership with me and, under the banner of the De Paauw Slaughterhouse and Meatpacking Co., to start experimenting PDQ.

It didn't take long for me to find him. Not out here in the flipping sticks, of course, this backwater of hayseeds and potato diggers. Not out here in this lawless hole where history had decided to dump our *mishpocha* as a sick kind of joke. We happened to live in the most crooked town in the nation; you wouldn't find a meaner nest of sharks anywhere. There was no point looking for a sharp-witted scientist around here, certainly not the kind of original, independent thinker I needed.

The man with whom I wound up starting the firm that was to grow into the first multinational enterprise in this poky, waterlogged, small-minded country lived in Amsterdam. A Prussian cosmopolite, which may sound like a contradiction in terms, but the truth is sometimes complicated; a man at least as sharp as I was, perhaps even smarter. I'm a practical man, creative and full of energy. This professor shared those same traits and was, moreover, upright, reliable, distinguished, and the only one in this country capable of realizing my dreams. His name was Rafaël Levine.

4...

Levine was a both realist *and* an idealist. Idealism is something a businessman can't afford, but as a man of science, it had helped him go far. He was born in Germany, but being a Jew, he couldn't find suitable employment in his own country. Germany had given rise to the most brilliant musicians, writers, and scientists, it was our most important foreign market, and yet, instinctively, I had never trusted the Germans, no matter how civilized they might appear to be. The fact that Rafaël was a Jew was a point in his favor, of course, but still, I was on my guard. I'd always had a foreboding, long before the shit hit the fan, that caution was in order when dealing with a people who, like a brainless mob, showed themselves ready to blindly follow the greatest villain history has ever seen.

Levine seduced me with his intelligence, his sense of responsibility, his indomitable drive, and his business acumen. He had a medical degree and had been teaching at a northern Dutch university since 1912. Yet when the First World War broke out, he had felt obliged to serve his fatherland. A man of honor, he had volunteered as a physician in the Imperial Army and was awarded the Iron Cross, second class, for his loyal service. In the nineteen-twenties he was appointed chairman of the pharmacology department at the University of Amsterdam, where he presided over his own research institute.

We had dinner together in the spring of 1923, joined by my brother, Aaron, sitting there like a sack of potatoes as usual, in Die Port van Cleve, a restaurant in the center of Amsterdam named after a town in Germany. The very choice of restaurant spoke to Levine's continued attachment to the land of his birth, even though that land had seen fit to spurn this learned man's erudition.

Levine's command of the Dutch language was so poor that people always begged him to speak in his mother tongue, since he was impossible to understand otherwise. He was an imposing gentleman of near middle age, with a striking, aristocratic bearing. His black hair, showing singularly little gray, was just starting to recede. Behind his round spectacles his dark, probing eyes seemed to pierce right through you. Adorning his upper lip was a fashionable little mustache which ten years later would acquire an unfortunate association with the fiend who was to have such a dire effect on our lives. I approached him with a healthy dose of suspicion at first. And indeed, there was that confounded accent of his, the incomprehensible syntax, Germanisms galore, but also, thank God, a sense of humor. During the first course, a beet and herring salad, he kept throwing his career accomplishments in my face, hitting the first and only raw nerve of my young life. Having only three years of high school under my belt was my sore spot, and he found it.

"I am in a noble profession," he declared; "nothing can compare with being chairman of the department of pharmacology at the University of Amsterdam, this beautiful city."

His words cut me to the quick. I was a rookie, just starting out, untested and able to call myself the boss only on account of my father's untimely death. I didn't yet have any kind of record to boast of, and was sensitive about my youth. I felt it was a strike against me; I was nothing but a green provincial salesman next to this egghead, who was obviously enjoying rubbing my nose in his own stellar achievements. Aaron sipped his wine and gazed at me, sensitive as he was to what riled me.

When Levine brought up the subject of insulin's discovery by that dratted pair of Canadians, it was with a tone of envy that I recognized. What he wouldn't have given to score that breakthrough himself! As the waiter served us platters of blood sausage, rillettes of braised baby back ribs in salsify cream, and a Jerusalem artichoke and giant-leaf tart floating in a "kitchen maid's tears" salsify broth, Levine proclaimed that he was confident he could be the first to make the newly discovered insulin commercially available on an industrial scale.

"I have the formula," he said, unable to suppress a triumphant grin. "I could be the first in the world to succeed in standardizing the product. To isolate the insulin from the pancreas is one thing. But for it to be made into medicine and save lives, it must be standardized. It can only be mass-produced if it's standardized. If I succeed, I'll be able to obtain an exclusive license for the manufacture and sale of insulin in the Netherlands; throughout Europe, in fact."

Right then and there he had me—this was exactly the man I needed. He droned on, and I greedily drank in every word of his monologue.

"However," Levine went on, "as an academic, I don't possess the means to undertake this research on an independent basis. I do have my own institute, but it is sadly lacking in every way. My laboratory is poorly equipped, the apparatus is outdated, and I don't have enough chemists or pharmacologists on my team of the caliber required to get a head start on this. We are up against the foremost scientists in the world; it's a race against time, which will only be won with a team of first-rate people and a state-of-the-art research institute."

Levine regarded me gravely, while Aaron blankly watched the waiter filling up his glass. Aaron doesn't much care for people who are very sure of themselves. I do. It was time to put my offer on the table.

"Professor Levine," I said, "I am your inferior both in years and in experience, and yet, as I listen to you, it's as if you are putting my own thoughts into words. It's fate: we are destined to work together on this grand undertaking. I am in a position to give you that research institute. A laboratory, a budget for personnel and research, and all the organ meat you'll ever want. I will give you carte blanche, as long as you give me your word you'll make the insulin ready for mass production as soon as possible. Insulin produced and marketed on a commercial scale, as a joint venture of business and science—it's never been done before. And once that's done, we can move on to the next project. I'll want you to work on isolating as many new substances from these organs as you can, anything that will result in commercially viable medicinal products."

By the time dessert was served, the general outline of our future partnership was already jotted down on the back of Levine's cigar box: a new company joining together our respective strengths. And by the time we'd enjoyed our coffees, an exceptional brandy, and one of Levine's exquisite Cuban cigars, parting with the promise to meet again in a few days to finalize the deal, the fellow had already come up with the perfect name for our new institute: Farmacom. A name that said it all:

a pharma-commercial partnership to produce medicines that hadn't yet been invented.

The fledgling concern that was to expand into one of the world's first multinational companies was conceived in an Amsterdam dining establishment with a German name, born of the union of an intellectual giant and a cutthroat businessman.

5...

Just as I was preparing to go to the partnership agreement meeting with Levine a few days later, Aaron walked into my office. He was chewing on his pencil, as usual: a nervous habit he never managed to kick and had probably acquired back when his stuttering was so bad that it ruled out normal conversation. That was one of the reasons my father had named me his successor in his will, dooming Aaron to live forever in my shadow. Strangely enough, it hadn't seemed to bother him at the time.

"Motke," Aaron said, lowering himself lethargically onto the armrest of the chair facing my desk, "you know, don't you, that with all the promises you've made to the guy, you have seriously undermined your negotiating position?"

That was Aaron to a T. Never so much as opened his mouth, sat through every meeting like a slab of beef on a meat hook; but he was always prepared to come up with a laundry list of objections afterward, pointing out where I'd slipped up. The annoying thing was that he was often right. I was used to his silent, watchful presence, and I have to admit that in some ways I relied on it. He was my disapproving conscience, always reminding me of my weaknesses.

It was true, I had promised Levine the moon, intoxicated as this mere sausage maker had been by the grand possibilities the fellow had rattled off. Naturally, I wouldn't give my brother the satisfaction of being right.

"Fools are always the first to judge," I said, fixing him with a withering stare. "Trust me, I know what I'm doing. We are at the start of something radically new; you've got to have the courage of your convictions, you have to go big, and put all your cards on the table. Collaborating with Levine is going to make us huge, I feel it in my bones, we're on the cusp of doing something truly groundbreaking, and you're whining about the chump change that's needed to make it come true?"

Aaron shrugged his shoulders, heaved himself off the armrest, and shuffled to the door. With his hand on the doorknob, he turned and said, "You're quite right, you have dug up an excellent candidate, and it's more than likely he'll make good on his promises. You're the one with the business instinct around here. I'd nevertheless like to give you a piece of advice, something I'm not often in the habit of doing: please make sure the De Paauw factories retain their autonomy, that we don't wind up shackled hand and foot to some professor who, aside from what's good for the company, has his own reputation and his future in academe to think about." Then he shut the door behind him.

• • •

My brother was right, of course. Rafaël—who proposed that we call each other by our first names, lulling me into thinking the negotiation was going to be a piece of cake (as I've already told you, I was just starting out in my career, and still somewhat wet behind the ears)—turned out to be a master negotiator, not at all inclined to be flexible. He knew he had stoked my greed with his vow to make my dream come true. I found myself unable to heed Aaron's warning. Never again in my life have I groveled the way

I did when drawing up that contract. Rafaël Levine and I became partners in the newly formed Farmacom. The De Paauw Slaughterhouse and Meatpacking factories were to supply Levine with everything he needed to turn his shabby University of Amsterdam lab into a world-class institute. Funds would be put at his disposal to hire scientific personnel and to furnish his laboratory with the most up-to-date equipment, to put him in a position to win the global race to be first. He was given free rein on how he chose to run the institute and his research program. Moreover, at our own site a new installation annexed to the De Paauw Slaughterhouse and Meatpacking Co. would be built as an additional research and manufacturing facility for the new hormones. In return, Levine would advise us on the best extraction and production methods, and would market his inventions only with our explicit permission. It seemed only fair to make him a shareholder and member of the new company's board of directors. Altogether a win-win situation, as they call it these days. I was reasonably satisfied with the way things had gone so far. But just as I was starting to lean back in my chair, thinking we had come to the end of our negotiation, Levine leaned forward in his.

"Just a few minor points," he said, taking a big pull on his Cuban cigar. "I assume you are aware that the generally accepted standard of scientific inquiry is that it should always steer clear of anything that isn't strictly pure, impartial research. The fact that I am prepared to stake my name and reputation on Farmacom and your meatpacking business is due to my sincere desire to make the new cures commercially available. That is why I have agreed to enter into a partnership for which I am bound to be heavily criticized. I am taking a big risk here. In return, I want you to give me the final say over the staff we take on at

Farmacom, as well as over any new hires at De Paauw involved with pharmaceutical production. Furthermore," he went on, "I insist on having a veto over any new drug that as a scientist I am unable in good conscience to endorse. And finally, I propose that we plow ten percent of Farmacom's net profits back into some scientific inquiry of my choosing." He gazed at me amiably. I could just see Aaron's triumphant grin, and opened my mouth to object, to protect the family firm's autonomy.

"As far as I'm concerned, my dear Motke," Levine went on before I could get a word in, "this is not up for negotiation. My honor and good name are of supreme importance to me. They mean more to me than my wife and five children put together. I have worked all my life to preserve them, and I shall never give anyone else the power to ruin them. So either you agree to my proposal, or we end this here and now and go our separate ways."

I gulped. Over the past few days I'd already been envisioning a factory floor humming with insulin production and an office buzzing with orders coming in from all over the world. Then I remembered Aaron's face just before he'd shut my office door behind him. Yes, I was taking a big risk in agreeing to these terms, but wanting to win means grabbing the bull by the horns. Isn't there always some risk associated with progress; don't you have to be prepared to play for high stakes if you want to succeed?

Rafaël sat back in his chair, puffed out a ring of smoke, and gazed at it thoughtfully as if it held the future. There wasn't a trace of anxiety on his face. I was offering him an entire research institute, a potential goldmine, but he looked as if he'd be just as happy to walk out the door—and, indeed, straight into the arms of another meatpacker. Would Bartelsma or Van der Vlis make him the same kind of offer? I couldn't imagine those dimwits having the imagination, the vision to take this on. Which was exactly why I had to act right away.

I could deal with Aaron's scorn.

• • •

A few days later—it was the summer of 1923—Rafaël Levine and I, in the presence of Aaron and a number of attorneys, signed the contract detailing the most stringent partnership I have ever entered into, a partnership that was to bring us spectacular success. And one which, thanks to the vagaries of history, I was able to wriggle out of some twenty years later.

Horace said it best: *"Make money, my son, honestly if you can, but make money!"* That is what I have done, without worrying too much about getting my hands dirty if necessary. It may not be altogether a fluke that I did not find the courage to terminate this groundbreaking partnership until Aaron's silent, reproachful presence had been snuffed out in a cloud of Zyklon B.

6...

Pain, paralysis, and the cussed helplessness that goes with it all. That's the worst. I, the guy who couldn't be pinned down, am finally forced to lie helpless, age ninety-seven, in Mizie's clutches. Her moment of revenge has come at last. She's had to wait a long time, but every loathsome, slow-moving second that I'm confined here on my stinking cot, not the conjugal four-poster but an adjustable hospital bed with metal rails, is balm to her wounded soul. Here I lie, imprisoned in a body that no longer works, in a bed that looks a lot like the cages that once housed our lab animals. She subjects me to my many daily treatments with barely concealed glee. My once pearly-white teeth are now yellowed and stained; every night I have to surrender the dentures stopping up the gaps in my formerly seductive smile. She holds out her hand with that haughty, condescending little smile of hers, which betrays both triumph and a glint of martyrdom as a widow-in-waiting. It must be a pleasure for her to see me lying here like this, with my fallen cheeks, my old man's chops. I can read her sense of victory in the twinkle in her eyes; her pretense at sadness doesn't fool me. I'm finally no longer in any condition to be unfaithful to her, at least not physically. Ah, these revolting diapers, they've turned me into an overgrown baby. That's why I am now obliged to allow the cute young thing, whom in my younger days I'd have hoist on my own petard, if you know what I mean, to soap my flaccid genitals with a pink washcloth under the watchful eye of my lawful wife. Next, once Mizie has turned me on my side, she'll get to work lathering my buttocks, and then towel off the whole shebang before slapping a clean giant diaper on my ass again. It is utter humiliation; it can't get any worse than this.

I've tried in my own way to live my life as a mensch, and I now realize that I've completely failed.

I console myself with the thought that even Mizie, still in the prime of her life, with her saintly airs that make me want to vomit, with her façade of decency and virtue, is driven by self-interest, by the need to dominate and gloat.

Oh death, where is thy sting, so that I won't have to go on seeing snatches of my deplorable life flash before my eyes—they come looming up out of nowhere, only to disappear again into this fog of gloom.

I do have the odd moment of solace when I recall something I can be proud of. The satisfaction of having lived at a time when there were still new things to be discovered, and my good fortune to have been in a position to facilitate those discoveries. I find myself returning to the days when the technology was evolving by leaps and bounds, and I was buoyed with the knowledge that my entrepreneurial spirit was making a difference, and leading to cures for fatal diseases. Those consoling memories make me smile and, just for an instant, resign me to my fate.

But far more often it's memories of the women that come and disturb my peace of mind—always the women. They were both my greatest joy and my life's most terrible curse. It was that blasted libido of mine that kept me endlessly chasing skirts. I was addicted to the thrill of the chase, which would sometimes propel both my conquest and me to the brink of disaster.

Now that my decrepit body's testosterone motor has finally sputtered its last, they loom up before me, always in my weakest moments, the Furies of my past. They take on, as ever, the face and form of Rivka, Rosie, and Bertha, the three great mothers of vengeance. They pound on the inside of my skull, screeching, giving me a tongue-lashing for the many times it seems I made the wrong choice.

I stretch out my arms toward Death, who's just sitting there smirking on the metal rail of my bed, and am forced to watch him turn around and slowly back away, calling to me from a distance, "Not now, not yet, your time has not yet come." I hear his cold laugh, and there is no place for me to hide.

7...

Women are the Achilles' heel of anyone calling himself a man. We all get taken in by them, somehow, sometime. We may *think* it's our brain that drives our body, like the diesel engine that drove the truck collecting the urine of pregnant mares, but in fact we are constantly at the mercy of our pecker, our dick, our cock. That self-willed organ dominated my mind and controlled the way I behaved—it got the better of my reason and simply took over. How I hated having those urges control my life! And yet how I loved it too! That's why it is with a mixture of relief and profound grief that I now behold my member in its current state, a soft, droopy, flabby, unresponsive little appendage dangling under a quivering hunk of belly fat like a decomposing bit of offal, emitting a steady drip of smelly dribble all day long, because, see now, I'm not the only one to have lost control; the beast has too.

I have never lacked for attention. Women are attracted to men who play it big; there's nothing more seductive than a man upon whom fortune has smiled. Women used to swarm around me, attracted like bees to honey. No wonder my name is De Paauw, the peacock! Such a proud creature, that likes to show off to the little woman in all its resplendent, glimmering glory! My own plumage comes down to a set of regular features: a powerful nose, a bold chin, a fine head of black hair, expressive dark eyes, and a well-proportioned body. And just as the peacock's splendid tail hides a trembling little *tuches* that can barely contain itself, so the beast, lurking deep within my bespoke suit, lifts its head, waiting for the moment when I'll set it free. I'm a hunter, I can't help it. Once I have caught my prey and devoured it from front to back and from top to bottom, it's time to go out again and stalk a fresh quarry; that's just the way it is.

If it had been up to me I would never have gotten married— why restrict yourself to a single dish when there's a whole world of delicacies to be sampled? Monogamy doesn't really exist; monogamy is the most unnatural idea ever to have made it into law. As far as the man goes, anyway. After all, the male is programmed to catch and pursue, it's our instinct, we're driven to do it. It isn't selfishness, it's a fundamental necessity— the species must live on. And it's the woman's job to nurture. Why else would she carry the child to term, endure excruciating pains pushing it out, and then nurse it? And if she were just allowed to scamper off instead of staying home breast-feeding the little nipper, the world would be teeming with neglected brats in no time, wouldn't it? There are of course some species, the emperor penguin for instance, where it's the male who takes on the responsibility of caring for the egg and hatchling. But the pathetic flap of flab dangling down over papa penguin's feet like an old crone's potbelly says it all. No wonder it's an endangered species on the way out. An evolutionary cock-up, and therefore doomed to extinction.

A man does have responsibilities, of course. I'm not the type to saddle a woman with a kid and then say it's *her* problem. You've got to take responsibility; if you get in a jam, you've got to pay up. Preferably for an abortion, although not every girl will agree to have one. Twice in my life I got into a fix where money wouldn't make an unwanted pregnancy go away. Sixty years ago, at the time when we were discovering one magnificent hormone after another, I got Rosie in the family way. There were circumstances that prevented me from helping her properly. And then of course there was Rivka, whom I met at a party at Rafaël's in the summer of 1923, when we had just forged our partnership.

Rafaël lived in a historic five-story merchant's house on one of Amsterdam's canals. It had lofty ceilings, drafty rooms, and a narrow staircase. It was the first time I'd been invited to his home. A maid let me into the marble entrance hall. As she was hanging up my coat, I noticed a gigantic four-story dollhouse taking up the entire back wall. It was a splendid replica of a stately neoclassical interior, one that had presumably graced the parental home of either Rafaël or his wife somewhere in Silesia. Climbing the stairs, I saw little evidence of that grandeur in the house I was now in. I was shown into two large, connected rooms with overstuffed bookcases lining the walls. The floor and coffee tables were strewn with fashion magazines, philosophy journals, and medical periodicals in various languages. In one corner stood an easel displaying a painting of a child's face. In the next room a pianoforte had pride of place, with a smattering of music stands and assorted violin and cello cases nearby. It looked like the rehearsal space for an entire chamber orchestra, but it turned out that the instruments belonged to Rafaël, his wife, and their children. The few spots on the walls not covered by bookcases were filled with pictures: a landscape by Van der Heyden, as well as an interesting mishmash of portraits, still lifes, and landscapes, quite skillfully done and probably the work of family members. Both in atmosphere and in decor it was unlike any other house I'd ever been in. I was used to luxury and the display of wealth as a token of personal success. In this house, all the glitz was confined to the dollhouse down in the entry hall. Upstairs, literature, science, and art reigned. Wealth was a means that enabled one to devote oneself to those important pursuits, and not an end in itself.

Rafaël welcomed me and introduced me to his wife, a short, stocky, severe-looking matron, her layers of fat squeezed into an old-fashioned black gown whose seams appeared ready to give at any moment. Her multiple chins billowed over the little black collar secured with an ivory brooch. Her gray hair was gathered in a tight bun by a comb whose teeth seemed to stick right into her scalp. I bowed.

"Motke, this is my wife, Sari, my dear Dauphine. That is what we call her, on account of her majestic, commanding bearing. Please tell her you're crazy about music, that you love to listen to piano sonatas on a daily basis, or she'll have nothing to do with you."

"He exaggerates," Sari said with a laugh, the stern expression on her face softening somewhat, "as he always does. It is fortunate, is it not, that I can contribute to this household something other than pancreatic enigmas? If it were up to my husband, our life would be nothing but hormones right now." She said it with some disdain. "Music," she went on, leaning closer to underline the importance of her assertion, "more than anything else in the world, expresses feelings in their most intense manifestation. Our ability to make music is what sets us apart from the animals. Without music we would live in an emotional wasteland. Can you imagine life without it?"

I had no choice but to shake my head no. I had had no musical education to speak of and was quite ignorant on the subject.

Fortunately, she wasn't expecting a reply and went on with her harangue: "Music expresses our desires, our attachment to things over which we have no control. As Gustav Mahler once put it, 'Music contains the pain and sorrow of life.' Mankind needs music, the way my husband needs his microscope." She fixed me with a piercing stare, as if she wanted to make sure that I agreed with her.

"See, that's just what I mean," Rafaël chuckled, "you haven't been here two minutes and already you've had to listen to one of the Dauphine's lectures. Sari, give the poor man something to drink, and then I can introduce him to our other guests."

To my surprise, it wasn't only the professor's contemporaries who were in attendance that night. Besides his own children, I was introduced to a number of other young people, whom I assumed to be students and laboratory colleagues. Rafaël had a wide circle of friends, comprising officials and politicians, musicians, artists, and scientists. He was also, apparently, an approachable, beloved mentor to his students and younger colleagues.

The professor introduced me to Sam Salomons, one of the top chemists he had hired to work at Farmacom. A contemporary of the professor's, he had a similar bearing—a stern-faced, Prussian dinosaur. They had known each other since their student years in Germany. After a short exchange of pleasantries, Rafaël continued steering me around to meet the rest of the guests.

We wound up at the circle of young people that included Rivka. She had an open face with twinkling, big brown eyes and a mouth that was prone to laugh; long, dark, curly hair; splendid tits stowed inside a black lace blouse with a rather impressive décolleté; and sturdy hips that belonged to a deliciously voluptuous body. With a wave of the hand Rafaël introduced me to the entire crew. Rivka, staring at me in surprise, exclaimed, "Rafaël, you didn't tell me your business partner was so young! I thought he'd be your age!"

To make a long story short, at the end of the evening, after a piano recital by the Dauphine—apparently an inescapable ingredient of any get-together at the Levines'—I offered to run Rivka home. It had been quite a night for me; I'd felt rather intimidated in the company of people who dropped the names of philosophers, writers, and scientists the way we might talk about different breeds of livestock. Rivka was clearly in her element there. I'd managed to snag a seat next to hers during the recital, and my whispered crack about the imposing dimension of the Dauphine's backside as she lowered herself onto the diminutive piano stool sent the girl into an uncontrollable fit of the giggles. It had been enough to overcome any initial misgivings, and she unhesitatingly accepted my invitation to take her home.

Frank, my chauffeur, was waiting in the car outside. I had been planning to drive home after the party, but meeting Rivka had made me change my mind.

"Have you ever been for a drive along the Amstel River at night?" I asked her as I followed her down the stairs.

"No," said Rivka, "I've never ridden in one of those things in my life. Do you really own an automobile?"

The sight of my Lancia made her giggle, and she insisted on shaking Frank's hand—a ridiculous thing to do, of course—then danced around the car three times before enthusiastically diving into the backseat. When Frank started the engine she got so excited that she grabbed my hand in a tight grip. But unlike the other girls I had lured into my car before her, she didn't put on a frightened little-girl act. She seemed to revel in the speed at which Frank negotiated the bumpy cobblestones and couldn't wait for him to really step on it once we were out of the city center. We zipped along the banks of the snaking river under a nearly full moon, the water showing barely a ripple in the crisp spring night.

It was the most romantic backdrop you could ever imagine; Rivka's childish enthusiasm, however, thwarted my efforts to create a correspondingly intimate mood inside the car. I found her extremely desirable and sexy, but she kept sliding open the little window between our compartment and the driver's cab to pepper Frank with questions about the engine, the RPMs, how often he had to fill up with gas or add oil. She could have been out on a date with Frank, for fuck's sake! But Frank knew me well; he was a loyal employee. And so, once we were well out of the city, he stopped the car at a discreet distance from a sheltered thicket along the river, announced that the engine had to cool off, and offered to spread a blanket for us at the river's edge on the other side of the bushes. I finally found myself alone with her, seated side by side on a blanket. I put an arm around her. She glanced at me brightly, then sighed, "This is so nice, two firsts in one evening! I've never been in an automobile before, and I've never sat on the banks of the Amstel at night. This is the life!"

It made her sound so innocent. A young thing full of dreams, without any concept of the struggle it is just to keep your head above water. A blithe little flapper who'd never yet been forced to take off her rose-colored glasses.

I smiled at her, brushing a stray curl off her face. "You're so darn gorgeous," I fawned, "that even the loveliest, most romantic setting doesn't hold a candle to your beauty." I started caressing her face, her neck, and then slowly drew closer, gazing deep into those lovely eyes, in which I read a mixture of excitement and surprise.

We kissed a few times—cautiously at first, just sampling, tasting; then my tongue sought hers. Pressing myself up against her, I gently pushed her down onto the blanket. With her hand resting lightly on my back, I slowly tugged her blouse out of her skirt, stroked her soft, flat stomach, then calmly moved my hand upward, slipping beneath the satin of her bra to find her breast, until my fingers encountered a well-defined nipple, which I began playfully wiggling back and forth. Her boob was firm, perky, just the way I like them. I was already incredibly horny, but I wasn't sure if she was as turned on as I was yet. Letting go of that heavenly tit, I pulled up her lace blouse and, tweaking her breast out of its cup, took it in my mouth, while my hand worked its way down to hike up her skirt and maneuver her underpants down. As my fingers entered her she began running her hands through my hair. I felt her stiffen. Letting go of her nipple, I moved my mouth lower down to kiss her navel. Digging my way through the roadblock of bunched-up clothing, I finally reached her bush, and started working her pussy with my tongue. Arousing the woman to the verge of orgasm, that was the way to break through the last bit of resistance. She was moaning softly now, her breath coming faster. She tasted of apples. Her soft, warm flesh was driving me crazy—that dish of delight my tongue was now lapping at frenziedly. Her suppressed cries were coming faster and faster. I unbuttoned my pants, pushing them down past my hips, and my beast, finally released from its cage, sprang up wildly. I started inching my way back up, continuing to stimulate her manually, until the beast found its way in. She opened her eyes and said softly, "I'm still a virgin, please be careful."

I kept myself quiet for a moment, kissed her, and said, "I'll be very gentle, all right?"

Running her tongue over her lips, she nodded; she was as hot as boiling water in a distillation flask, and it wasn't long before I was able to really get going. We both came at the same time. I stayed inside her for a few seconds, gazed at her, and smiled.

"*Three* firsts in one night, that's a record," she said.

8...

Eight weeks later Rivka walked into my office unannounced. I hadn't seen or spoken to her since our dalliance on the banks of the Amstel, although I had written her a little note telling her that I thought back on our romantic car ride with considerable pleasure. Actually, I'd decided I wouldn't mind getting together again sometime. I had a notion we might very well hit it off in the future. But I was up to my ears at work, what with the construction of the new lab on the top floor of the meatpacking plant, and the intense negotiations Levine and I were conducting with the Canadians to secure the European licenses. Levine and his team were already very close to developing a standardized form of insulin that could be mass-produced, and there was no time to lose. Competitors in France and Germany were snapping at our heels, and it was vital for us to win this first battle. I was just dictating a telegram to Agnes when Rivka burst into my office without knocking.

"I have to speak to you—alone," she said, looking at Agnes, who can be relied on to follow my orders, but not those of a strange woman barging in unannounced. Agnes, not budging, looked away, waiting to see what came next.

"Rivka!" I said affably, hiding my perplexity over her unexpected arrival. Until you know what you're in for, never show your hand. "This is *such* a surprise," I went on by way of welcome, signaling Agnes to leave us. My loyal assistant stood up, but not without giving me a surly pout to express her displeasure at this interruption of our work session.

As soon as Agnes had shut the door, Rivka marched up to me and, before I could take her in my arms and kiss her, said in a whisper—she, at least, wasn't sure that Agnes would honor her boss's request for privacy—"We have a problem. I'm pregnant." She looked at me wide-eyed.

I tried to hide the shock her announcement gave me. "Yet another first; that makes four, right?" I smiled, my mind racing, trying to think what to do. Rivka did not respond. I put an arm around her, steered her to the sofa, and, kissing her, helped her out of her charming summer jacket. "Relax," I reassured her. "Don't worry, we'll find a solution. Would you like something to drink?"

I rang for Agnes and asked her to bring us tea and cookies, and also not to put through any calls. Then I pushed the button on my desk that turned on the red lightbulb outside my door, to make sure no one would come in, and sat down next to Rivka on the sofa.

"What exactly do you mean by 'a solution'?" asked Rivka as we sat there balancing our fine China teacups after I'd helped her to two lumps of sugar. She turned down the cookie.

"Darling," I said, "pregnancy isn't the end of the world, you know. There are perfectly good ways to get rid of an unwanted fetus. And it isn't dangerous; at least, it doesn't have to be," I said when I saw her open her mouth to say something. "Do you think I'd expose you to anything dangerous? Of course I wouldn't! But

I have connections, I can arrange for it to be completely safe. It'll cost quite a bit, but you're worth it to me."

She stared at me, aghast.

"You aren't Orthodox or anything, are you?" I asked, thinking it would be the ultimate irony if, of all the broads in permissive, promiscuous Amsterdam, I had knocked up the one girl who objected to abortion on religious grounds, while out here in the puritanical sticks I'd been sneaking around with wenches of all faiths and persuasions.

"Motke, my parents know. My father is furious. He works in Levine's lab and he says he'll ruin Farmacom if we don't get married."

She began to cry. That's when the panic set in; it wasn't her tears but the news of her father and his threat that made my blood run cold.

"What's your father's name?" I asked, staring at the weeping puddle of misery. I lifted her chin with my finger and she looked up at me through teary eyes.

"Sam Salomons."

That's when I knew I was really in trouble.

9...

Salomons was an old schoolmate of Rafaël's, a chemistry professor, and, like Rafaël, a German Jew. I had met him at the soirée in the Levines' canal house, when he had just accepted a position at Farmacom. Levine had told me that he recruited Salomons because the man had untold influential connections in the scientific world. Soon enough, once we had won the licensing battle, we were going to need the help of his German contacts to launch our insulin products on the European market. I just couldn't risk getting in trouble with this important, highly respected man, who, I suspected, would cling to his old-fashioned moral principles. A disgruntled Salomons could scuttle our entire operation. Besides, I didn't know how I could face Levine if Salomons made trouble for Farmacom as a result of my randy behavior. I still considered Levine my mentor back then; I looked up to him a great deal. I might have arrived at a different decision some years later, when our relationship had cooled somewhat, but on the day Rivka came barging into my office, I didn't want to rouse his ire and cared deeply about what he would think about my philandering.

I knew I had to act quickly to appease Salomons's wrath; I'd have to pay a visit to Rivka's father as soon as possible. I had a few urgent pieces of business to dispose of before I was free to take care of it, so I sent Rivka home in the car with Frank, with a letter to give to her father, a letter that, for once, wasn't dictated to Agnes. Using my own fountain pen and a sheet of Farmacom's brand-new stationery, I humbly begged Salomons's forgiveness for being responsible for the state his daughter was in, rhapsodized about her irresistible charms, and declared that, given his permission, I would be honored to marry her.

Years later, Rivka complained bitterly that no one had ever asked her what *she* thought about getting married. Since she had come to my office as her father's messenger, I'd always assumed that she agreed with her father's ultimatum. Besides, we had no choice in the matter. Rivka had gotten herself knocked up, and once you've made your bed, you just have to lie in it. There were only three options for a girl in her condition: you could get rid of the unwanted child, your mother could adopt it and pretend it was one of her own, or you got married; there was no other way out. Today there is a fourth alternative—you can raise the child yourself as a single mother, but as far as its being an improvement over those first three choices, I have my doubts. After seeing what happened to Rosie, I know it can lead to all sorts of problems.

• • •

As far as my marriage to Rivka, however, we actually made a good go of it for a surprisingly long time. Of course we were young; I was twenty-seven, Rivka just eighteen. Matrimony had never appealed to me, even as a child, and I had been determined, with every fiber of my being, to hang on to my freedom. But once I found myself in this impossible situation, I resigned myself to the inevitable. And I have to confess that the times in my life when I've actually managed to remain monogamous, as I was during the first months of my marriage to Rivka, have been few and far between. It wasn't twinges of so-called conscience or decency that caused me to be faithful at first; I've never been very much bothered by those, luckily. It was quite simply because having her was enough for me. Rivka was energetic, funny, and sensual, and, in spite of her pregnancy, she had such an inexhaustible enthusiasm for sex that, coming on top of my busy and exciting work life at the factory and with Farmacom, it left me with no energy for further sexual escapades. It wasn't until the birth of our daughter Ruth, when Rivka seemed to lose interest in our love games a bit—understandably so in light of the sleepless nights, the feedings and colic and other afflictions requiring endless consolation, sapping her energy—that I turned to other women. I have never—almost never, anyway—been faithful to one woman again since. But the very fact that Rivka didn't leave me until twenty-two years and four children later proves that, in spite of everything, I was always able to satisfy her needs. I'm not the type to be with a woman and then ignore her. I'm a man with a big heart, with a great deal of love to give. It's simply more than one woman can handle.

10...

All my working life I've had a framed picture of those two bloody Canadian geniuses hanging on my wall. It's a sunny day, and they're posing in front of a low building with the dog whose pancreas they've removed. You can tell it's windy from the ballooning lab coat of the bespectacled forty-year-old and the rippling necktie of the fresh-faced student, still wet behind the ears but confidently smiling into the camera. The one who looks unhappiest is the dog, evidence that it isn't much fun having to go through life without a pancreas. The dog should have been given the Nobel Prize for his ordeal, but the prize went to those two smug-faced Canadians instead. That photograph makes my blood boil every time I look at it, which is why it's hanging in such a prominent spot. It's the perfect goad, the fly in the ointment. Having those two windbags looking down on me every single day provoked the hell out of me. What kept me going was knowing the day would come when I'd triumphantly toss that photo in the trash—the day Rafaël, accompanied by me, of course, would fly to Stockholm to collect the coveted award. I'd have the Nobel diploma mounted in the same frame and hang it right there on my wall, to trumpet the world's recognition of our work. The fact that, lying here in my bed, I'm still forced to stare at those two assholes, who've never grown a day older, means that my dearest wish has never come true. I may have only three years of secondary school under my belt, but I've been awarded an honorary doctorate; I've sat with government ministers on advisory boards; I've been received by the queen; I was part of the prince consort's inner circle and was given the proud title of "royal merchant." Not bad, is it, for a boy from the sticks? But that one distinction I most wanted always eluded us, and it still makes me spitting mad.

• • •

I can't remember ever feeling more elated than the day we inaugurated our own laboratory at the De Paauw plant. Not only had Rafaël's Amsterdam lab been equipped with top-of-the-line apparatus, but a floor of our factory was now dedicated to a second Farmacom laboratory, furnished according to the professor's specifications. Here the discoveries explored in Amsterdam were to be developed further, and the new hormones readied for commercial production.

What a contrast there was between the lab and the rest of the plant! I was used to the hustle and bustle of the factories, where everything was aimed at delivering the most merchandise to the widest possible market. Our industrial site had always been a din of clashing sounds. The hiss and whistle of the train ferrying in the livestock to be slaughtered. Trucks with their racing engines and claxons, either bringing in raw materials or being loaded with the finished product for delivery. The loading carts pushed by big bruisers in overalls, their hefty wooden wheels clattering across the cobblestones. All day long the bellowing cattle and men's shouts provided a deafening jangle, punctuated by the shrill report of the bolt gun shooting a metal pin through a pig's skull while the dull thud of the sledgehammer sending some calf to its maker produced a steady background hum, accompanied by the crack of the woodcutters' axes chopping the firewood for the many ovens, the hammering from the carpenter's shop, and the sigh of the glassblowers' bellows. Their mournful notes underscored, in a minor key, the shrieks of the pigs smelling death before the pin pierced their brains or the butcher's knife slit their throats. There was also the clang of cleavers from the slaughterhouse floor, where butchers were busy breaking down the carcasses, and the clatter of typewriters floating out of the offices of the secretaries and accountants (the latter wore white coats for no other reason than to distinguish them from "ordinary" workers), all of it contributing to the sense of urgency and energy pervading the plant.

But how different it was in the laboratory, our first improvised "hormone factory," still so vulnerable and new that you felt you had to close the door to the sanctum very gently behind you, afraid the entire place—nothing but a rickety assemblage of glass, cork, rubber, and a few support stands on wobbly tables—would otherwise collapse like a house of cards.

Nowhere in the company was time of greater essence than here, where the rattle of the teletype machine might at any minute sound the alarm that the hormone we were so desperately trying to find had been discovered by some other lab somewhere else in the world.

But if there was any such pressure, there was no outward sign of it; the sparsely furnished space was a sea of tranquillity that instilled a feeling of calm and serenity, and I loved to spend time in there. Whenever I stepped into that lab I felt my chest swell with pride, gratified to see my bold initiative playing out here in my own factory, in the form of a squadron of scientists bent over distilling flasks, microscopes, steam baths, and scales. Their white lab coats were spotless in contrast with the workers' coveralls, which were usually spattered with blood, fat, and feces. To distinguish the biologists from the lab technicians, the former's coat collars were notched. Leaning against the wall, I liked to watch them work, monitoring the bubbling, fermenting, odorous concoctions while jotting down the odd notation. Invited to peer through their microscopes, I couldn't make heads or tails of what was on the slides. The squirmy, slithery, wriggly organisms in those minuscule droplets only gave up their secrets to those who had learned to decipher them. Sometimes I'd feel a stab of regret, and perhaps anger, at the fact that these gentlemen (and even, yes, even the occasional female, for crying out loud!) had been given the right to analyze this stuff, whereas I was dependent on their knowledge, their noodles, their brains.

I liked to walk past the cages housing the lab animals. This living rabble was nothing like the stacks of pig and beef carcasses dangling in our slaughterhouse. The rabbits, mice, and rats and, later on, roosters, dogs, and apes were confined inside small cages. Depending on what had been injected or surgically removed, they might be either agitated or semi-comatose, some of them whining softly from horniness or pain.

I have never taken pleasure in the slaughter of animals, but I am not sentimental about it either, the way some people are nowadays. To me killing animals is just as much a part of life as shitting, eating, or making love. All four are necessary, in ascending order of gratification.

I lived next door to the plant as a child, and so pigs being driven to slaughter was something we took for granted, just as we thought nothing of the fact that in the morning, when the factory opened, a crowd of scruffy men would be gathered outside the gate, like sperm cells milling about inside the fallopian tubes waiting to strike when the time is right. My father would pick out a few of the sturdiest and least filthy men from the throng of yokels and offer them a job for the day. Once his selection was made, he ordered the foreman to tell the rest of the bums to scram; he didn't like people loitering outside the gates. The dejected look of those fellows as they trudged off reluctantly, muttering darkly and dragging their feet, reminded me of the way the calves moved as they were being led to slaughter. From a young age I understood that there wasn't any point resisting the law of survival of the fittest, and that you had to make sure you were one of the ones coming out on top.

Aaron was different; he felt sorry for both the animals and the unemployed scum my father sent packing. Once, when we were very young, as we stood watching, each clutching a sandwich in a clammy little hand, one fellow kept insisting, begging my father to give him a job. "My kid's sick in bed and he's starving."

The gaunt, emaciated man tugged at my father's sleeve with one hand and held out the other beseechingly. As the foreman slapped his hand away, Aaron darted forward to offer the man his sandwich. The poor devil reached for it, but my father knocked it out of his hands, sending it flying into in a mud puddle. Aaron received a box on the ear for his trouble, and as the beggar bent down to retrieve the bread, the foreman kicked him in the butt, landing him facedown in the mud. My father and the foreman turned and walked back inside the gate, leaving Aaron standing there bawling, more upset about the man than his own smarting ear. I grabbed my blubbering brother's hand and dragged him back into the house.

43

11...

We did eventually manage to secure the licenses for the insulin. It was mind-boggling, the effort Levine and his team put into getting it done. Levine was unstoppable in his determination to turn Farmacom into a world-class outfit, the first to make the insulin drug commercially available in Holland and the rest of Europe. He worked day and night, barely allowed himself time to eat or rest, and demanded the same total commitment from his coworkers.

His passion for research knew no bounds. For countless days and nights Levine and his assistants rammed massive amounts of animal pancreas through a simple fruit press, twisting the screw a couple of turns tighter every so often to wring out the essence drop by precious drop into a flask placed underneath. Someone had to stay in the lab all night to check that the pressing went on uninterrupted, and Levine did not excuse himself from that duty.

He was likewise first in line to try out the rudimentary insulin preparation once it was ready to be tested on humans. He had no hesitation about injecting himself with the serum, which could have sent him into a potentially fatal coma. I did try to stop him, chiding him that he was too important to the business to risk his life. He looked at me, smiling, and shook his head.

"For your age, you are remarkably clever and quick on the uptake," he said, "and I do appreciate your concern, but the proof of the pudding is in the eating, as they say. We are about to make this drug available, and we are going to ask physicians to administer it to their patients. Those patients, by volunteering for this trial, will help us to tweak and improve our product. Then does it not behoove me, as the drug's developer, to assume some of the same risk myself?"

Levine was a man with a strict nineteenth-century Prussian military sense of ethics. His good name, as he had told me that first evening in the restaurant, was more important to him than his life. Fortunately, the injections didn't wind up sending him into hypoglycemic shock after all. Later I did ask myself if he had always known he was going to be fine. Was he really the hero I thought him to be, or had he been pulling my leg? I was never quite sure of his true motives. I never knew whether he was playing me for a fool or not. An unpleasant thought. A shadow over what had started off as such an exhilarating collaboration.

Maybe it would all have turned out differently if there hadn't been the interruption of the war—the great cataclysm that was, even in the best of all possible cases, a problematic disruption in the lives of the Chosen People of Europe. It set us back at least five years, an eternity in our murderously competitive field, where every second counts. But in actual fact our hands were already tied by 1933, the year those blind, benighted Germans elected the odious goon, which meant that besides dealing with a financial crisis, we faced the danger of losing our biggest export customer. Of course, the fact that the bastard next door was clamping down so hard on our neighbors did bring us an influx of very capable people: all those Silbersteins and Rosenbergs fleeing to the Netherlands from the east. Poor sods, thinking they'd be safe here with us. With such enthusiasm they devoted themselves to the work here in our lab, hoping to get their disrupted careers back on track! Farmacom took in the very top echelon of Europe's scientific establishment. Highly experienced people we could never have recruited before threw themselves into our hormonal experiments with great gusto, content with just a pittance, so eager were they to leave the humiliations of their fatherland behind. Of course, they were still blissfully unaware that the storm of abuse, accusation, and stigmatization would soon sweep across these chicken-livered lowlands as well, forcing them to their knees once more. And this time for good.

• • •

I can get all nostalgic thinking about the early days of my partnership with Levine. Lying here in my metal cage, I can sometimes feel the admiration I had for him then running up my decrepit spine like a shudder, a tremor delivering a stab of pain. Our collaboration had let me hone my inexperienced brain on that formidable intellect, and he in turn seemed to enjoy satisfying my curiosity.

In business too, we were an unrivaled team. Levine wasn't merely the instigator and motivator of the scientific research; even though his clinician's soul was devoted to making the lifesaving insulin available as quickly as possible, he was never blind to the commercial aspects of the business.

Before the ink was dry on the contract that was to bind us so intricately together, he had already started working on a number of articles on the Canadian discovery of insulin for domestic and international medical journals. He didn't fail to mention, naturally, that his lab, in a joint venture with Farmacom, was the first to make the drug commercially viable. He also started a medical journal of his own, published simultaneously in French, German, and English. A platform to publicize his discoveries around the globe, it attracted a wide readership from the very first issue.

The extraction of insulin was indeed a masterful achievement, considering that insulin is a protein that's mixed in with other proteins, and therefore very difficult to isolate. Insulin is as well camouflaged as a cloud in an overcast sky. And as if that weren't complicated enough, the stuff turned out to be extremely sensitive to physical and chemical contaminants, which often damaged it and rendered it useless.

The Canadian eggheads had come up with a biochemical test to identify and isolate the insulin. They had further devised a method that allowed them to measure the blood-sugar level of the dog without a pancreas after injecting it with the stuff. Levine and his team took this a step further; by experimenting with various methods they were able to do some fine-tuning and come up with a preparation of consistent strength from batch to batch. This was a crucial step, for until then the insulin could be either too weak, and fail to prevent a diabetic coma, or else too strong, resulting in death by hypoglycemia. Hundreds of rabbits with the dubious distinction of being the designated guinea pigs in these experiments came to a sad end after being injected with either too weak or too strong a dose. Nor did all of the human patients in the various medical trials survive the experimental insulin. Scientific breakthroughs happen only by trial and, more often than not, error. In those days there were no rules or guidelines governing medical experimentation; drugs didn't even require a doctor's prescription. At the time we were introducing the insulin drugs to the market, it was left up to the scientist, in consultation with the physician, to decide when to move the inquiry from lab-animal experimentation to human trials. This did provide a great measure of freedom, unthinkable nowadays; you could experiment to your heart's content, far more than is permitted today.

• • •

As I said before, we were a terrific team at first. Once we had the licenses in hand, we decided to approach Bayer, already a huge pharma concern. And, impressed by Levine's reputation, despite the fact that Farmacom consisted of just one laboratory in Amsterdam and a space on the top floor of the De Paauw Slaughterhouse and Meatpacking Co. plant, they did give us a hearing. Genius as he was at manipulating protein, Levine likewise knew how to play our opponents by giving them just enough information to whet their appetites. Their arrogance, however, won out over their greed. They were convinced they didn't need our piddling little company to market the coveted drug in Germany; they thought they could do it without us. A serious mistake, which they soon came to regret. For the Bayer directors were to discover to their dismay that Levine and I had already set up a German subsidiary, which held the exclusive rights to insulin in Germany.

Levine's way of exciting interest for his products was no different from the way he had worked his spell on me in Die Port van Cleve. He knew how to arouse people's greed to such an extent that they felt they just had to take their chances with him, come what may. Once he'd reeled them in, it was my turn to strike with hard-nosed negotiating tactics, and to hammer out a lucrative deal for bulk sales of the insulin. This team effort was the commercial foundation upon which we built our empire.

12...

It took some time for Rivka to feel at home in these godforsaken boonies. It was quite a change for her, from her life as a schoolgirl growing up among the intellectual and cultural elite of the big city to the unrefined rusticity of our depressing backwater, with its dirt roads and the stench of poverty seeping out of every hovel, the hardened face of the woman on the street corner with her meager array of fruits and vegetables displayed on a ragged mat, the slurred voice of the man who'd spent his miserable weekly wages on drink and was stumbling home to his slum without any food to offer his starving brood, or the gangs of delinquents staging raids on local farmers not much better off than they were.

My blithe coed appeared to have no problem saying goodbye to her carefree school days and soon cheerfully slipped into the role of young mother and wife of one of this hick town's leading citizens. She energetically took charge of our home next to the factory, an elegant villa equipped with all modern conveniences, and took obvious pleasure in overseeing the small army of maids and other servants who had been running the household. After my father's and mother's passing, I had remained in my parental home, leaving the decor exactly as it was, and had also kept on the servants, headed by Marieke, the trusty house-keeper. Marieke, who had started out in service as a shy young thing, had grown into the sturdy, energetic commander in chief of my bachelor household. The moment my young bride stepped over the threshold, Marieke took to her hook, line, and sinker, and did her very best to answer her every whim. Rivka's arrival on the scene brought with it considerable changes to our plodding daily routine. When she first walked into the house, she'd exclaimed, "How vulgar! What tasteless schlock!"

I'd stared at her, taken aback. I had never met anyone who wasn't suitably impressed by these elegant interiors, and her blunt criticism hurt me more than I liked to admit. At the same time I admired her candor. Rivka was a girl who didn't mince words.

"If you want me to be happy here," she said, running her hand over her slightly swollen belly, "you'll have to let me do a little remodeling."

And so it came to pass. My parents' pride, their castle, proud embodiment of their newly acquired wealth, their victory over poverty, was completely dismantled. The murals disappeared under stark geometrical wallpaper patterns, the ceilings were replastered after being stripped of their ornamental medallions and cornices, and almost all of the neoclassical furniture was replaced, so that for the first several months after the renovations I felt like a stranger in my own home. My indefatigable wife introduced our backwater to the latest in modernist style. With tables, sofas, lamps, chairs, and coatracks by artisans and famous designers like Piet Kramer and H. J. Winkelman, our entire house was turned into a model interior of the Amsterdam School. It led to quite a bit of eyebrow raising, which bothered Rivka not a bit.

The birth of our first child, Ruth, affected me more than I had expected. Children had never much interested me, but to my surprise, I was fascinated to see Rivka's body swell and to feel the life kicking inside her belly. It was with anxious anticipation that I awaited the baby's birth, and watching my daughter grow, and in quick succession a second and then a third little girl, gave me more pleasure than I had ever thought possible. That fatherhood could produce such strong feelings of connection, that it would awaken the protective instinct in me, was something I'd never expected.

Rivka did sometimes miss the excitement of the city. The solution she found to her homesickness was to invite lots of guests to come and stay. She made sure our spacious, comfortable home was always ready to accommodate her university friends from Amsterdam, who were only too happy to be invited to spend time in such modern, elegant surroundings out in the countryside (to them an exotic locale), next to the ever-bustling factory.

Rivka organized musical performances, readings, and theatrical soirees, and with the help of our cook prepared exquisite spreads for her dinner parties. Aaron was often one of the guests. He tended to stay in the background, slumped in his chair with an alcoholic beverage in one hand, observing the proceedings. I never caught him showing even the slightest interest in any of Rivka's many girlfriends.

Hard to understand; I often had trouble controlling myself. What an effort it took to keep my hands off all those smart, well-spoken, shapely girls! But I restrained myself, because there's a limit; I knew seducing my wife's girlfriends was wrong. If only because it was just asking for trouble.

13...

In addition to the complex problems we dealt with daily involving the insulin production and further hormonal research and production, it was important to drum up public support for our endeavors. The employment opportunities our meatpacking plant provided had made us well liked by the locals. But the growing range of drugs Farmacom was beginning to market had to be handled with caution in this Roman Catholic hinterland. For that reason, I actively sought to improve our relations with the local notables, and one of the most important players among these was, of course, the new parish priest.

I invited the man to my office for a meeting. The curate was a reedy, brittle-looking person. He was young, but his face was ageless; he had sparse, limp, and already receding ash-blond hair, a fuzzy little beard that hardly deserved to be called such, and an oily voice so soft that it was hard to believe that in church his sermons could be heard by the whole congregation. He spoke carefully, as if his every word might arouse the wrath of God. He had been sent to our town straight from the seminary, and he told me how much he enjoyed being the shepherd of his flock. When I asked him which aspect of his wide-ranging job he found most interesting, he replied, "The contact I have with the people in my parish, both young and old; that is a great blessing to me. They have so many problems, and it gives me great satisfaction to lend them a sympathetic ear, and to help them accept their heavy lot."

That's exactly the sort of platitude you'd expect from a priest, and it's why I can't stand the Church. If there's one thing I've refused to do all my life, it's to accept things as they are. I am not some lame believer who meekly bows his head and accepts the fate allotted to him from on high; far from it. I like to grab fate by the horns the way a butcher reaches for a slaughtered steer, and turn it to work in my favor. But it was important to have a good relationship with a cleric venerated by the majority of my workforce, in light of the fact that our company was planning to produce increasing numbers of drugs that might appear to fly in the face of Our Lord's commandments. Besides, I'm never averse to buttering people up if I have nothing to lose by it.

"Father, would you mind describing to me the nature of their struggle? I suspect that a great many folks around here find themselves in straitened circumstances on account of having too many mouths to feed and insufficient means to take care of them; isn't that the main problem?"

The black-frocked prelate looked at me pensively, as if weighing my interest. A mirthless smile split his face from ear to ear. He took a sip of the watery tea that Agnes had been instructed to make weak on account of his "delicate stomach," and then he spoke. "Indeed, for many folks poverty is a tribulation, a terrible cross to bear. But it has always been so, has it not? No, the issue of greater concern to them right now is a more recent development: the fact that so many young people now troop off to work in the factories. Many of the parents are fearful about the young girls in particular—they are being exposed to crude behavior and harassment at work, which they are often power-less to resist."

I nodded gravely.

"I understand," he continued, "that in your factory the men and the women do have separate changing rooms, and that the sexes are kept apart wherever possible on the shop floor and in the canteen, yet it appears that there are still a great many instances where the young girls are forced to put up with cer-tain improprieties, which, innocent and inexperienced as they are, they are often incapable of rebuffing. Worse, some of them may take the indecencies to which they are subjected for well-meaning attentions, which in turn may tempt them to indulge in unbecoming conduct, with all the tragic consequences that may entail."

Even though our region had seen industrial development for well over half a century, it seemed that industry was still regarded as an intruder liable to jeopardize the area's once-pristine innocence. People do like to place the past on a romantic pedestal, like some treasured Christmas ornament, conveniently forgetting the hanky-panky and fornication that has always been rife in the open fields or the hayloft. Who hasn't heard the raunchy stories about rolls in the hay? They just go to show that barns aren't only for housing the livestock and their fodder.

"We take every aspect of our workers' safety extremely seri-ously," I replied, "and do all we can to save the young girls from themselves, as well as guard them from the boorish behavior of the male personnel. But surely the parents must accept some of the responsibility too? And the Church, naturally. You yourself just acknowledged that we have tried to keep the sexes apart wherever possible. What more can we do? After all, this is a commercial enterprise, not a finishing school."

"We do what we can, of course," said the priest, slowly tapping the tips of his emaciated fingers together, "but in this case we need everyone to step in. In my parish, we offer informational sessions; we get women of unimpeachable repute to prepare the girls for their future housewifely duties, instructing them in the arts of housekeeping, cooking, and virtuous conduct. It would be to your credit if your company could assume some similar role in educating your workers. There are other firms in our country—not yet very many, I'll admit—that have shouldered that responsibility. It would benefit not only your employees but your own interests as well, since it would do a lot for your firm's general success and reputation. All in all, I know the people around here would very much appreciate that sort of initiative."

I didn't think much of the idea, but promised the padre I'd mention it to the other directors, and that I would keep him apprised of our decision.

When I told Rivka that night about it, she was immediately enthusiastic. My young wife had the knack of befriending folks from all walks of life, even out here in this class-conscious rural society. I had noticed this propensity of hers that first night in my Lancia, when she'd been so chummy with Frank; she always managed to win people over. In the beginning I found it quite charming; later on, her coziness with my factory girls very nearly destroyed me.

My energetic young bride wasn't prepared to cut herself off from the outside world and stay home like some broody mother hen. Her vivacious, free-spirited nature—the quality that had so attracted me when we first met—proved to be the very essence of her makeup. I was away a great deal, of course, mostly on business, though there was also the occasional extramarital fling.

Rivka didn't seem to mind very much. She wasn't the type to sit around moping, waiting for me to come home. On the contrary; a women's-libber before the concept even existed, that was my Rivka.

The priest's suggestion found a receptive ear with her, and she immediately set out to organize instructive evenings for my workers. I doubt that my bride was the one the cleric had in mind to carry out his plan, not being of unimpeachable virtue herself (he, like everyone else, had kept a careful tab of the number of months we'd been married before her delivery). And besides, she wasn't even Catholic. An unbeliever and a Jewess, could it be any less suitable?

Rivka wasn't conscious of class or racial segregation. In the circles of the Amsterdam intelligentsia to which she belonged, what counted was schooling, intellect, and a sense of humor, and although most of her friends and her parents' acquaintances were Jewish, background wasn't considered relevant. It may have been guilelessness, a willful ignorance of the class system that reigned in these parts, or perhaps simply her gut instinct that led her to hitch the right ladies in our firm to her reformation wagon, but whatever it was, she managed, to my surprise, to assemble a motley crew of all denominations—Catholic, Protestant, and Jewish, the uneducated factory rats who streamed into our plant every day in their shabby coveralls and threadbare aprons. There was particular focus on the young girls, who were instructed in a lighthearted way in the kinds of things a young woman ought to know. The subjects included how to prepare healthy meals with little cash, and the rudimentary hygiene these future housewives should try to maintain, even if they had to do so in drafty, ramshackle huts barely a step up from the peat shacks of the past, places with neither plumbing nor fresh air. There was also some mention, without getting too explicit, of ways a girl might ward off a hot-blooded beau, provided that was what she wanted. It should come as no surprise that these instructions, doled out by my enthusiastic darling, weren't taken all too seriously. Most of the shiksas were smart enough to count to nine, and there were few people in the factory unaware that our first child must have been conceived sometime before our low-key wedding. But that fact only made them more inclined to accept my Rivka.

During a dinner at our house, Rivka enthusiastically told some of her former schoolmates about the teaching sessions, and a plan was soon hatched not only to educate my employees, but to organize cultural activities for them as well. These cultivated alumnae loved the theater, and one of Rivka's complaints was that she hadn't been able to get there very often since her marriage. At school they'd had an inspirational classics teacher who had challenged himself to make his students see that the language of the ancient Greeks could inspire the young people of today. Rivka had often described in colorful detail how they had staged *The Twelve Labors of Hercules*. It had been one of the high points of her school days. (Actually, the story of Hercules has always intrigued me, especially the way it begins: Alcmene gives birth to twins with two different fathers. It was just a myth, of course, for the idea that two eggs could be simultaneously fertilized by two different men was implausible even in ancient Greece. Still, I considered it to be the best explanation yet for the fact that Aaron and I had turned out so very different in every respect.)

As the company around our dining room table grew jollier and jollier—I have always prided myself on being a generous host—it was agreed that some of them would devote one evening a week to helping Rivka mount a production starring factory employees. No Hercules for them, of course; that wouldn't have gone over very well with these former peasants. It would have to be a revue, lavishly produced, and all the local yokels, even workers from rival factories, were to be invited. It would definitely be a novelty in this district, a pioneering endeavor in what's now known as sociocultural work, and it was at first roundly mocked by outsiders. Some of my co-industrialists even accused us of harboring socialist sympathies, but I didn't see the harm in it, frankly. On the contrary, I had a notion that Rivka and her Amsterdam friends were building goodwill for our firm.

In the late spring of 1930, a large audience gathered in the converted workmen's canteen to watch the first and only performance of *Tittle-Tattle*. It was a cabaret show: Marius and his Mice, Toontje and his Carboys, Belinda the Mystic, and Karl the Butcher-Knife Juggler. Toby from export turned out to be a gifted comedian and trumpet player, lab technician Maria played the singing saw, Has and Hanneke twirled around the stage, and Rosie pulled a test rabbit out of a top hat that looked suspiciously like one that belonged to me. Felix the foreman, assisted by a group of lab workers, staged an elaborate goat-circus act; Saartje gleefully declaimed some comic verse, and for the finale, Rivka and her friends had rounded up the would-be performers without special talents into a chorus: the Song-Singers, who didn't even sound all that out of tune. The show was a great success, and it started a long tradition of theatricals at our plant.

14...

"Religion is the opium of the people." That's the only thing that troublemaker Marx ever said with which I am one hundred percent in agreement. Religion is the anesthetic of mankind, the ultimate excuse to remain ignorant.

Three things in life have motivated me and given me the energy to accomplish what I have: one, run a successful business; two, seduce the women who appeal to me; and three, explore and unravel nature's mysteries. For years I thought it was just a matter of time before all the riddles were solved. Silly of me, of course; it shows how naïve I was back then, for neither Mizie nor I will live to see the day, not even if Death continues to get a kick out of making me lie here in my human cage, endlessly drawing out my torment. Neither my legal offspring nor my bastards scattered around the globe—not even their children or their children's children—none of them will be around for that glorious day. No, the human race will have gone to the dogs, dragging Mother Earth with it, long before the last mysteries are revealed.

If there ever was a God, he must have been a schlemiel, just a lousy endocrinologist who never figured out how to fix the flaws in our DNA. I'm telling you, if this schlepper had worked in our lab, I'd never have renewed his contract, I'd have thrown him out on his ass myself, because this so-called God is just a failed biochemist with damn little creativity and even less brains who gives up too easily and has never managed to eliminate all the mistakes in the human formula. He's had millions of years to fine-tune and experiment, and yet his alleged creation, man, is and remains a god-awful mess.

Levine and his team also needed time, of course, to locate, map, and purify the insulin, the estrogen, the testosterone, and all the other secretions. But they got it done within a couple of years, which was fortunate, since it would have been prohibitively expensive otherwise. God is a total failure from a business point of view as well—a rank amateur who has been allowed to go on tinkering for far too long without doing a proper cost-benefit analysis and without being accountable to anyone. If there is a heaven, they forgot to set up a proper finance department up there—big mistake. It astonishes me that in today's world, where reason and commerce are so highly prized, billions of people still can't seem to recognize how bankrupt that global enterprise Heaven & Co. really is.

• • •

I was the infidel in our family. Aaron had always left open the possibility that there might be something more after death. As certain as I was that I was right, both in business and in my private life, that's how uncertain he was. Aaron was a bit of a ditherer. He often said he hated certainty, because it only obscured a fear of life's unpredictability, to which I'd respond that his waffling only masked a fear of making decisions.

He was extremely skeptical of my marriage vows to Rivka. Seated in the front row in the town hall, chewing on his pencil, he grinned when I promised to be true to my wife until death did us part. When his turn came to congratulate us, he wished Rivka good luck and whispered in my ear, "If you remain true to Rivka, as you just promised, I'll eat a kilo of raw pancreas. I'm giving you a year."

Perhaps he was simply jealous of my captivating little wife, or of the fact that she was carrying my child. Although I never caught him showing the least bit of envy; he never appeared to have the hots for her, which worried me. I wondered if he might be a faggot, one of those nancy-boys, or even a pederast—a rather mortifying thought.

How had Aaron and I, with nearly identical genes, having shared the same womb for nine months, grown into such dissimilar people? It was as if our respective character traits had been concocted from two radically different formulae, so that on a cellular level there wasn't a smidgen of genetic compatibility between us. In some primitive societies a multiple birth is regarded as an abomination, the work of evil spirits, or even proof of spousal infidelity. I can't imagine my mother being guilty of the latter; I've never known a colder, less passionate woman. But in indigenous societies it's not uncommon for the weaker of the twins to be killed. In that sense, I suppose the law of nature did win out in the end. I was incontestably the stronger one. Aaron's number came up the year he turned forty-eight. My brother keeps popping up in my thoughts now that I'm shackled here to my prison bed; I no longer seem to have any control over it.

I never contributed to his happiness; I did contribute to his downfall. But in the end, you have to make your own way in life. And if you don't, you run the risk of falling into the trap that someone else, or history, has laid for you.

• • •

Those were hectic times. My dream of conquering the world pharmaceutical market demanded an all-out effort and considerable manpower. Opening up export markets for the insulin, as well as any future products, was essential to Farmacom's growth. Our sales territory had expanded exponentially when we acquired a German subsidary; within a few years its sales were four times those of the parent company.

With our insulin on its way to conquering the world and the money pouring in, Levine was already on to the next big thing. Hormone research, he explained to me, depended on being able to come up with a reproducible test result. American scientists had discovered a method of determining when female mice came into heat. The mouse's vagina gets swollen and moist when the female is ready to mate, as in all other mammals. In a neutered mouse, of course, this reaction will not occur. But the Americans had found out that just one milligram of the substance they had isolated, a certain secretion of the ovaries, was enough to make ten thousand neutered female mice hot to trot.

Levine and his team pounced on this discovery and, thanks to some fanatical researching, and with the help of thousands of live rats, mice, and rabbits, the placentas of innumerable cows, sows, and mares, and a handful of human placentas thrown in for good measure, they became the first in the world to standardize the invisible ovarian ingredient and make it ready for mass production.

Ah, the rutting hormone, that wonderful secretion that makes the female behave in ways men find so delightful! It is that elixir, hidden inside the female organs, that prompts her to open up, that makes her spread her legs, that makes her nipples swell, that makes her pussy wet, that breaks down her resistance. A single milligram is enough for ten thousand mice! Can you blame me, a full-blooded male, for having visions of paradise when I realized the possibilities of the stuff?

The raw material required for this estrus preparation turned out to be most readily available in the urine of pregnant mares. We collected thousands of liters of the stuff, a massive undertaking that had to be repeated every winter.

The farmers we approached were suspicious at first. Four and a half cents for a liter of horse piss? Jaspers, who managed our raw materials department, gave me the gist of the first few conversations he'd had with the farmers. After optimistically setting off on his bike, he'd covered miles and miles of dirt road, only to get the same reaction wherever he went: "They stare at you, their jaws slowly dropping; at first they frown and then they begin to snicker. 'Has that meatpackin' Jew gone right off his rocker? That's a good 'un...four and a half cents fer a liter of horse piss, that's more'n we get fer a friggin' liter of milk. So what you gonna do with it, the piss? Turn it into champagne? No need fer food coloring, anyhow.' " Uproarious laughter, and a jerk of the head suggesting Jaspers get the hell out of there if he didn't want a kick in the backside.

The request for horse piss must have stirred up some vague, atavistic trepidation in the farmers' hearts. Their poverty was great; the depression had affected them as it had everyone else, on top of which a long-standing milk price war had further nibbled away at their already paltry earnings, and so some extra income from collecting what to them was a worthless waste product should have been more than welcome. But they could not fathom why we were so interested in the urine, and it made them wary. After all, make a pact with the devil and you can never go back. The request that sounded so meshuggah to them must have awoken some seed hidden deep within, a fear planted there by their forefathers' dark whispers about the Jewish race and its occult practices. To a simple farmer, there couldn't have been all that much difference between horse piss and the blood of Christian children.

Thanks to the intervention of the local veterinarian, we did in the end manage to overcome their misgivings, and for many years they kept their pregnant mares isolated for a number of gestational weeks, collecting the urine via a special drain into barrels provided by us. The vats were collected at specific sites, then conveyed to the factory in an old jalopy. Sometimes, when the sandy paths got flooded, we'd have to get a day laborer in thigh-high waders to walk ahead of the vehicle to make sure it didn't hit a sinkhole and disappear in the muck with its precious cargo.

It was quite a smelly job, boiling and then filtering twelve thousand liters of horse pee; you had to pour in gallons of alcohol from wicker-wrapped carboys until you wound up with a semisolid mass that might in the end yield just a handful of pure, very fine crystals, which, after being sterilized, could produce amazing, though variable, results.

The farmers' mistrust was rekindled ten years later, when the country was mobilizing for war. Sinister rumors about the purported practices of the Chosen People began to circulate once more, and the farmers started passing up their four and a half cents a liter on account of the whispers—doubtlessly started by the brownshirts, who'd started crawling out of the woodwork and throwing their weight around in public ever more brazenly—that we were using the stuff to make poison gas. Now *that* was what you'd call chutzpah, in light of the genocide to come.

15...

Even in the wild years of the stock market crash and the economic recession that followed, we managed to keep our heads above water. By the time the crisis broke, I was fortunately no longer an inexperienced young whippersnapper but had grown into a tough businessman unafraid of making the hard decisions. During those stormy years, when I'd finessed the handing off of the oil, fats, and soap production to one of our rivals, we also made the decision to diversify by going into canned goods, thus creating a new sales avenue for ourselves. Thanks to such measures, we managed to keep both our well-regarded meatpacking business and the fledgling Farmacom afloat.

Our insulin exports had steadily increased before the market collapse, thanks in no small part to Aaron's efforts; that can't be denied. He had actually succeeded in getting a foothold in Argentina. He had gone there to make a deal with a firm that had thousands of kilos of pancreas to sell us. The "sweetbreads," as we called the gland, had to be deep-frozen for the trip to the Netherlands. We were forced to start importing the stuff because of the growing demand for insulin; the amount produced at our own plant was no longer anywhere near adequate. Then, having made the Argentinians curious as to what on earth we needed their waste product for, Aaron, capitalizing on that interest, created a demand for our insulin in that country.

Furthermore, I didn't shrink from taking draconian measures when necessary. So for several years in a row I would fire a large segment of our workforce just before Christmas, only to rehire them in the new year. It wasn't very nice for them, but had I not done so, I wouldn't have been able to offer them any work that year.

• • •

After many successful experiments on animals, in which sterilized young mice and rabbits went into heat after being given the new substance, and those squirmy little creatures showed themselves ready and willing to procreate, the moment was at hand when the white powder was ready to be tested on humans.

"A critical juncture!" Levine announced, explaining to me that the compound, sterilized and packaged in a special "clean room," would first be administered to women with menstrual problems. The first vials would go out to a select group of clinicians, with instructions to administer it in minute doses. These trials called for the utmost prudence, since one couldn't be certain that a real, live woman would react the same way as a mouse or a rabbit.

The physician was asked to carefully record how many units the patient was given, what changes occurred in the woman's body, and to note any side effects, since it was difficult to ascertain these in lab mammals. Through this process Levine and his team would gradually achieve a better understanding of how the preparation worked.

Levine's extreme caution in these clinical trials severely tried my patience, never one of my strongest qualities. Of course innocent people ought not to be frivolously exposed to unacceptable risk, but still, it was the De Paauw Slaughterhouse and Meatpacking Co. that was bankrolling all this research, a huge investment that had to be recouped as rapidly as possible. Levine always put his rigid dedication to science and his moral principles ahead of everything else; commercial considerations often came last as far as he was concerned.

I was exceptionally interested in the testing of our rutting hormone. Providing the world with life-giving drugs would put us on at least an equal footing with God. Would it really be possible to resuscitate a barren womb, to repair a set of faulty ovaries, and to eventually help an infertile woman conceive? And—holy cow!—would we someday have a way to prevent a pregnancy? After all, our own Ruth wasn't the only kid to come into this world unplanned. How many people are there who started off in life as an accident, the result of a moment of lust or lack of self-control, the living result of an expert seduction or a brutal rape? Hasn't mankind attempted since time immemorial to find a way to forestall pregnancy? All over the world women have tried every method under the sun to prevent conception—stuffing their nether parts with leaves, fruits, or even crocodile dung, for instance, in hopes of being spared yet another mouth to suckle, feed, and protect.

• • •

Levine one day asked me to join him at his favorite Amsterdam establishment, the restaurant with the German name, to give me an update on his research on hormones, which he had started calling "soul glands." The more that was known about these compounds, the clearer it became that they not only were responsible for the organ's own function, but had a marked influence on the overall workings of the human body as well.

"I'd like to name the rutting compound 'Genesis' —as in 'creation,'" he clarified.

I stared at him, appalled. "Genesis? What in hell has got into you? A direct reference to God—it's unthinkable!" I could just see the frown on the pasty visage of the pastor, who had already been around several times asking anxious questions about the drugs we were developing, and had implied that with our most recent discoveries we might be stepping on God's toes, contravening the meekness that behooved mankind.

"Exactly," Levine chuckled. "We are unlocking the secrets of creation. The name Genesis shows that we are taking over God's racket..." He took a sip of his cognac, observing me through half-closed eyes.

"Rafaël," I said, "you may enjoy your little joke, but I'm the one who has to get the stuff sold. A product invoking the work of God doesn't stand a chance of succeeding on a global scale. I'm having enough trouble as it is trying to allay the clergy's mistrust, and it's essential that we avoid drawing their attention to our work. So no, Genesis doesn't exactly strike me as the ideal name for it."

Levine chortled. "Too bad; I just thought I'd give it a try." He promised to find another name. We were calling it Preparation 288 for now, since in Rafaël's lab both the experiments and the test subjects had numbers assigned to them. Then he told me there were indications that the new drug might cure women's menstrual pains, help young mothers with lactating problems, and ease or even overcome the menopausal complaints of older women. And it probably had even more benefits that had yet to be discovered.

• • •

On the same occasion he told me of the latest breakthrough, from Germany. There a scientist had established that the pituitary gland, that little appendage of the brain no larger than a chickpea and until now thought to have no particular function, exerted considerable influence on our rutting hormone. Small pieces of the frontal lobe of a cow's pituitary gland had been implanted into immature female mice. A hundred hours later, all the mice were in heat.

"This might just be the Master Gland," said Levine, pronouncing the last two words as if he were talking about Alfred Nobel himself. "That ugly little appendage could very well be the pilot in the hormonal world's cockpit. Pivotal, this! We must get to work on it immediately. It's a fantastic discovery, quite definitely up our alley; we haven't a day to lose, and I'll need more manpower."

This was par for the course. The De Paauw Slaughterhouse and Meatpacking Co.'s contribution to Levine's laboratory, as stipulated in the original contract, turned out to be just an initial down payment on a never-ending stream of orders and requests for more money to fund further research and augment the team of scientists. One chemist for each new drug was Levine's motto. He seemed to think of our firm as some fat milk-cow, his own personal gravy train.

Both in Amsterdam and at our factory, dozens of experiments were being conducted at once; one group worked out of the university lab, while a scant fifteen men in white coats with notched collars on the top floor of the De Paauw Slaughterhouse and Meatpacking Co. were trying to figure out the exact composition of the secretions capable of producing such amazing results.

In her office next door to our improvised lab, my perky and able Agnes was busy all day dispatching letters and telegrams to every corner of the world and forwarding lab results to Amsterdam. But she had to spend even more of her energies on a constant flood of demands and admonitions reaching us from Amsterdam by mail, telephone, and telegram needing immediate attention. There was no end to the shopping lists: rat cages, incubation boxes, aluminum containers, pressing bags, stone pots, meat presses, hundreds of live rabbits, mice, and rats, tons of yeast, dried blood, pigs' bristles and pork liver, chicken genitals, adrenal glands, horse ovaries, bovine follicular fluid and pituitary glands, powdered thyroid and placenta, bone marrow, mucous membranes, deep-frozen bovine pancreas—every other minute, it seemed, a new demand would come in for something the university lab needed straightway. All this took up a disproportionate amount of our employees' time. It wasn't just the effort required to track down the materials; every order tended to come with its own set of problems, since finding the best ways to conserve or convey the stuff was still a question of trial and error.

But that was nothing compared with the way Levine treated us. He was never happy with our efforts; he was always criticizing our research methods, which he considered too slapdash or sloppy, or else he was unhappy with the promotion campaigns, or with our global marketing strategies, or our domestic or foreign outreach. We kept hearing that we weren't running enough by him, that we weren't heeding his directives, and that we were doing it all wrong. He wanted to be consulted on every trivial decision. He expected to receive an extensive account, or "business report," as he called it, several times a week from us, to keep him abreast of everything, every single little detail, under consideration. His obnoxious meddling was starting to turn my initial gratitude into a growing sense of irritation. It wasn't only me; everyone at Farmacom, all the workers putting their heart and soul into making our firm succeed, felt that way. I went through several very capable directors in those years, people I'd have liked to keep on, who quit because they did not like being constantly second-guessed and treated like schoolchildren by the slave driver in Amsterdam. Never in my life have I known anyone who was as much of a control freak as Levine. Besides, it galled me that he had so little faith in me or my people, and that he hardly ever showed any appreciation of my success in getting his inventions sold as far afield as Indonesia, China, and South America.

And yet I just couldn't let the enormous potential of the pituitary gland slip through our fingers. Levine always knew how to whet my hunger, and time and time again, dependent as I was on his expertise, I ended up acceding to his demands.

16...

My talks with the priest turned into a tradition that I consciously kept going. The clergyman never brought up Rivka's activities, probably because the casual, nonsectarian gatherings she organized were not conducted in the strict Catholic spirit he'd originally had in mind.

And yet we did reach a certain measure of trust in our relationship. We met several times a year in the privacy of my office to discuss any problems with the workers, as well as any items of concern to his flock. Our conversations thus provided me with some useful insight into how our products were perceived by the Church. The insulin and the vitamins we manufactured could reasonably be expected to bring a certain amount of goodwill, but Preparation 288, which had recently come on the market, was being greeted with a great deal of mistrust. After all, the Lord moves in mysterious ways, and it was felt that deciding whether someone is fertile or not ought to be left up to our Maker; interfering in that domain was tantamount to blasphemy.

One day the prelate told me he was sometimes called upon to counsel young brides or wives who were having trouble conceiving. If his advice did not result in a pregnancy, he would recommend that they resign themselves to their fate. Another group suffered from the opposite affliction (and here the padre gave a rather sour smile): an overabundance of offspring. In that case he always tried to convince them that having a large brood was a blessing.

As I listened to the priest's hokum, it occurred to me that I did not have to rely solely on Levine—who was growing more demanding and arrogant by the minute—for experimentation. My own factory was teeming with human guinea pigs! Saartje in export, Milly and Rosie and all the others doing their stinking best down there for nine hours a day, could be more than just a docile herd of meatpackers. I had never before viewed the frumpy wenches working on the shop floor as real people, women with typical female problems. My workforce and Farmacom's innovations had been two quite separate entities to me until then, but the black-frocked priest's lisped confidences suddenly brought them together, opening up a world of possibilities. Just as my factory's generous supply of pancreas had been a bonanza to Levine, so my female employees could be used as test subjects in my own experimental Garden of Eden. A fertile paradise to which Levine would have no access, and where I could garden to my heart's content.

• • •

You might say that my experiment was a hobby that got a little out of control. My intention was to conduct a small, private research project. I now explain it as the weakness of a young man coping with many stressful responsibilities on a daily basis. Just as my youngest, my Ezra, hasn't seemed able to control himself at the pinnacle of his career, so you might characterize my actions in the early years of the rutting hormone as my own personal Waterloo. They set off a string of events that brought me to the edge of the abyss, and left my reputation dangling by a thin thread. But it was Aaron who stepped over the edge and tumbled into the void—no, leaped of his own volition. And I got out of the experimentation business before anyone could kick me out. Knowing how to hang on, that's what's important.

My own experimentation with that fascinating rutting hormone, the one that seemed to have the ability to cure the poor girls and women in my factory of their ills, began as a sincere attempt to alleviate their suffering. At the same time, the opportunity to make my own observations and draw my own conclusions without being subjected to Levine's constant carping was too tempting to resist. It was a clumsy effort to clear at least a small space for myself where I might operate independently from Levine and gain some insights of my own into an area where otherwise I was utterly dependent on the Prussian prof.

From Rivka, whom I didn't tell of my plans, I found out which of the women at the plant had fertility or menopausal problems. I decided to focus on the young married gals who longed for motherhood but were still childless after several years. Can you blame a young man for zeroing in on that particular group instead of tired, flabby old hags complaining of hot flashes or insomnia? Besides, it's hard to teach an old dog new tricks. I was, after all, an amateur researcher, working on my own, and there was only so much I could do.

Even though Aaron was in charge of personnel—just one of the many responsibilities we had divvied up between us back then—I did sometimes have occasion to summon an employee up to my office myself, usually only in the case of some serious misdemeanor. I was top man at the firm, after all; I knew how to deal with the miscreants. I usually sent them packing with a thundering sermon, telling them I would make it my personal business to make sure no other firm in the area would hire them either.

I approached my embryonic project with proper caution. First I informed Aaron I wanted to get a better picture of our factory workers' circumstances. We were in the throes of the most serious economic recession the world had ever seen, and since in those uncertain times a reorganization might become necessary, I wanted to be in a position to make the right decisions when the time came. I would therefore be asking individual workers to come up to my office for an interview from time to time. As I was explaining this, Aaron stopped chewing on his pencil and gave me an icy stare.

"What are you up to?" he asked coldly.

"Just what I said," I replied, and stared back at him poker-faced. "We live in uncertain times, and I'm the one in charge here. I feel responsible for each and every employee of ours, therefore I want to know a little more about them before making any decision about their fate. At this difficult time, if you lose your job in these parts, you're cooked; you know that as well as I."

"Indeed," said Aaron. "I am only too aware that these are rotten times for our people. What bothers me is your sudden concern. The present crisis isn't something new to them, you know, as it is for our directors. Our people down in the slaughterhouse, the ones slicing and packing bacon nine hours a day, the ones manning the ovens and carting off the waste, they've never known anything except trouble, misery, and want. They've been down and out all their lives. People living in these parts have always had the wolf at their door—nothing new under the sun, really. I've never seen you getting all softhearted about them before. So, Motke, what the hell has gotten into you?"

For a moment I toyed with the idea of taking him into my confidence. Aaron couldn't stand Levine, and he could probably relate to my fantasy of getting rid of him. But we weren't there yet, not by a long shot, and I wasn't sure Aaron would condone my idea of experimenting on our employees. Also, I was a little embarrassed about wanting to start my own project, since the secrecy required and my lack of scientific know-how couldn't help but make it amateurish. I decided I'd rather not have my brother's scrutiny. And Aaron? He didn't trust me one bit, grumbled and pouted, but in the end let me do as I wanted, as usual. He always let me have my way, no matter what the price.

• • •

Annie Bakels from packing was the first shiksa I called up to my office: married two years ago at age seventeen to Klaus Bakels, a butcher likewise employed in our slaughterhouse, and still childless. She entered looking pale and nervous, ushered in by Agnes, who had been asked to fetch the girl from the factory floor. Annie stopped just inside the door, where she took off her white cap and bowed her head. I walked up to her, led her to the chair across from my desk, then went to sit down in my own armchair, with its elaborately carved wooden backrest crowned with a peacock, and nodded at my loyal secretary to leave us. Agnes took her time moseying out of there, obviously dying to know what this was about; something told her it wasn't going to be the usual scolding.

Annie sat hunched up like a frail little bird, her eyes on the floor, waiting, a sight not all that different from that of a quivering laboratory rat cowering in a corner of its cage after an injection, as if trying to make itself invisible. I attempted to put her at ease with some friendly small talk, which only seemed to alarm her even more. It wasn't easy to bring up the subject with that little heap of misery, who'd apparently been driven into a panic by the mere fact of having been called to my office. I cursed the fact that my only interaction with my workers heretofore had been to play the bad cop.

"Don't be scared," I said, smiling my most charming smile. "You haven't done anything wrong, that's not the reason I sent for you."

"But Mr. De Paauw," she whispered, "then why am I here? I'm always on time, never out sick."

"I am aware of that," I quickly reassured her; "no, I sent for you in order to discuss something of a very personal nature. It's about the problems you and your husband are having. I realize it might seem a bit alarming, the boss wanting to speak with you about this, and of course I don't wish to be disrespectful, but I believe I may be able to help you."

She raised her head for the first time, tears glinting in her eyes, the panic now full-blown.

"Problems? Me and my Klaus? But we ain't got no problems, us!" Her eyes darted wildly around the room, as if she might have missed something she ought to have noticed. She went on uncertainly. "He's a good man, he is, ain't he? He don't beat me, he don't drink, we're good together."

Even that statement came out sounding like a question. I quickly went on. "I am delighted to hear it, that's fortunate. Still, I think there's something in your marriage that isn't all it should be, am I right?"

I'd expected the tête-à-tête with my employee to be a little less work. I'm just not cut out for tiptoeing tactfully around a subject. Seducing a woman was one thing, but getting one to agree to take part in a scientific experiment required quite a different approach, one at which I'd had no prior experience. I was used to practicing my arts of seduction on a more sophisticated type of woman. This timid, vulnerable little thing was quite another kettle of fish. I cleared my throat.

"As you may know, at Farmacom we've been working on developing new kinds of drugs."

She nodded almost imperceptibly, as if the slightest movement on her part might set off some terrifying cataclysm. I felt a surge of impatience. Goddamn it, I was in a position to supply this little minx with the brat she so longed for—as long as that bastard Bakels didn't put the kibosh on it. But for that to happen, she *would* have to be just a little more cooperative. I didn't have all day, I had a board of directors meeting scheduled in half an hour. This little bundle of misery had to be gone by then. I decided to push on and get to the heart of the matter.

"We have come up with a drug that may overcome barrenness, and if you'd like, I could provide you with some. For free."

She raised her head and stared at me like a deer caught in the headlights. I could tell from her dazed look that what I'd said had gone completely over her head.

"A home without children is like a church without an organ," I went on, hoping that the analogy would lead to greater comprehension. She did now seem to get it, because a tear was beginning to trickle down her pale cheek. The subject was out in the open. I staunchly continued. "Tell me, are your periods regular?"

She looked down again and, with the barest of shrugs, shook her head no. My heart leaped.

"Fine," I said; "in that case I can help you. I'll give you a package of tablets to take back with you; swallow one of these three times a day for two months. Then come back here in eight weeks and tell me if you've started menstruating. If so, there's a good chance that if you keep taking the pills you'll soon be pregnant. Understood?"

She nodded slowly. You could practically hear her brain creaking as she tried to take it all in, which took quite some effort.

"One other important thing," I continued. "I don't want you to mention this to anyone. Not to the girls in your department, not to your parents, and not even to your husband. Just think how surprised he'll be when you tell him there's finally one on the way. So that's the deal. Break the deal, and—no more pills for you. Not only that, but both you and your man get the sack, is that understood?"

I slid the carefully prepared packet of tablets across the desk and gestured for her to take it. She turned it around warily, opened it, and sniffed at the pills. She pulled a face, since the horse urine tablets definitely had a bad odor. We hadn't yet come up with a solution for that.

"It ain't dangerous, is it, sir?" she asked.

I reassured her it wasn't and told her the stuff had been tested on thousands of lab animals, and that a famous Amsterdam professor had been giving this remedy to some big-city doctors to treat their rich lady patients. And that she was the only girl in our town right now lucky enough to have her female problem cured for free. Then I asked her to do something for me in return: keep track of whether there were any physical changes in her body and note these every day. Any discharge, bleeding, dizziness, stomach cramps, excess or lack of energy, appetite—any little thing could be of interest. I gave her a little notebook and a pencil with which to jot these things down.

"Because," I said in conclusion, "rabbits can't give us that sort of information, but smart girls like you can."

Her wan little face was flushed bright red as she left my office with the packet of pills, the notebook and pencil tucked into the pocket of her smock.

It's gone now, the feeling of excitement I got from seeing the little wench leave my office with those tablets, and I don't think I'll ever get it back. The triumph I felt then has been completely crushed by the events that were the eventual outcome of that afternoon.

17...

My condition worsens by the day. Not all at once; on the contrary, the deterioration seems to be progressing in near-imperceptible increments, gradually weakening me like the doddering white mouse in its metal cage in a corner of the lab, the researchers' canary in the coal mine. When the poor animal, with a gasp, breathes its last and collapses onto its back, its legs sticking up in the air stiff and cold, the researchers know it's time to air the place out because there's been a lethal buildup of fumes in the lab. Since I haven't yet kicked the bucket, Mizie can tell that her ploy to postpone the bitter end is working.

Here I lie in my jailhouse bed, my mind as clear as the alcohol in our demijohns. My mind seems determined to remain sharp, so that I'll have all my marbles as I'm forced to watch every physical part of me break down bit by bit. My stomach no longer tolerates solid food, and my beast has given up the ghost.

Once I thought it would be different. I'd have preferred to die in the saddle, so to speak. Tommy Cooper, the well-known comedian, keeled over onstage of a heart attack, and the audience howled with laughter. I can't think of a finer death for a person in his profession. I'd always imagined that I'd croak while making love, right at the grand, overwhelming, and glorious climax. Could there be a more gratifying send-off? I snake my right hand under the plastic edge of the diaper, fumbling for the pathetic remains of my beast. Limp, quivering flesh, a hopelessly sad case; my decrepit old engine has sputtered its last.

But my ticker keeps beating, and Mizie refuses to let me go. Is it because she's afraid of being left behind, or is it because this is her revenge, to make me pay for all the miserable years she spent at my unfaithful side?

Right after we were married she conveniently forgot the fact that when we first started going at it hot and heavy—I no longer in the flower of youth, she still fresh and juicy—I had also been seeing a whole slew of other women. It is man's nature to play the field, as everyone knows. Did she really think I would shed my reputation like some useless old overcoat the moment I was lured into marrying her? Oh, to hell with marriage, that detestable institution. I've always been dead set against it, and the only reason I fell into the trap again was to calm my old man's fear that my seductive powers would dry up someday. But as I said yes for a second time, I secretly swore to myself (not in vain, as it turned out) that this second marriage would not put a damper on my escapades either.

Mizie was only too eager to step into the spot vacated by my first wife. I was candid about letting her know beforehand that faithfulness was never part of my repertoire, and that I had no interest in being caged in. Young and smitten as she was, she probably chose not to take my warning seriously, hoping she'd be able to tame me in spite of it. She has suffered bitterly as a consequence. Now that I have grown totally dependent on her devoted, loving care, I am cut down to size, reduced to some kind of infantile monster, the physical wreck I never wished to be. What was the fucking point of signing that living will?

I know she's locked it away in her desk somewhere two floors down from my own prison.

Was it revenge that drove her to engage this provocative tootsie with the big tits to wash me, knowing full well I can't get it up anymore? Like waving a slab of bacon under the nose of a toothless cat and getting a kick out of watching it suffer. Mizie could end my torment right now; it's in her power to do so, if she'd just stop force-feeding me her revolting pureed vegetables, the bland soups and horrid nutri-drinks. But it's clear she'd rather put it off for as long as possible. Her smile oozes love and venom by turns as she strokes my leathery face with an ice-cold finger or pinches my decrepit old-geezer's mug roughly, impatiently, forcing me to open up for her so she can stuff her disgusting baby swill into it, or else push the spout of the plastic beaker in to make me swallow some repulsive brew.

And yet, even under these deplorable conditions, I have managed to eke out a small victory. I have succeeded, I am happy to report, in winning over the cute young thing. My physical body may have deserted me, my magnetic smile may be sitting in the water glass next to my bed like some daft Cheshire cat, and my witty banter may be reduced to inarticulate mumbling, but apparently I'm still capable of making a wench come running at my beck and call, even lying here dressed in nothing but baggy striped pajama pants instead of a custom-made suit. I assume my PJs don't look that different from the ragged prison pants in which Aaron probably spent the last freezing months of his life.

I have always hated pajamas, and I never wore them in my life. Why should I? My beast was cooped up often enough as it was, and at the time of my return to the Netherlands from my luxurious London exile, striped pajamas were as abhorred as the

"Horst Wessel Song." But these days Mizie likes to hoist me into a pair in order to keep the giant diaper in place.

The sexy young thing has noticed my interest in Ezra, who is now a front-page news item, and has taken it upon herself to show me the papers the moment my loving prison warden leaves the house, since Mizie forbids any stimulus that might lead to overexcitement.

The wretched but still pulsating mechanism that is my heart skipped a beat when I caught sight of the photograph: my proud boy, my own vain, greedy, pushy blood, looking unshaven and unkempt, his graying hair disheveled, being led off like a common criminal, in the city that should have been the stage of his greatest triumph. Handcuffed, hands crossed in front, as if they were afraid he might kick a policeman in the balls. Utter humiliation.

The strength of one strand of female hair is mightier than any rope; its pull can bring down an entire career, as evidenced by my own life as well as by Ezra's downfall.

Ah, that thing that seems to have a life of its own, that can wreck both your peace of mind and your professional life—the irresistible lure of the contours of a secretary's breasts poking through her flimsy summer frock during a meeting about some bulk insulin shipment, or the coffee lady's backside rising in the air as she bends down to take a fresh can of milk from the lower shelf of her cart, a glorious tush that in all its shapely plumpness seems to shout at you right through the tight black stuff of her trim little dress, *Touch me, hug me, pinch me!*

Or, say, the intimate chat in my office with one of the young women taking Preparation 288, some with great success, some with none. If after several months of treatment there was still no baby on the way, I'd be looking at a little puddle of misery, the legs slightly ajar, the eyes brimming with tears, begging me for another chance. " 'Cause Annie and Bertha, they're in the family way now, Mr. De Paauw, so why ain't it working for me?" The pleading look, as though beseeching the Messiah himself, that moved me to rise from my chair, walk around to where she was sitting, and console her with a pat on the head, a hand on her back, as it occurred to me that the cause of her infertility might very well be her husband's semen count. And then, pressing her teary face to my torso in a comforting hug, I'd feel my beast rise up like a hound on the scent, straining to be let off the leash.

Self-control has simply never been our strong suit. Playing with fire, that's another thing my youngest spawn and I have in common.

18...

So it came about that in the period when the rutting hormone was being used in the development of an ever-growing number of drugs for female problems, the red light outside my door would come on with increasing regularity, indicating that I was not to be disturbed.

I was aware that stories were making the rounds about my magnanimous impulses; it was whispered that you could get a lot more from Mr. De Paauw than just pills. Girls from the factory floor were starting to find excuses to come up to my office and offer themselves to me, either subtly or less so, and not always because they were longing for a child. Although I did not as a rule like to disappoint these willing volunteers, I preferred to pick the girls out for myself. Sometimes, on one of my factory rounds, some young chick would attract my eye, and I'd stop to chat with her to get a sense of whether she was interested in taking our acquaintance to the next level. It was their eyes that told me they were willing, even if they didn't even know it themselves. Of the ones I invited up to my office, some would simply offer themselves up to me, as it were, on a platter, whereas others, reticent at first, might need a little more persuasion. I must confess that their inhibitions didn't always hold me back. There's something titillating in a little resistance, I find; a bit of a struggle, a head shaking no, a hand fending me off, a tussle, until the wench accepts the inevitable and lets you have your way, limp as a lab rabbit receiving an injection. Then, when it was over, I always knew how to make the girl feel okay about it, reassuring her with a loving pat on the rump before sending her back down to her workstation.

All of this didn't have a lot to do with scientific research, naturally. My Garden of Eden was my own private domain, however. I didn't have to report to Rafaël about it, and by rights it should also have fallen outside of Aaron's morally superior oversight. But Aaron was starting to grow more and more suspicious about the parade of young girls trickling into my office and the red light blinking outside my door. His gloom seemed to be deepening by the day too, and as time went on I felt increasingly uncomfortable in his presence. The telling looks that signaled he was watching me made it harder to convince myself I was doing something good not just for myself, but also for my female visitors. Sometimes I wished I had a bit more of Aaron's detachment, and that I wasn't always ruled by the will of my rod. It would certainly have been worth it to be able to concentrate on the countless essential tasks demanding my full attention instead of being constantly distracted. That sex drive of mine—I wouldn't want to be without it. Yet at the same time it was a curse I could not escape.

I was usually the last one to leave the administrative floor. One evening, noticing that the light in Aaron's office was still on, I knocked on his door and went in. My brother was seated at his desk. He looked up at me darkly.

"What's keeping you here so late?" I asked him.

He shrugged, raising his hunched shoulders even higher than they already were. His eyes, the same brown as mine but without the purposeful gleam, stared at me dully.

"There isn't much for me to rush home for," he muttered list-lessly. "Whether it's here or there, the silence is the same. At least in here I can pretend I'm making a difference. Even if all I'm doing is propping up your house of cards."

"Do you mean you're lonely? That you wish you had a wife?" I asked, puzzled. It was the first hint I'd ever had that he wasn't happy being a bachelor.

"Does it surprise you?" he asked rather sardonically. "Never thought your brother could be anything other than your handy little helper, did you? Never suspected that poor, bumbling old Aaron might be a man with needs and desires, have you? Never considered that I might dream of a woman waiting for me at home, even if she's only half as good a catch as the trophy wife you bagged for yourself by banging her?"

"No," I said, "or rather, yes, of course I've thought about it, and I've never understood why women seem to leave you cold. At first I used to wonder if you were more attracted to men, but I've never seen you show the slightest inclination in that direction either."

Aaron laughed. "You don't know me at all, little brother," he scoffed, his gaze traveling outside the window. "I think that I see through you far better than you see through me. It isn't hard for me to figure out what you're up to with the girls you call into your office, you know. Whenever I catch myself in a moment of weakness, like right now, I only have to think about you, and how you're cheating on your lovely wife, to squash every bit of desire I have. I wouldn't for the life of me want to turn into a despicable bastard like you!"

I looked down at the ground. Aaron and Levine were pretty much the only ones in the world who could make me feel bad about myself.

"I do struggle with it, and try to stop myself," I said sullenly. "Still, I don't see that I'm doing anything wrong. I'm giving them the child they so dearly want, or helping them get over their sexual frustration."

Aaron let out a loud and bitter laugh. "A factory boss who fucks the young girls in his employ, and then has the *gall* to claim with a straight face that he isn't doing anything wrong! Motke, you're a disgusting piece of shit."

"And you're a frigid, gutless schmuck who doesn't have what it takes," I fumed, and stormed out, slamming the door behind me.

In the days following this episode, Aaron's words kept coming back to me. I was in the process of purchasing a tract of land across from the plant, since I envisaged that we'd need to expand soon and wanted to provide Farmacom with its own research and lab-animal facility. It was an exciting prospect, but the thought of Aaron's rebuke soured my mood. I couldn't help thinking somberly that my brother was right. I was constantly cheating on my "lovely wife," Rivka, and abusing my position of authority in the company.

I resolved to rid myself of these bad habits and to be an irreproachable husband and boss from now on. I made a concerted effort to remain faithful to my Rivka and to leave the factory girls alone, even sending away the ones who came to me voluntarily, trying instead to focus all my energies on the two companies, which took so much work to run.

I kept it up for two weeks. Like an alcoholic who's on the wagon and can't think of anything but the damn bottle, I found those days an interminable hell. I just wasn't up to handling our German subsidiary with my usual sangfroid or decisiveness as they tried to wriggle out of our price agreement. My normally sharp mind seemed to be wholly and obsessively occupied with female buttocks, boobs, and pussy. My common sense was in thrall to my beast, which would get hard at the most inopportune times. Jerking off provided only temporary relief. At night, as soon as the children were in bed, I'd try to get Rivka to have sex with me, but I was so importunate and impatient about it that one fine night she pushed me away and announced she wouldn't sleep with me anymore. She banished me to the guest room and, from that day on, avoided all physical contact with me.

• • •

On the seventh day of the second week I gave up. I rang for fat Bertha, who wasn't one of my test subjects but a zaftig, willing tart from meatpacking only too eager for my attentions. As soon as she walked into my office and closed the door, I pushed her over to the sofa, unbuttoned her white smock, and thrust my way in.

"Gee, Mr. Motke," she exclaimed in surprise, "ain't you got ants in your pants! I never seen you this horny!" She looked up at me, amused.

I stayed inside her a while longer, my tormented soul slowly calming down. Once my breathing had returned to normal, I began petting her solicitously, more lovingly than I had ever done before with the broad, and then I took her another time. Afterward I thanked her and, before she left, slipped an unnecessarily generous sum into her apron pocket. I was genuinely grateful to her for giving me the opportunity to recover my old, inescapable self, and decided I'd never attempt to deny my true nature again. Living up to my brother's standards was impossible; it would have derailed my marriage, my business, and my life.

• • •

And so it began all over again. Of course I had to take care that my activities did not become common knowledge. I knew Aaron would never have the guts to give me away, but caution was in order. My position as head of the firm required a great deal of integrity, naturally; a bad reputation would be bad for the entire company as well as for my ever-growing network of important connections. I was regarded as the point man for the Dutch meat industry. Not a Nobel Prize winner, certainly, but nothing to sneeze at either, for a high school dropout. My stellar reputation led to an invitation to chair the Netherlands Pork Board, an organization founded after the crash to bolster the national meat industry. I was delighted, naturally, to accept the position. Four years later, however, after a government inquiry into alleged conflicts of interest, I sadly had to resign. It had actually been quite a nice little sideline, and it was too bad that a few unusually vigilant politicians had made that glitch come to light. But since I had stepped down without a murmur of protest, I was invited to join the Council of Government Commissioners in return for being such a good sport and, on top of that, was appointed commercial adviser to the Dutch government on agrarian affairs. Those prestigious posts eventually led to an invitation from the Royal Palace. In time I became a welcome guest there, and was honored with the title of royal merchant, purveyor to the queen. I was gaining more respect abroad as well, and became adept at making friends in all the high places in the global business and diplomatic worlds.

I made it quite clear to the girls that the reason for their visits to my office were to remain our little secret, and if even a whisper came out about the encounters on my "Cozy Corner" (the tasteful sofa Rivka had picked out for me), it would mean instant dismissal for them as well as any other family member in our employ. The threat was enough to do the trick. The depression had not yet run its course, and not one of the bimbos was prepared to jeopardize her job or those of her relatives. Besides, the wenches usually felt complicit. After all, hadn't they been warned, both by the priest and by their parents, not to provoke a man's lust? And I'd remind them ever so subtly that I had read an unmistakable invitation in their eyes, even if it hadn't been conscious on their part. Finally, it was still a common adage in this provincial backwater that it was easier to watch a passel of fleas than to keep a young maid in line. So any girl who was a victim of sexual abuse must herself be partially to blame.

• • •

I hadn't realized how dangerous my little game was until, some months after my failed attempt at self-restraint, I heard Bertha, who was waiting outside my door to be invited in, tell Agnes: "Just gonna go in there an' earn meself a new summer frock..."

She walked in still grinning at her own little joke, but her smile froze when she saw my icy stare. She tried to give me a hug, but I slapped her arm away. "You've broken your side of the bargain," I snapped. "Not a word to anyone; that was the deal."

I glared at her. The slap seemed to have made little impression.

"Gee, Mr. Motke," she wheedled, contrite, wagging her nicely filled ass, "ain't *we* in a bad mood. Now don't get yer knickers all in a twist... It was just jesting, an' Agnes ain't blind to the hanky-panky goin' on in here, surely? I never done talk about it to no one else, promise. I wouldn't dare..."

I told her to get out and thought about firing her, but decided not to, because a girl like that might create a stink once she was no longer dependent on me for her paycheck. No point digging myself into a ditch. I did have another talk with her later and made it clear that there would be no more rendezvous on my sofa. I warned her again that if she whispered so much as one syllable about what we'd been up to, I would sack both her and her father, a glassblower in our factory. All I could hope for was that she would soon get embroiled in other escapades, and the trysts on my sofa would fade into the background.

"Playing with fire means you'll eventually get burned," I mused that day, thinking of the risks I brought onto myself through my capers with the factory girls. But as I read the mail, as I went over the monthly figures—which were up in spite of the recession—I decided that, in fact, my work was likewise nothing but a dangerous game that I played all day long. It's what you do if you're a successful entrepreneur. You have to throw your weight around, toot your own horn, score points, walk the finest of lines, lick people's boots, make a big splash, bluff, gamble, and brag; short of that, you won't get anywhere in a world where everyone is out to crush the competition.

The race had acquired a new dimension now that Rafaël was on the verge of tracking down the male hormone. We'd been behind the eight ball on insulin and the rutting hormone, secretions that had initially been isolated by others, but now Rafaël and his team of expert scientists appeared to have a real crack at beating their German rivals and becoming the first to isolate the male hormone. I couldn't have asked for a more satisfying payback for all the cash, sweat, and tears we'd put in over the years than to see this discovery being made in our name. That was why I let nothing get in the way of Rafaël's work. Despite my profound irritation at his exacting demands, I provided him with everything he needed to pry that precious little hormone out of those bull pizzles.

Running a business venture is playing with fire. If you're scared of getting burned, you'll never make it big. In my business life I ran one risk after another, all the livelong day. So why, of all things, give up those private moments of relaxation and bliss with my cuties? No, I had tried, and I couldn't. The price was still much too high.

19...

One day in the summer of 1935, I received an urgent request to come to Rafaël's lab. When I got there he showed me a robust, proudly crowing cock that was restlessly pacing the confines of its small cage, waving its glossy tail and shaking the splendid bright-red comb that crowned its head. The rooster's comb is the testament of male performance, the showcase of male virility. Like a man's business suit, the cockscomb shows the little woman that if she takes her chances with him, she won't be sorry. She can tell from the flamboyance of the headgear that its wearer is a superlative choice, guaranteed to deliver the finest offspring. Here, in Rafaël's cage, was an extraordinarily fine specimen, crowing at the top of its lungs.

"Good-looking bird," I commented, looking at Rafaël quizzically. I live in the countryside, where roosters are a dime a dozen; I didn't need to waste precious time traveling to a lab in Amsterdam to admire one.

"Good-looking bird?" Rafaël scoffed. "An exceptional bird, this is. The finest cock I've ever seen in my life. This bird is our prize achievement. And do you want to know why?"

It had to be something to do with the search for the male hormone. But exactly what, I couldn't say. This was typical of

Rafaël, to rub my reliance on him in my face. Was he doing it on purpose, did he get a kick out of revealing my ignorance? Or was I just being oversensitive?

"This, my dear Motke," Rafaël went on, taking no notice of my annoyance, "this superb specimen, that given the chance will go for its rival's jugular, that makes every hen that comes near go weak in the knees, this animal was, not so long ago, a capon, parted from its balls right here in the lab. And, as you may know, a capon's flag droops at half mast, the comb vanishes, the cock becomes a lame duck, stops crowing, and turns into an emasculated wimp."

I looked at him, incredulous. Was this it? Had they actually managed to isolate the male hormone?

"We've done it, Motke." The words were uttered with such force that Rafaël might well have swallowed a dose of testosterone himself. "We have worked out the composition of the stuff. Behold this brilliant creature, risen like the phoenix from its miserable capon ashes; here is the apotheosis of our first wholly independent scientific discovery. For two weeks we've been injecting it with the bovine testicle extract, and behold, the neutered bird is transformed into this splendid, aggressive, crowing cock, sporting the world's most spectacular comb. The article has already been sent off for publication. The world will very shortly hear about it. We *won!*"

We fell into each other's arms, Rafaël enfolding me in his imposing girth. I had never been so warmly embraced by another man. My father wasn't one for physical contact; he found it disgusting. When we were little, Aaron sometimes tried snuggling close to me, especially when he was scared or had been chewed out by my father, but I would invariably push him away. I hated the idea that my father might see us, and that the sharp gibes normally reserved for Aaron would also be directed at me.

Now I felt Rafaël's heart beating against my chest, and, strange to say, I was flooded with a profound sense of peace. All the usual stress seemed to fade away, taking with it the burden of the heavy responsibilities that normally weighed me down. The economic crisis that was still raging, capable of sinking the entire global economy, the shouts of the bully across the border threatening to bring our whole world to an end, our firm getting panned for charging market prices for our medical products, the Church's mistrust of our latest discoveries, which the papists claimed were blasphemous evils—all of it seemed to melt away like snow in the sun. Just for a moment, as I leaned against Rafaël's chest, he became the father I never had. A powerful man, a winner, but one who didn't need to prove his manhood by keeping others at a distance. No, he was the father with an unstinting heart. With that hug, Rafaël, the incomparable colossus from Amsterdam, the Prussian soldier, the Jewish Maecenas, allowed me, Motke, to share in his triumph. In that remarkable moment I felt a sense of connection stronger than I have ever had with a woman. Never would I feel closer to anyone in my life. A moment of total bliss, born from our combined near-superhuman effort, the absurd pressure we'd been under, and our daring, groundbreaking alliance that was about to bring us worldwide fame.

We had done it! We were the first in the world to isolate the male hormone!

20...

One evening not long after that memorable day, Rivka and I set out for Amsterdam to celebrate with Rafaël, his Dauphine, his colleagues, and a few other friends the testosterone discovery as well as the publication of the related article in a scientific journal. Aaron stayed home. He seemed to be growing more morose by the day. My brother's lethargy sometimes worried me, but on this particular occasion I didn't care. I did not insist when he told me he'd rather stay home in his cold, lonely house, with its ingrained smell of cigarette smoke and stale whiskey.

The mood in Rafaël's crowded house was exuberant, the dinner abundant, the consumption of alcohol prodigious. A grand opportunity to let our hair down, at a time when, aside from this triumph, there wasn't much to celebrate.

One guest after another made a heartfelt toast; there were many predictions of a trip to Stockholm, since everyone there believed the Nobel Prize was in the bag. Rafaël reported on the League of Nations conference in London, where his discovery had received attention from the Health Committee. Salomons, my father-in-law, raised his glass to the late Dr. Brown-Séquard, the eccentric and much-maligned scientist who, in 1889, at the age of seventy-two, had injected himself with blood taken from guinea pig testicles, suspecting it contained a substance capable of reversing the aging process, whereupon he said he felt thirty years younger. After some weeks of treating himself with the guinea pig blood, the old codger, who literally had one foot in the grave, was apparently able to run up and down stairs like a youngster, to put in long days at work, and, to his inexpressible delight, to get his rocks off again. His shrunken pecker seemed to have regained its ability to get up and go. The fellow had been drunk with joy. Even though the scientific community wrote him off as a charlatan and the articles he published were derided, especially on account of the sex, he did get the popular press interested, resulting in a veritable stampede to his Paris institute by graybeards eager to be injected with the elixir purported to restore their youthful vitality.

"To Brown-Séquard," said Salomons, rising from his chair, "who was not deterred by the narrow-mindedness of the Philistines, and paved the way to the male hormone's discovery, even if he couldn't explain how it worked!"

The male hormone is capable of many things. But in my present state, a second youth, a miraculous resurrection from my metal cage, is no longer in the cards. Older than all those eager French geezers hoping for a new lease on life, and also wiser in the wake of a whole century of scientific progress, I know that for me there's no turning back the clock.

At Levine's party the possibilities of the new discovery were extensively debated. Wild fantasies about cures for all kinds of unlikely diseases flew back and forth across the table. It was pure speculation, of course; so far the stuff had only been tested on the caponized cocks and castrated mice, all turned into potent fertility machines after they were given the miracle drug.

It didn't take long for the conversation to turn to the eunuchs of the past—the poor sods who were mutilated in ancient Egypt, Greece, and many Islamic countries, in order to guard the sultans' harems. Castration was considered an effective precaution against any fornication between sentries and concubines.

"Incidentally," Rafaël snickered, "whether the sultans were correct in their assumption is questionable. There are known cases of eunuchs—a minority, to be sure—who remained capable of having erections, even orgasms. So they may have been having a wild old time in those harems, especially since the ladies didn't have to worry about getting pregnant. This was possibly the seraglio's best-kept secret."

The Dauphine, our walking music encyclopedia, mentioned that in seventeenth-century Italy, boys were castrated at the age of eight or so, usually in the hope that the castrato's voice would bring the mutilated child's family untold wealth, although in reality that seldom happened. If the boys did manage to survive the horrific surgery, performed without anesthesia, all most of them had to look forward to was a life of hardship. Easy to spot by virtue of their luxuriant locks crowning an otherwise hairless, excessively long-limbed body that gave them a tottering, unsteady gait, sooner or later they all wound up obese. Most of the castrati lived out their lives shunned by society.

"In 1904," said the Dauphine, looking pointedly around the table, for she did so like to show off her exhaustive musical training, "I attended a performance by the castrato Alessandro Moreschi in Rome's Sistine Chapel. He was not, sad to say, a particularly great singer; his 'Ave Maria' was a startling feat rather than a truly moving interpretation. I think the man—perhaps that's not the right word for it; what do you call such a creature?—well, anyway, I think he owed his fame largely to the fact that he was one of the last of his kind, because castration has quite fallen out of fashion."

Her voice held a note of regret. The company peppered her with questions: What did he look like, how big was his rib cage, did his face have feminine features, and how would she describe his voice?

"It's almost a pity," mused Samuel Klein, a pharmacologist who had been a major player in the breakthrough we were toasting, a little peanut of a fellow whose appearance belied a quick, sharp wit, "that those Italian castrati are no longer around. We could have been of considerable help to them, and we'd have had a whole bunch of clinical test subjects thrown into the bargain."

"We do still have access to some neutered men," Rafaël reassured him. "There are plenty of accidental castrations, as well as cases where the testicles are amputated for medical reasons. And then of course there are the virtual eunuchs, men who, even if the gonads are intact, don't have the normal sexual drive. That affliction is caused by a deficiency of the same testes hormone; we know that now. So we'll have more than enough customers for our clinical trials!"

We all drank to that.

Silberstein, a chemist whom I had turned down for a permanent position in our firm and who had fled Nazi Germany a year earlier, told us how in his fatherland homosexuals were being pressured to get castrated to cure their "disease," which ran afoul of the Aryan ideal of manhood. Would Farmacom someday be able to help these unfortunate creatures by giving them back their sexual apparatus? The conversation now took a different turn, from discussing hormones to bemoaning the barbaric practices that were becoming increasingly common across the border.

After dinner the party moved into the living room, where we were offered coffee, cognac, and Rafaël's Cuban cigars; for the ladies there were filter cigarettes in the sterling silver case on the coffee table.

The company included a number of recent refugees from the Third Reich. Most had fled to our country alone, hoping to build a life for themselves here before sending for their families. They were all extremely worried and distressed by the reports reaching them of what life was like for the ones they'd left behind; the situation was getting more desperate by the day. To make matters worse, there was no guarantee that the reluctant Dutch government would grant them and their threatened family members permission to remain in the Netherlands.

• • •

Setting up a German subsidiary ten years earlier had been an excellent move. Germany was a big country, and it had become our main export market. But the current dictatorship and growing reign of terror over there made me less and less inclined to invest another cent in Farmacom Deutschland and someday run the risk of having it confiscated by that piece of shit and his followers, the ones who had declared outright war on our people. Besides, a worldwide boycott of German goods had already put the kibosh on our export operation. I thought the boycott was a rather surprising knee-jerk reaction, by the way, probably owing more to political expedience than to sympathy for the victims. After all, the Chosen People haven't ever been all that popular anywhere in the world. It's no wonder that one of the Jews' favorite jokes is the one in which Isaac sighs, *Isn't two thousand years of being the Chosen People enough, Lord? Couldn't you give some other race that honor for a change?*

Because we had a branch in Germany, and also because we had given all those German-Jewish refugees jobs in our Farmacom operation, there was a growing perception that our company had links to the Third Reich. There is as little room for nuance in business as in politics. The refugees were mainly friends or colleagues of Rafaël's; people who turned to him or his Dauphine for financial help, employment, or introductions that might lead to a coveted residence permit—and they never seemed to come away empty-handed. Rafaël simply assumed that I was just as anxious as he was to offer help to these erudite men, reduced by dire circumstance to penniless beggars. Our waterlogged country, which had always had a reputation for hospitality and tolerance, and once upon a time had been a haven of refuge for my own forefathers, was in these crisis years turning into an increasingly inward-looking, provincial place, afraid of both a flood from the west and a deluge of refugees from the east. A fearful nation, it allowed itself to be intimidated by the thug across the border, and was therefore not keen on letting in more of the persecuted outcasts. Besides, the brownshirts in our own midst were growing more vociferous, spewing their hateful invective all over the place, and our own citizens were starting to hear them out with increasing enthusiasm. In uncertain times folks tend to be drawn to ruffians who, by shouting simplistic slogans and wild accusations and by dragging up ancient prejudices, manage to heap the blame for all their problems on some innocent scapegoat. A fearful populace wants to see blood, and the demagogues provide plenty of ammunition, first in word and then in deed, as they set upon the black sheep in an orgy of bloodletting.

My position as CEO of a fast-growing company was rather precarious. I was responsible for keeping my workforce employed, and for that I needed the goodwill of the world at large. And it really stuck in my craw to find the notion taking hold that our company, Farmacom, born and nurtured on good Dutch soil, was actually a German concern, or at least intimately linked to Germany. I had to use every means at my disposal to dispel that idea. For that reason I sold the German subsidiary, and I put new policies in place to stop doing business with our eastern neighbor and not to employ any more foreigners, especially German nationals. Besides, it showed we supported our government's efforts to bring down the high unemployment rate.

Rafaël and I disagreed on this issue, although he himself had taken Dutch citizenship some years earlier, just before that dirty bastard seized absolute power. Prompted by his desire to distance himself as much as possible from the abhorrent goings-on in the Third Reich and to show his loyalty to his new homeland, he may also have been motivated to some extent by a desire to please me, knowing how patriotic I was.

However, Rafaël's sense of loyalty to the asylum seekers streaming in from his former fatherland kept growing stronger. He tried to find a job for every poor, persecuted Yid who came knocking on his door with some sob story, and kept importuning us to take on more German Jews. As if our firm wasn't practically a Jewish ghetto already.

The more dire the situation inside Germany, the more Rafaël's once-shrewd business sense abandoned him, as his indignation about what was being done to his people intensified. He did everything in his power to sever all links with Germany. As a member of the faculty, he put considerable effort into getting the university to boycott an important Munich conference. The way he saw it, participating in that conference was sleeping with the enemy.

Of course I shared his anger at what was happening, but I was finding it increasingly difficult to accede to his over-the-top demands, motivated as he was by the urge to be the savior of anyone who needed his help. I had to do what was best for both Farmacom and the De Paauw Slaughterhouse and Meatpacking Co. Never bite off more than you can chew. A firm that allows itself to be governed by emotions is doomed to fail.

And so that evening in Rafaël's living room, I found myself in a rather difficult spot. The emotional, tipsy exiles were growing more and more belligerent: Why wasn't I offering more of them jobs? I was the only one at the party in a position to do so, and they sensed my reluctance, although I tried to be as noncommittal as I could.

"If we Jews fail to do everything we possibly can to rescue our brothers from Hitler's clutches, and to help them where we can, how can we expect the rest of the world to do so?" said the Dauphine tartly, topping off the brandy snifters.

"But we are already doing all we possibly can," I replied defensively, sensing the eyes of the entire company glaring at me. "We are in the process of divesting ourselves of our German subsidiary; we have offered lots of people positions in the company; we have donated generously to the refugee organizations; but I do have to remember that my first responsibility is to the firm. If Farmacom should come to be viewed around the world as a German concern, it's curtains for our business, and that means the bread line for all our workers, Jew and non-Jew alike. We're in a difficult quandary and have to be extremely careful how we handle it."

"But, Mr. Motke," said Silberstein, "don't you understand how serious this is; don't you see how easy you have it, compared with us? To you it's just about employment opportunities and corporate profit margins. To us and our wives and children back in Germany, it's a matter of life or death."

There were nods of agreement all around.

Rivka had been following the discussion intently, and now she put in her two cents. "Motke," she said, "a German firm or a Jewish firm, surely those are two very different things? Surely the world can be made to understand that taking on asylum seekers means taking a stand against that despicable regime? Surely if Farmacom and the De Paauw Slaughterhouse and Meatpacking Company are seen to be helping the *victims* of Hitler's tyranny, it will generate goodwill for the firm around the globe, and open up new markets abroad?"

The buzz that greeted my wife's comments made clear that she had a receptive audience. I suddenly saw red. My own wife trying to teach me a lesson, here at this gathering; how dare she?

"Talk is cheap," I retorted haughtily. "What do *you* know about running a business, Rivka? My responsibilities are far greater than any of you can possibly comprehend." I stood up. "Come, Rivka," I snapped at her. "I have to be at work again in the morning, unlike some of the people here. Have a pleasant evening."

Rivka hoisted herself from her chair with visible reluctance and a pointed shrug, went up to the Dauphine to kiss her goodbye, and gave the company around the table a smile and a little wave. Rafaël followed me into the hall to see us out.

"It's a shame," he said, helping me into my coat, "that it had to come to this. I wanted this evening to end on a festive note. I do very much appreciate, Motke, that you have made Farmacom possible. And I am over the moon about our latest achievement. But surely you see that we are now at a point where commercial considerations ought no longer to be the key motivation. This is about life and death, as Silberstein said, and we all know that evil doesn't need much incentive. If humankind just stands by and does nothing, it's enough to let atrocity prevail."

"Ah, but nice guys finish last," I responded, and stomped outside without waiting for Rivka, who, when she finally came out, got into the passenger seat next to Frank. In a silence more deafening than any provoked by our sporadic fights over twelve years of marriage, we drove home to our mansion in the sticks.

21...

The thirties were bleak years in many respects.

The months following the party fiasco saw me working even longer days at the office than before, up to my neck in negotiations, contract signings, and expansion plans, or else away on increasingly frequent business trips that took me, and sometimes Aaron, to England, America, South America, and China—territories where it was necessary to nail down new and existing business contacts and get subsidiaries off the ground. My intensive workload was occasionally lightened by a fling with a factory cutie or a diverting seduction in the lobby of some foreign hotel.

Rivka was kept busy looking after our four girls. She was a cheerful and enthusiastic mother, and I admired her for not taking out on the children the coldness that had arisen between the two of us. She also continued running her enrichment programs for the factory girls. Since our visit to the Levines, she had thrown herself into volunteer activities, assisting refugees who had managed to reach our country despite the strict border controls and the country's fractious mood. Whenever we happened to run into each other at home, she'd insist on telling me their tragic stories in a reproachful tone of voice, as if *I*, and not the Satan across the border, were the one who'd been mistreating all those poor schmoes.

• • •

The discovery of the male hormone did not bring us the success we were expecting from the get-go. It was a big headache at first, because a major German company had registered some premature patents that could conceivably block us from putting Levine's invention into production. Moreover, the fact that the discovery had been the brainchild of a Jew goaded the German government into doing everything in its power to claim it as an Aryan achievement. That nest of crooks was in the habit of appropriating Jewish discoveries and chalking them up to the master race.

To lay claim to a scientific breakthrough is an extremely complex matter. I was well aware of how difficult it was to obtain a patent for our kind of discovery. If you were an inventor, it wasn't all that hard to win the right to stop others from commercially exploiting your invention for a certain length of time; an inventor comes up with something from scratch, something that's never existed before. A scientific researcher, on the other hand—for example, one who isolates a new substance from existing matter, such as animal organs—was often informed by the patent office that his product did not meet the criteria of an original invention, and thus did not qualify for a patent. It always took great amounts of red tape to protect our discoveries, but it was critical to do so in order to recoup our costly investment.

These efforts were further complicated by the fact that we had to divest ourselves of our German division. As it turned out, the most convenient way was to sell the business to one of our major German customers—none other than the sharks who'd beaten us in snagging the patents for the hormone. The most Byzantine negotiations of my business life resulted in the end in an agreement by which our subsidiary was sold for a pittance.

However, thanks to some crafty moves on my part—a huge consolation—we did manage, in the face of fierce opposition from our Aryan rivals, to set up a corporation in the United States, thus creating a huge new market for our products. And in 1937 we finally obtained the necessary patents for the substance Levine and his team had discovered, and which he now endowed with a new name: testosterone.

Aside from having to cope with all these vicissitudes, I was getting increasingly concerned about Aaron, who seemed to be growing more depressed by the day. He would often show up late for work, or not show up at all. Once, hearing his sluggish, shuffling tread on the stairs leading to our office floor, I confronted him and chewed him out right in the administrative office hallway. I let him have it within everybody's hearing, scolding him for playing hooky, something an executive in his position could not afford to do. Staring at me with his dull, droopy eyes, as if my tirade registered no more with him than the sound of the bellows from the glassworks, he shambled right past me into his office, not even bothering to stand still and hear me out.

He neglected his work, made errors in drawing up foreign contracts, disregarded proper dismissal procedures, failed to follow up on decisions made at board meetings; everything he was supposed to be responsible for was getting bungled. Although he had never been much of a cheerleader for our company, he had previously always done what was expected of him, joylessly and perfunctorily, the way he did everything in his life. But since he had started dropping the ball, I could no longer count on him; I felt things were spiraling out of control, that his unreliability was imperiling the firm. This could not go on. I decided one afternoon that something had to be done.

I marched into his office without knocking and found him sitting at his desk, staring out the window overlooking the busy courtyard. At the sound of the door opening he listlessly turned his head in my direction, then looked away again when he saw who it was. I perched on his desk and gazed down on his pale, stooped form. It was hard to think that he really was my twin. Tangled, unkempt hair; dazed, absent eyes; pasty skin; flushed cheeks that signaled copious alcohol consumption; hunched shoulders; and that flabby, sagging torso—sitting there like Job on the dunghill. *Christ*, he looked terrible.

This was my brother, my unfortunate twin, the one who shared my entire history, who was so much a part of me that it was like having a third hand, or another foot. My twin sibling had always been there and would always be; life without him was unthinkable. But if that was so, why did we have so few things in common, aside from those nine months in the womb and a childhood dominated by two unloving parents? I suddenly remembered something—an article I'd once read that I'd dismissed as pure nonsense before consigning it to some subterranean repository of useless information. It was a report about the Yoruba people of western Africa. They believed that twins possessed one soul between them. An utterly galling thought, but suddenly I couldn't get it out of my head. Aaron and I had been accidentally conceived from two separate eggs at the same exact time. Aaron had been the first to squeeze through the birth canal, paving the way, and all I'd had to do was slide out after him. My brother and I were as different as day is different from night. But—to share one soul, what a horrifying thought! It meant we belonged together like two sides of a coin, like a photographic negative and positive. It would explain why I had turned out the way I had: enterprising, quick on my feet, and purposeful. Aaron, meanwhile, was my inner voice, my silent conscience, my better self. And so he could just sit there brooding and suffering, knowing I would do what had to be done, for myself, but also for him. Two bodies, one soul.

I shook my head to get rid of that crazy, troubling thought. Of course we weren't one. He was my lost-soul twin, a man totally cut off from the real world, and so beset by loneliness and inertia that he just couldn't seem to snap out of it. I needed to step in and make him get ahold of himself so that he'd be able to resume his part, however minimal, in the gigantic task facing us.

"Aaron," I said, "you've been dropping the ball on everything; we can't count on you anymore. What's the matter with you, for chrissakes?"

Aaron went on staring out the window, gave a slight shrug, and said nothing.

"Aaron," I said, now raising my voice, "if something's wrong, buck up, man, pull yourself together. We need you."

Slowly he turned his head toward me, with a listless "You need me?" He went on with a sneer. "Yes, I'm handy to have around, aren't I, as your flunky? All those nasty but necessary little jobs that have to get done. A contract here, a dismissal notice there, but does it make a damn bit of difference? A bungler, a dolt, a dope, that's what I am. No one needs me. Not here at the factory, and even less out there in the world at large. Nobody even notices I'm here. If I had to be born, why did it have to be in this godforsaken dump, why was I born with *you* as my twin, why into this wretched firm, and, worst of all, why at this abominable time in history?"

He picked up the pencil stub lying on the desk and started gnawing on it.

"Jesus, Aaron," I said, getting up to pace about the room, "you really are depressed. That's the kind of thinking that will drive you mad. Sure, times are bad, but we are fortunate enough to be largely in control of our own lives. Make something of it! Just remember what a lucky dog you are. Count your blessings, give yourself a good kick in the backside, go take a trip. It's a big world out there, with lots of sales territories left to conquer. Get yourself a beautiful woman—there are plenty of them out there, you know—and try to get the most out of all life has to offer!"

He didn't respond.

"You've said it yourself," I went on; "you need to find yourself a girl, get yourself a nice piece of ass. A man who doesn't do it on a regular basis will forget how."

"I may not 'do it' enough, but you 'do it' far too much." He looked straight at me for the first time. "Just for a moment back then, I thought you had taken to heart what I'd said to you. For a few days I clung to the illusion that my words might have brought out some decency in you, that I had at the very least saved some girls from your dirty shenanigans. But no, you're still the perv you always were and always will be."

He stared at the floor.

"I did take your words to heart, Aaron," I said. "You did have a point. I wish I was better at controlling myself, that I wasn't subject to these urges that seem to overtake me like a raging fever. I did try, but I simply couldn't do it. I go nuts if I can't let off steam every once in a while. And trust me, those girls, they're asking for it. You act as if I'm some kind of rapist creep, but I'm not. Sure, I like the thrill of the hunt, to feel in my guts that I have the power to seduce some broad. Knowing I can have whichever girl I want, knowing she'll spread her legs for me, that she wants to offer herself, that's what gives me the energy to do what I do, by which I mean my business exploits, not the ladies. No, it isn't the girls I'm worried about; I'm worried about *you*."

Aaron stared somberly into space, gave a deep sigh, and muttered under his breath, "Me, I don't have any desire for a woman, the way you describe it. I don't even have any idea what that feels like." Tapping his pencil on the armrest of his chair, he took a deep breath and went on in a louder voice. "There, now you know how it is with me. Now you can despise me even more than you did before." He leaned his head against the window pane with a look of total defeat.

Those last words struck a chord; suddenly it was clear to me why my brother had been floundering all his life. I remembered what Levine had said at dinner about unsexed men whose genitals appeared to be in working order. Aaron's listlessness, his lack of aggressiveness, the disinterest in women; I had always misread it. My brother had been contending since boyhood with a secret he'd had to keep from everyone, in order to escape my father's derision and my scorn. How ironic! My brother, one of the directors of Farmacom, an enterprise that for more than ten years had been on the hunt for various "soul hormones," suffered from an insufficiency of the very thing Rafaël had so recently discovered! Aaron had been going through life with a colossal testosterone deficiency.

22...

I realized I was the wrong person to tell my brother of this diagnosis; it required someone who could first confirm medically whether Aaron was lacking in the sex hormone department and, if so, persuade him to accept treatment. Regular injections with Levine's new potion might boost his testosterone and, indeed, might even transform him into a bold, sexually active, happy man. Wouldn't that be great! If he got cured, we might wind up sharing responsibility for the firm on a more equal basis. I'd have a real partner at last, a true comrade.

Not wanting to waste any more time, I approached Rafaël. The clinical trials for the male hormone were in full swing. Rafaël had asked us to stockpile every last damn bull testicle the Netherlands had to offer, for use in preparations of various strengths and combinations. He was also trying to collect as much male urine as possible, following the example of the German scientist who, when the testosterone race had still been in full swing, had got his hands on an enormous supply of the most aggressive male pee in the Reich: the urine of young SS soldiers in a military barracks in Berlin.

Without revealing that it was Aaron, I mentioned to Rafaël that I had met a man who bore the hallmarks of a castrato, as described during the party at his house, and asked him to recommend a physician who might treat the unhappy soul with the new miracle cure. He gave me the name of a doctor in Nijmegen who had enthusiastically embraced the clinical trials. Without mentioning the therapy I had in mind, I managed to persuade Aaron to go see this doctor.

My dispirited twin took the train to Nijmegen. I had confided to the good doctor in a phone conversation that my brother was, in all likelihood, suffering from an insufficiency of the manly hormone. Aaron returned from his visit without breathing a word about what he and the doc had discussed, and I couldn't tell if he had started the treatment or not. I kept a close eye on him the next few weeks, curious to see if I could detect any change in his energy or mood. The fact that he was making the trip to Nijmegen several times a week gave me hope; it could well mean he was receiving a course of injections. He seemed to trust the doctor; however, my patience was being sorely tried, since in the first few weeks I detected no difference in him. His somber mood and inertia did not lessen; ever since our last conversation, he'd clammed up again like a bivalve determined to shut out every last drop of seawater, and I was starting to have doubts both about my diagnosis and about Levine's wonder drug. If he was indeed being treated with the soul hormone, was the prof's potion really all it was cracked up to be? Or was Aaron being given too insignificant a dose? The trials were still in an early stage, and there was quite a bit of uncertainty as to the proper dosage, the ratios required for optimal results in humans as opposed to roosters.

Blame it on Levine's excessive caution regarding the dosage, his reluctance to take any risks as long as the therapy's clinical effect on humans wasn't yet known. My impatience with the

glacial pace of his methods had already led to several alterca-
tions over the past few years, since I felt that he showed too
little concern for the financial aspects of the business. After all,
we'd poured a small fortune into every discovery and every new
drug. Of course I could see it was necessary to test their effec-
tiveness on humans, and that each new preparation had to be
produced in sufficient quantities to provide insight into its basic
workings and side effects. But Levine tended to be excessively
prudent and scared to death of harming his reputation. I thought
it only fair, considering the enormous financial investment we
had made, that he stick out his neck a little and speed things
up just a tad. But the dosage instructions he gave the doctors
were always so conservative that it took ages to come up with
any conclusive results, let alone a viable drug that we could sell.
Speed and impatience, as I've said before, are my middle names.
There's anger in there too, since Rafaël's chickenhearted methods showed that he cared more for his precious good name than
for our firm's sound financial footing.

After several weeks with no obvious results, I decided to pay
a call to Aaron's doctor myself in order to get some answers. He
received me courteously and respectfully, as most of Levine's
contacts did, since they felt honored to belong to his circle of
trusted associates and knew that the preparations they were
being given to try out were manufactured by my company. Participating in the trials was a way to make a name for themselves
as physicians on the cutting edge, more able than their less fortunate colleagues.

The doctor received me in his surgery in the late afternoon.

"I have come on condition that I can trust you not to breathe
a word to anyone about this," I began. "I would hate to have my
brother or Professor Levine hear from you that we've had this

little talk. Aaron keeps me informed about his treatment, naturally, but I'd nevertheless like to hear from you if there is any chance he can be cured."

The doctor gave me a reassuring smile and reminded me that he was bound by his Hippocratic oath. In any case, his lips were sealed. When I asked him if he agreed with the diagnosis I had initially shared with him over the telephone, he nodded in the affirmative.

"Well now," he eagerly began, despite his sworn adherence to the Hippocratic oath, "your brother presents as a typical case of a man suffering from a low sex hormone condition, and it has probably affected his life grievously, as you more than anyone else must know. It's a blessing that we now have a remedy for it, and he seems to be tolerating this brand-new drug exceptionally well."

"But it isn't having any effect," I blurted out.

The doctor carefully shook his head from side to side, trying to suppress a smirk. "As you are no doubt aware, I have been emphatically instructed to increase the dose by the smallest of increments only, since the preparation is still in the experimental stage. Although there have been practically no significant negative side effects, it nevertheless behooves us to proceed with caution. Surely I don't have to explain that to you?"

"I am only too aware of Professor Levine's conservative approach," I replied, "and of course I completely agree that unreasonable risks must be avoided at all costs. But my brother's depression and his inertia are so extreme that I am very worried and live in fear every day that he might harm himself. I would give anything to see you step up the dosage a bit, so that he'll be cured sooner. The professor's prudence is often somewhat exaggerated."

The doctor looked a bit troubled. He'd apparently thought that Levine and I were of the same mind.

"If you were to hurry the whole thing up a bit, and boost my brother's medication by some significant amount, you could be the first in the country to come up with a concrete, positive result! It would be a way to make a name for yourself. You'd be able to publish your results, and gain instant fame all over the world."

I can spot a man seething with frustrated ambition a mile away, one who wishes he could set himself apart from his colleagues as he plods through life in a stuffy consultation room.

"I would be *most* grateful, and in recompense, you may be assured that in the future Farmacom will always be giving you our new products to try out first, before distributing them to any other practitioners."

The doctor had to give it some thought. The room grew quiet. I waited. I can be patient as long as I know it's worth it. The doctor squared his shoulders and answered, as I'd expected, "Fine, I will up the dose significantly. On one condition: you may not have a professional oath to abide by, but I trust that you will not breathe a word of this to anyone."

I stood up and shook his hand firmly. "Naturally. And I promise you won't regret it."

"I trust that I won't." He shut the door quietly behind me.

23...

The next few weeks saw a noticeable change in my brother's behavior. Little by little his step grew more energetic, his expression livelier. He was starting to not only speak up in meetings, but also express disagreement, which he had never done before. He came up with new suggestions for increasing our exports, and took steps to improve working conditions in the factory. I gave him plenty of elbow room, happy to see the change in him, and chuffed that Rafaël's discovery did indeed work the way he had said it would.

I had asked the girl Rosie to come and see me in my office one day. A cute little thing with long, slightly wavy black hair; big, dark eyes; full lips; even white teeth; a well-proportioned body with small breasts; and startlingly large hands. At first she'd resisted my advances, nervously shaking her head, twisting her mouth, and fluttering her long, sturdy fingers incessantly, as if the strangled words hidden inside were struggling to come out in the form of some kind of sign language. A strange dance of the hands. She seemed to regard our brief encounters on my Cozy Corner sofa as necessary insurance against unemployment. I assumed, however, that she enjoyed the passion with which I took possession of her. In any case, she must have been flattered by my attentions. That day, just as I was seeing her out of my room after a short but satisfying intermezzo, Aaron happened to walk by on his way to his office. He stared at Rosie, who lowered her eyes bashfully, greeting him in a low voice. It was the first time I'd ever seen Aaron's eyes light up. I winked at him, upon which he turned his head away and darted back into his room.

• • •

Some days later the priest asked to see me. That surprised me, for our twice-yearly conversation had taken place three months earlier. What did he want with me?

After greeting me warmly, he took his usual place on the sofa. He gazed at me beatifically, tapping his long, emaciated fingers together, a habit of his, as if he felt the need to rehearse the rhythm of his sentence first.

"Mr. De Paauw," he said, and swallowed, "I am obliged to raise a delicate subject with you." As he tried to find the right words, a faint blush spread across his pallid visage. "It feels like I'm sticking my nose in someone else's business, and I had to do a great deal of soul-searching before I finally screwed up the courage to come here. There's no worse venom than evil tongues. One of my parishioners has been telling tales about you, and what she is saying worries me."

He leaned forward and looked at me sternly. I felt a surge of adrenaline shoot through me. Had one of those little sluts spilled the beans? I quickly tried to recall which girls had spread their legs for me recently, right there, on the very sofa where the reverend now sat stiffly perched. And as the pastor lisped on in his roundabout way, unable to get to the point, I cast about for ways to save myself. A substantial donation to the Church. It would probably have to come down to that.

The clergyman took a deep breath and seemed finally ready to come out with it.

"Mr. De Paauw, there appear to have been some improper activities in these parts." As he spoke he didn't dare look at me. "I have therefore spoken sternly to my parishioner and have made it very clear to her that such unsavory situations arise only when the alleged recipient has given some provocation thereto. I know the young people in their teenage years well enough to understand how difficult it is for a man to resist temptation when they flaunt their bodies at us as they do. I do not know if it is yourself or your brother who has failed to control himself. You are a happily married man, and I must therefore assume that these lapses are your brother's. I would urge you to admonish him. Please regard this conversation as the warning of a friend, one who would not wish your enterprise anything untoward."

I let out a deep sigh of relief. If I had understood him correctly, the padre had some secret peccadillos of his own that he didn't want to come to light, and so he wasn't about to shout this kind of gossip from the rooftops. Whether he was really unsure whether the stories were about me or he just wanted to spare me the embarrassment didn't matter right then.

I assured him that I would reprimand my brother and that there would be no further improprieties. But which of the little bitches had let the cat out of the bag? I thought it better not to ask. I ended the conversation by thanking him for placing such trust in me, and saw him to the door. I decided that for the time being I had better restrict my dalliances to just the girls who were most receptive. And to Rosie. After all, with her I had nothing to worry about, since she never set foot in the priest's house of worship. Rosie belonged to my own race, the Chosen People, the ones who in these turbulent years were feeling the noose of hate tightening ever more snugly around our necks.

No need for hush money, then—for the time being.

• • •

In February 1938 we convened a lengthy board meeting to deal with a packed agenda, including, to mention just a few items, the construction of a new laboratory on the recently purchased tract of land; a strategy to deal with the effect the evil prick's likely takeover of Austria could have on our foreign trade; and the renewal of Levine's contract, which ran out the following year. Levine decided to make the most of the opportunity by demanding an absurd increase in his already exorbitant salary, an unreasonable cut of the profits, and an even greater say over the way we manufactured our products. Tensions were running high among the board members, and there were many angry exchanges. Levine's bitter accusations that we were unwilling to meet him halfway made me seethe. Aaron, who much to Levine's surprise and dismay was taking an active part in the debate, parried that if the proposed contract did not meet his expectations, he was free to resign from Farmacom. Although I was happy to see Aaron taking my side so energetically, I did have to do some deft backpedaling to ensure that Levine did not pack his bags right then and there. I had been fantasizing about ending the relationship, but was all too aware that Farmacom did not yet have the necessary know-how, and hadn't yet built up enough of a worldwide reputation, to stand on its own without him.

Another concern was that Levine, with his gold mine of international contacts, might pack up his wife and his five children any day now to abscond to the other side of the world and throw in his hat with some big multinational corporation. After all, how can you ever be sure that a foreigner who's been kicked out of his own country will remain loyal to the nation that took him in and gave him both work and recognition?

When the other board members left the room, Aaron stayed behind, which was unusual for him. I offered him a glass of whiskey, thanked him for his feisty intervention, and pointed out that I too longed for the day when we'd be able to show the Prussian the door, but asked him to hold his horses just a bit longer, since we were going to need more time to extricate ourselves from our involvement with the professor.

Then I looked at him pointedly and asked, "I have the feeling your therapy is starting to work, is that true? You seem so much more active and involved. I'm seeing very little sign of the depressed, apathetic man you were just a while ago."

Aaron took a sip of his whiskey. He sighed.

"Something's definitely happening," he said after a while. "The awful depression, the feeling I'm dragging my body through some sticky morass, yes, that's definitely getting better. And I'm not finding it as hard to get up in the morning these days."

He sighed again. I remember that conversation as if it were yesterday. It was a brief exchange but pivotal for both of us. I probably shouldn't have let my enthusiasm carry me away; maybe what he said should have raised a red flag. But what's the point of stewing over that now? It's just one of the endlessly useless thoughts coming at me out of nowhere as I lie here in my iron cage.

"It sounds as if the treatment is doing you some good," I said, "both mentally and physically."

Our relationship, which was slowly but surely improving, was still too rocky to allow me to come clean and tell him I knew more about his treatment than he thought.

"Maybe," he said, "it's one thing leading to another. The soul gland is what our Prussian pasha calls it, and not for nothing. Something in me is definitely changing, Motke, and it scares me sometimes. It feels like some kind of rage boiling up inside me, something so strong that I fear it might just overpower me. Do you know the feeling?"

"But that's fantastic!" I cried. "That, Aaron, is masculine energy. Congratulations!"

I slapped him enthusiastically on the shoulder, but Aaron's expression remained troubled. "Well, we'll see, Motke," he said, getting up and draining his glass. He smiled awkwardly and then, without another glance, left the room.

24...

On March 11, 1938, the news came that we had all feared: Austrian Chancellor Schuschnigg had resigned and the Nazis were goose-stepping through the streets of Vienna, where until recently their party had been banned. I was at a Ministry of Economic Affairs conclave in The Hague when I heard the news. I returned to my office in a despondent mood, since this meant we were now barred from doing business with Austria too. I was also worried, naturally, about what other plans the brutal pig might have for Europe.

As soon as I walked into the reception area, I knew something was wrong there as well. Instead of the usual sedate atmosphere, the monotonous rattle of countless typewriters and the quiet murmur of bookkeepers and secretaries conferring, there was a suppressed buzz of excitement in the air. I surprised some visibly agitated employees in the hall, who scurried hastily back into their offices, leaving their doors ajar.

When she saw me, Agnes came running. Her usual composure was gone; she was in a state of total panic.

"I'm so relieved you're here, Mr. Motke," she stammered, glancing nervously at Aaron's closed door. "Something dreadful has happened. Please, let's go inside."

She dragged me into my office and as soon as the door was shut burst into tears.

"Your brother, there's something terribly wrong with him. He went after Rosie; he's brutally assaulted her."

"What?" I exclaimed. *"Aaron?"*

Agnes looked at me anxiously and went on with her story. "He ordered me to fetch her up from export. I did think it was a bit strange. What does he want with Rosie, I asked myself. But hey, he's the boss, isn't he, so I went and got her and when she went in, I hung around outside the door for a bit, because I didn't really trust it."

I had always known that my loyal Girl Friday possessed a healthy dose of curiosity, but never before had she admitted it to me so openly.

" *'Come here, you!'* I heard him bellow in a loud, scary voice I'd never heard him use before. Then it was quiet, then Rosie cried *'No!'* and after that I heard a crash, as if a chair fell over. Your brother growled, Rosie screamed, there was more crashing around, it sounded as if they were fighting and smashing things. And then I heard noises that sounded like they, well, *you* know..." Agnes blushed, shrugging her shoulders. "Rosie kept yelling *'No!'* I just didn't know what to do; I called the others out of their offices. But no one dared to intervene, we just stood there listening to your brother bellowing from time to time. Then after a while the door flew open and Rosie ran out."

Her voice grew so quiet that I had a hard time hearing her. "Her apron was torn to shreds, she was bleeding, Mr. Motke. The devil's got into your brother, that's the only explanation." Agnes was now sobbing loudly. "I didn't know what to do. Nobody knew what to do, Mr. Motke."

Panic seized me by the throat. Goddammit, what had that nitwit done? When an angel turns into a devil, he's the vilest of them all.

"How long ago was this," I snapped at Agnes, "and where the hell is Aaron, and where the hell is Rosie?"

I had to act quickly. This was a complete and utter catastrophe.

"Mr. Aaron hasn't come out of his room," said Agnes, glancing anxiously at the door, as if he might burst in at any moment. "You can still hear him roar once in a while," she whispered, leaning closer to me, as if it had suddenly occurred to her that the monster might have heard the whole thing. "And Rosie—I ran after her. I lent her my coat and sent her home."

"*Damn!*" I exclaimed. A badly bruised and battered Rosie, leaving the office in full sight of the administrative staff, and going home to her poverty-stricken parents in a hysterical state—it was the worst possible scenario.

"How long ago did she leave and where does she live?"

"She lives on the other side of the tracks, not far from here," Agnes replied, looking at me nervously. "I couldn't send her back down to export in that state, Mr. Motke, now could I?"

"No," I said, "you're right, you couldn't. Listen to me, Agnes. Go after Rosie immediately and tell her to come back here, and her parents too; if they're home, that is. I must speak to her or all of them before they decide to take any other steps. Tell them I am just as appalled as they are over what happened, and I don't intend to sweep this thing under the carpet. Justice will be done. But in order for that to happen, she must come see me. I promise she will not have to see my brother. Go, right now. And not a word to anyone."

Agnes left, glad to be able to get out of the office and do something useful.

I took a deep breath and sat down at my desk in order to organize my thoughts. What a catastrophe. Aaron finally gets a bit of spunk in him, and what happens? He goes and screws it up—big time. I tried to recall our exchange of a few weeks back. Hadn't he mentioned being afraid of the new power that was being unleashed in him? It should have set off all kinds of alarm bells, and I'd simply missed it. How *could* I have been so blithe about it all, so blind to his struggle?

The sheer number of witnesses to Aaron's testosterone explosion meant there was no hope of keeping it quiet. An overdose of the soul hormone had delivered a Trojan horse into our midst. My God, a brutal rape! Aaron was caught like a rat in a trap. I didn't see how I could rescue him now; the whole debacle had been too public and too violent. I had to get my brother out of the office before Rosie and her parents got here.

Entering his room, I recoiled in horror. His usually immaculate office had turned to havoc. Tumbled chairs left and right, the carpet crumpled and covered in broken glass (from the looks of it, it was the amber-colored designer vase Rivka had given him on his last birthday), files and papers strewn everywhere, everything pointing to a fierce struggle that had taken place there. And in the midst of all the mess, Aaron lay facedown on the carpet, his trousers down around his knees. He reminded me of a stranded whale on some filthy beach. My brother was bawling, loudly and wretchedly, with long, choking gasps. Was there anything I could do to turn this disaster around?

I shut the door carefully, walked up to him, and kneeled down by his side.

"Aaron," I said softly, touching his back, "come on, get up, man, let me help you pull your pants up."

Aaron's bellow turned into a howl of despair, like a wolf letting the rest of the pack know he's in grave danger. He stared at me, dazed. His face was covered in blood; Rosie must have fought back like a wildcat. Brusquely, he shook my hand off his back. My presence seemed to whip him into an even greater fury.

"You and your soul glands! Is this what you wanted for me, you schmuck? You've finally done it, I've finally turned into as big a creep as you. Now we are one, the same lousy piece of scum, only in two different bodies."

I tried to pull up his trousers, but he slapped my hand away hard. "Don't touch me, don't you dare lay a finger on me," he roared, but then hauled himself to a sitting position, pulled up his pants, sobbing and groaning, and buckled his belt. I poured him a glass of water and handed it to him. Refusing to look at me, he took a sip and, staring at a large amber shard from the broken vase, started mumbling to himself in an expressionless voice. "I didn't want to, I didn't mean to. I tried to resist it, with all my might." He raised his head and looked at me with eyes that did not see me. "She was so scared of me, so terrified. No, not of me. It wasn't *me*."

And as he spat out those last words, his voice growing louder again, he stood up, picked up the broken piece of glass, and started waving it at me. I got up too, and began backing up slowly, not daring to look away, toward the door.

"It was *you*," he thundered, stabbing the shard in my direction, "it was *your* voice. You were there all the time I was doing it, you were laughing, urging me on, I mean, you were inside my head." Dropping the piece of glass, he began hammering his fists against his forehead, as if trying to brain himself. "Inside my body. *You* forced me to, you were turning me into *you*. *I* didn't want to do it!"

Then he collapsed again, banging his head on the parquet floor, howling at the top of his lungs.

I realized I had to get out of there. I wasn't the right person to calm him down; on the contrary, I was the wind fanning the flames. Quietly I left the room, closed the door behind me, turned the key in the lock, and dashed into my office. There I rang Rivka, who was fortunately home, and informed her without going into detail that Aaron was in a bad way.

"Alert the doctor and ask him to come here on the double, with however many rapidly working sedatives he has on hand. It's an emergency. And please hurry over here yourself."

Once Aaron was sedated, Rivka and the doctor would be able to get him home, which would give me the chance to talk to Rosie and her parents in peace. I picked up the carafe I kept in my office and poured myself a glass of water, then sat down at my desk and tried to think what I should do next.

25...

Agnes returned empty-handed; Rosie hadn't been home. She had encountered only the mother, who'd been greatly alarmed to find the executive secretary on her doorstep in search of her daughter. What had that girl had done now? she'd wanted to know. Agnes had said something noncommittal and left in a hurry.

She was looking at me anxiously; I felt my panic rise. Where *was* that little bitch? Had she gone straight to the police? It seemed rather unlikely, since the Rosie I knew was the guilt-ridden sort; she'd be too ashamed to have her disgrace be known. Maybe she'd gone off someplace to hide. Or, God forbid, she was licking her wounds at the house of a friend.

I drummed my fingers on the desktop. Had the entire office staff not witnessed Rosie's spectacular flight, I could have tried to hush up the whole affair. I could have tried paying the girl off with a tidy little sum, but since the whole office had seen her in her distressed state, it was too much of a risk. *One person's secret is shared by God alone; a secret shared by two soon to all is known.* There was nothing else for it: unless I wanted to be dragged down with him in his fall, I would have to sacrifice my brother. Sometimes one has to give up one's beard in order to save one's head. Yes, I'd go to the police and report to them what had happened, and do everything I could to save Aaron. Everything, that is, except jeopardize myself or discredit our first real scientific breakthrough.

• • •

As I walked into the police station my heart sank. The fat sergeant, seated at a desk dwarfed by his enormous bulk, was busy jotting something down, and across from him sat two women with their backs to me. I immediately recognized Rosie's skinny, huddled form shivering in Agnes's coat, jiggling the fingers of her startlingly large hands more nervously than ever; it looked as if she were typing on an invisible typewriter. And, what do you know? Next to her sat that devil spawn Bertha in all her glory. Could it get any worse? The fact that sweet little Rosie had apparently run into that tart Bertha—it was the worst possible luck. For a moment I was tempted to turn and run, but Bertha looked up and saw me. She jerked her chin and nudged Rosie with her elbow, saying "There he is." Then, addressing me with a note of triumph in her voice, she said, "Yer gonna get it now, Jewboy, like a tomcat getting its nuts lopped off."

Rosie cringed, and the sergeant looked up. He hauled himself to his feet and came forward, shushing Bertha with a hand gesture.

"Mr. De Paauw," he said, coming up to me with his hand outstretched, "it's good of you to come. I was just about to send some of my men to your office to investigate the situation. Please, take a seat."

He pointed to the chairs in front of his desk and then realized they were already taken. "Girlies," he said, "I've heard enough for now, you can go. You'll be hearing from me."

I saw Bertha bristling. She glared at the fat officer and exclaimed indignantly, "Ain't you gonna lock 'im up, the kike? Are you gonna let him blow smoke up yer ass, this prick who can't keep his dick in his pants?"

The sergeant's face grew red. "You don't talk that way to Mr. De Paauw. Get out!" he reprimanded the devil-bitch.

Rosie hurried past me on her way out the door, refusing to look at me. Bertha slowly hoisted her fat ass out of the chair and stalked past me with a haughty look, mouthing, "Oh, yeah, how could we ferget, rich birds uvva feather stick together."

I looked her straight in the eye and said, "Don't bother coming back to work, you little bitch. Girls who talk about their boss that way aren't wanted. And don't ever let me hear you've been spreading more dirty rumors, or your dad's a goner too."

Bertha went as red as a tom turkey, and stomped angrily outside, yelling, "Jest go to hell, you bastard!" She stuck her head around the door one more time to scream at the police officer, "Whatever he tells you, he's lyin' through his stinkin' teeth!"

In the ensuing silence I went and took a seat. The sergeant sighed.

"Mr. De Paauw, I'll get straight to the point. This is an extremely serious situation we have here. Even if only a fraction of the hogwash I was just told turns out to be true, the whole town's gonna be up in arms, you can bet on that. I cannot let this slide. That heavy one, the fat tart, she clearly has a bone to pick with you, and I'm going to take anything she says with a grain of salt."

As he spoke, he picked up a sheet from the stack in front of him and started tearing it into little pieces with a triumphant look in my direction. He stood up and let the scraps flutter into the wastebasket, then rubbed his hands as if to cleanse them of the filthy words written there. Taking his seat again, he went on.

"But that quiet little girl, she's been dreadfully misused; that's something we cannot ignore. It's going to have to go to court, without a doubt. Your brother cannot escape punishment."

I let his words sink in. If I read him correctly, this swaggering cop had just admitted, before I'd even tried justifying myself, that he was prepared to go along with the very strategy I had worked out on my way over! The statement fat Bertha must have given him in gory detail about our disports on my sofa (although she'd almost certainly omitted the fact that my exertions had taken place with her full consent) now lay in shreds in his wastebasket. Only Rosie's complaint still stood. It remained to be seen if the poor abused girl had confined herself to reporting only that afternoon's rape, or had also mentioned my own habit of fooling around with her, which she, unlike Bertha, had never openly encouraged.

The officer did not leave me in the dark long. "That bitch tried to get the poor little thing to say that she had been abused by you as well, but the victim herself has given no indication that this is indeed the case."

I managed to suppress a sigh of relief. I seemed to have dodged the bullet. As far as Aaron went, I'd have to try to salvage what could still be salvaged, being careful, however, to avoid any publicity that could negatively affect Rafaël's discovery. Otherwise we might as well kiss the testosterone drugs goodbye.

I explained to the officer that my brother had always been an open book, a man with a sterling reputation. In the past few months Aaron had sunk into a deep depression, and had been taking a number of different medications, a poisonous cocktail that must have set off this blind frenzy. A physician would be called in to confirm this explanation, and would determine that my brother had not been in control of his faculties and therefore was not fully accountable for his actions. The policeman seemed relieved to have the matter resolved so easily. We agreed that Aaron would come to the police station the next day to give himself up, thereby avoiding the mortification of an arrest at work or at home, which would only invite further gossip. I thanked the fellow for being so understanding, assuring him that if I could ever be of service to him in the future, my door was always open.

Once outside again, I took a deep gulp of the fresh night air. Depressing as it was to know that my brother would have to spend the foreseeable future behind bars, I couldn't help but feel relief over the way the interview with the cop had gone.

26...

In the weeks following that catastrophic day, I was forced to pull out all the stops to save my own skin and the firm's good name.

After my productive visit to the constabulary, I hurried back to the factory, where the night shift had just come on. To forestall further gossip, I summoned the factory foremen and supervisors and gave them a short, businesslike update on what had happened. The ladies and gentlemen listened to my story in a state of shock. Aaron was a beloved figure to the workforce, and, like Agnes, no one could even imagine the moody but kindhearted pushover being capable of such an outburst. I disclosed that the authorities had been informed, and that my brother would be going to the police station the next day to give himself up. He would not escape punishment. I asked them to spread the word to their workers and said that gossip about the incident would not be tolerated. Then I rushed over to Aaron's house, where I found the G.P. and Rivka, who was extremely upset. The good doctor had injected my brother with a healthy dose of tranquilizer and, when that hadn't had the required effect, sedated him with a strong narcotic. Aaron now lay stretched out on his bed like a corpse, temporarily released from his tormented soul. Both the doctor and Rivka were mystified as to how my lethargic brother could suddenly have turned into a brute capable of raping a girl known in the factory as a sweet and rather unremarkable young thing. I told them the same story I had told the police about the drug cocktail Aaron had supposedly taken to cure his depression. That made the doc look up, since my brother had not been to see him in over a year.

"What sort of drugs?" he asked suspiciously.

I assured him I had no idea. The conscientious medic said there must be some pill bottles lying around to tell us what medications my brother had been taking. I told him I had already looked and had not found any, neither in Aaron's office, the scene of the crime, nor back here at the house. But the doc wouldn't let it go. Like a dog refusing to surrender its bone, he demanded that I give him the names of the doctor or doctors who had written the prescriptions. I promised the fellow I would do everything in my power to find out, and finally got him to leave. The obstinate quack insisted he'd come and have another look at his patient in the morning, before Aaron gave himself up to the police. That meant I would have to get Aaron out of there before the pit bull's return. I shuddered to think what might happen if anyone got wind of the true story. I thanked the doctor warmly and shut the door behind him with a sigh of relief, only to have to face Rivka, standing there demanding answers.

"What in God's name is going on, Motke?" she said, staring at me with a mixture of distrust and worry. "Aaron raping a girl? There's no one on earth more good-natured than your brother. Surely he would never, ever do anything like that! What's come over him? And what was that crazy story of yours about the pills? Did you give him something nasty to swallow? That new preparation, perhaps, since that's all you know how to talk about these days? Did he get injected with that testosterone crap

Rafaël's been working on? Is Aaron one of your guinea pigs? Has Rafaël been experimenting on him? Tell me it isn't true!"

That was one of those times when I regretted having married a smart woman who wouldn't let me pull the wool over her eyes. I asked her to make us a cup of tea, and then sat down at the kitchen table with her.

"Rivka, I'm going to tell you something in the strictest confidence. A secret I trust will never pass your lips. You're making me come clean with you, because your guesses are not that far off. You're right, but you're also wrong. Rafaël has nothing whatsoever to do with this. He knows nothing about it and it's crucial he never does. Aaron was given that stuff by a specialist he consulted, because all the signs were pointing to the fact that his body was producing too little testosterone, and it was ruining his life. Something must have gone wrong with the dosage. I had at one point suggested to the doctor he might want to step the treatment up a bit, since Aaron was in such a bad way. But if it gets out that my brother was receiving a bigger dose than the one prescribed by Rafaël, all hell will break loose."

"So Aaron and Rosie are now the victims not only of that *brilliant* discovery of yours, but also of your everlasting impatience? Christ! Why do you always have to have it your way? Why can't you ever accept the fact that someone else may know better?" Rivka jumped up, snatched a sponge off the counter, and wiped the table clean for the second time.

"Well," I admitted, "I really did think I was doing Aaron a favor. I was wrong, I now know that, to my chagrin. But if a word of this leaks out, it's curtains for the company. A catastrophe, not just for myself or for our family, but for the hundreds of workers who will lose their jobs and become beggars. So if only for their sake, Rivka, you'd best keep quiet about this. I shall do everything in my power to contain the harm this will do to Aaron."

"And Rosie?" she asked. "That poor girl, what are you going to do for *her*?"

"I'll give her whatever help she needs, rest assured of that."

"Tell me, though, Motke," she said, looking at me coldly, "give me one good reason why I should stick up for you. I've been raising our four girls, I run your household, but that's about it. There hasn't been much else to keep us together these last few years. Why should I go to bat for you?"

The coldness of her tone shocked me.

"You're not the only one who's upset that we seem to have drifted apart," I said quietly. "I too wish we could get back to being as close as we used to be. How the hell did we end up here?"

Rivka had sat down again and was staring darkly into her teacup. She stirred it with her spoon and then looked up at me earnestly. "You're miles away," she said. "Sometimes I have the feeling that we're living on two separate continents that are drifting apart. There's a wide and savage sea between us preventing me from reaching you. It's as if I can just catch the occasional glimpse of you standing over there on your iceberg, pontificating. I often find myself thinking that somewhere inside that arrogant prick, surely, there must be the man who once swept me off my feet. The winsome lad I wound up marrying because my father insisted on it, to spare my family the scandal. And even though no one ever asked *me* if I wanted to get married, our marriage did make me happy at first. Where is that Motke, the man who showed me the Amstel River by night, who bewitched me with all his charm, and taught me there is nothing more thrilling than two beings in love becoming one? Where did that man go? I miss him."

I think I felt sort of sorry for her then; she looked so terribly sad and lonely. I got up, kneeled by her chair, and gave her a hug. Her body stiffened at first, as if steeling itself against me, but then she snuggled her head against my shoulder.

"I'm so sorry, darling," I said, caressing her gently. "You don't deserve this. The boy you fell for, or, I guess you might say, the boy who fell on you"—here I chuckled softly—"is still here, I promise. Here, feel."

I took her hand and placed it over my heart. "He's still in there, always. Except that of late he hasn't been coming out as often as he'd like. He has to act tough, he's shouldering heavy responsibilities, he's under a lot of stress; there are so many people who depend on him. If he were to show his open, vulnerable side, the wolves out there would tear him to pieces in a heartbeat. He's had to harden himself; he has to keep fighting. Otherwise, they'll just walk all over us—me, you, and the girls."

Rivka lifted her head and shook it in denial. "No, Motke, I'm not buying it. You say you wouldn't be able to get through life showing your softer side. That the only way to survive is to fight, to make others obey you, to crack the whip. I don't buy it, I refuse to accept it. Loving others, having compassion—those are our greatest strengths."

I took her head between my hands. "You are a woman, Rivka, of course that's the way you feel. Your life is at home with our little girls; your job is to teach them how to love. But I'm standing out on the prairie where I can hear the hyenas howling, ready to pounce. I'm guarding the entrance to our lair, to stop wild beasts from devouring you and the children. That is the man's role, the role of the boy you once fell for."

"I believe there's another way," she insisted. "I want there to be another way; I can't accept this. I say we stand shoulder to shoulder outside our lair and set an example of how to face the world with love and kindness."

We looked at each other as if we were really seeing each other for the first time. Her frown slowly relaxed into a smile, and I found myself smiling back. Slowly, slowly, with almost painful deliberation, we leaned closer and kissed, long and passionately. Rivka pressed her body against mine, and, with our lips still locked together, we stood up and I led her to the room with the guest bed. Aaron was in the room next door, oblivious to the fact that this was his last night of freedom, and I made love to my wife in my disgraced brother's house. It was the best time I ever had with her, the best sex I ever had with any woman.

That night, sometime during those pitiless, endless hours after my twin brother's life was destroyed by a testosterone overdose and both my business career and my company were hanging in the balance, one of my sperm bored its way into one of Rivka's egg cells, and Ezra, my only son, my youngest child, was conceived.

27...

It was still dark when in the chilly and bleak early-morning hours, I walked Rivka home. We strolled along the dank, deserted streets, still dazed from the experience of the past few hours, when we'd been closer than ever before. When Rivka kissed me goodbye at the front door of our house, she said, "Tonight I felt he was with me again, the boy I once fell in love with. I can't say I know where we go from here, but it's nice to know that boy is still in there somewhere under all the body armor."

She shut the door softly, and I hurried back to Aaron's house. There I took a shower, brewed a pot of coffee, and, gathering up all the scattered glasses of stale whiskey, overflowing ashtrays, and dirty plates, stacked them on the kitchen counter. Then I quietly went into Aaron's bedroom. He was still in bed, wrapped in a blanket. His eyes were open; he was staring at the ceiling and didn't react when the door opened. I returned to the kitchen to pour him a cup of coffee and carried it back to the bedroom, then sat down on the edge of the bed and offered him the hot brew. He sat up slowly, as if every movement cost him extraordinary effort, took a few sips, and then gave the mug back to me.

"How are you doing, kid?" I asked.

He gazed at me with half-closed eyes, but it was as if he didn't see me. He was somewhere else entirely; I imagined he was drifting through some dark and dismal ghost world, haunted by swarms of demons.

I wished I could have sat with him like that all morning, waiting for him to come back to earth from that distant realm, and let him calmly get used to the idea that this would be the last time he'd wake up a free man, at least for the foreseeable future. But there was no time for dawdling. My brother had to be delivered to the police station before the pit-bull doctor's return.

"Aaron," I said carefully, unsure how he'd take what I had to tell him, fearing it might bring out the madman in him again, "I spoke to the police yesterday. Rosie had gone to see them, and I schmoozed until I was blue in the face to get you off. The officer in charge wasn't unsympathetic, but there's such an uproar about what happened that we can't just sweep it under the rug. You'll have to go to the police."

Aaron lifted his head. His voice sounded hoarse, as if the previous day's bellowing had strained his vocal cords. "Are they coming for me?"

"No," I said softly. "I promised I would take you in. But I'm going to get you the very best lawyer in the business."

"No," he said firmly. "I don't want a lawyer. I deserve my punishment, the harshest punishment there is. I'm prepared to serve my time. There's no denying I did what I did, and no excuse for it either."

He made a move to get out of bed, but I held him back with a gentle push. I would have tried to persuade him that he had the right to a defense, that he should not deprive himself of the opportunity, but he had spoken with such fierce determination that I just didn't have the heart to insist. There was some other urgent business to get off my chest, however.

"We do have another thing to discuss, Aaron, before we go," I told him. "About the doctor who gave you those injections—I'm afraid that was what made you behave the way you did."

"I'm sure that it was," Aaron said, starting to fold the blanket painfully slowly. His hoarse voice was barely audible as he went on. "As it turns out, our esteemed professor's heaven-sent discovery possesses satanic powers. Are you intending to go ahead anyway with producing that tripe?"

"We'll have to see, naturally. Something went terribly wrong, and you were the victim. And Rosie too, of course," I added quickly, since Aaron was about to interrupt me. "But," I went on, "if word gets out that you were being treated with that stuff, our goose is cooked. And, well, it's obvious the doctor gave you an overdose, but I beg you to go easy on him. Yesterday I put out the story that you'd been stockpiling a whole slew of different antidepressants, and that those had been responsible for everything going awry."

"You're a rat, Motke," said Aaron, for the first time looking at me, with narrowed eyes; "you are the most despicable sleaze-bag I know. I'm ashamed to have you as my brother. I'd bet my life that the reason you're all in a sweat right now isn't so much because of what I've done to that poor girl, or because I'm going to jail, but because you're worried this little ruckus might expose your own dirty hands in this whole sordid affair, am I right?"

I looked him straight in the eye, and he stared right back at me. A staring contest, to see who would back off first. It took everything I had not to look away. Aaron's eyes bored stonily into mine. Looks can kill, they say. It was agony. In the end I had to avert my eyes from his. I looked down at my feet, thinking that Aaron did not even know the half of it; he had no idea how involved I had been in his downfall. I considered making a clean breast of it, but before I could make up my mind, he spoke up.

"It would serve you right if word got out about the way you've abused your position. I have committed a single, heinous wrong, and I am ready to atone for it. But *you've* been getting away with one dirty deed after another, and you go about it in such a sneaky way that the victims don't even realize it's not their own fault. I've known you long enough to have an idea of how you get those girls to think they're just as guilty as you of whatever obscene thing you're doing to them."

I wanted to interrupt him, to beg him for the sake of the firm not to reveal any of this. He put a hand over my mouth and went on. "Now you're going to try to persuade me not to do anything to endanger Farmacom's survival. That if people knew, your house of cards would come tumbling down and the whole workforce would be out on the street. You're good at that; you always hide behind the 'greater good,' which allows you to get away with your shenanigans. But you don't fool me, Motke. It's all about you, always. You are the center of your universe, and everything else is only there to serve your interests."

He paused for a moment and then continued. "But the scales have fallen from my eyes. I will never again defer to your wishes. I could make a huge stink about what you've done, which would land you behind bars. But no, I want to have as little to do with you as possible, I don't want to be locked up next to you in the clink. I'll keep my mouth shut about your proclivities, not to spare you, mind; you don't rate my clemency. I'll keep silent because I am just as guilty of your sins as you. All this time I knew what you were up to, and I turned a blind eye to what I saw. I was just another of the millions of chicken-livered cowards in this world.

Because of people like me, people like you get away with your evil behavior. A wimp who doesn't dare open his mouth isn't any better than the one doing the dastardly deed.

"I am going to jail. I won't deny a thing, I won't assist in any investigation whatsoever, and I'll pay the ultimate price. And only you will ever know that I'm atoning not just for my own sins, but also for yours. On one condition, mind, and don't you ever forget it: these indiscretions of yours have got to stop. If, while I'm in the slammer, or later, once I'm out again, I ever get a whiff indicating you're still fooling around with those girls at work, I won't rest until I've sent you and the whole caboodle down the tubes. And believe me, if you ever so much as lift a finger to touch some innocent thing, I will make it my business to find out about it. I want you to swear, both on the graves of our coldhearted parents and on your Rivka's goodness, that from now on you'll never lay a finger on any of the girls in the factory."

His words seemed to be coming from very far away. I stared at him, and after a pause, I said, "I swear, on the graves of our coldhearted parents and on the goodness of my wife."

Aaron nodded and swung himself out of bed. I extended a hand to help him up, but he shrugged it off. "And another thing, Motke," he said, unbuttoning his tattered and torn shirt, "after today I'll have nothing more to do with you. You are my brother no longer. Once I've done my time, I am never coming back to this shithole. And you'd better make sure that Rosie gets whatever she needs. Now I'm going to get washed, and then you may escort me to the police station, and after that, we'll each be a man without a brother."

Without wasting another glance at me, he disappeared into the bathroom.

28...

After dropping off Aaron at the police station, which he'd entered without bidding me goodbye, I rushed back to the office. I didn't have time to stop and think about the morning's events; the ship was still floundering, with a huge gash in the hull.

First I rang the doctor in Nijmegen and informed him of what had happened. I managed to assuage his panic, assuring him that I wouldn't breathe a word to anyone about Aaron's testosterone overdose. I pressured him not to tell Professor Levine about it either. This seemed to calm him down. The poor quack must have felt duty-bound as a scientist to fill the professor in, but at the same time he was scared shitless of Levine's wrath. My directive relieved him of that obligation. It's astonishing, really, how people will agree to a request if you make them believe it's an order. It's rare that they'll find the strength to resist an assertive demand and hang on to their own sense of what's right.

After putting down the phone I asked Agnes to gather together the office personnel who had witnessed Rosie's escape and heard my brother's brute bellowing of the previous day. Standing in the hall, I gave a short speech in which I apologized for Aaron and his transgression, brought about, I explained, by a harmful concoction of medications. He was already locked away in a cell, I told them, awaiting punishment. Moreover, I said, my brother was racked with remorse and wished more than anything that the dreadful episode had never happened. I sent the employees back to their desks, but not before warning that this was to be the last word spoken about this affair, and that I would not stand for any gossip. I also asked them to do all they could to nip in the bud any rumors undoubtedly already circulating on the outside.

"Farmacom belongs to us all," I said in conclusion, "and slander and scandalmongering affects all of you just as much as it affects my own family. Blackening the name of the firm is tantamount to besmirching your own. I hope and trust that by pulling together we can rid Farmacom of this blot on its otherwise sterling reputation. I thank you sincerely."

There was a smattering of applause from the white-coated employees, and some quiet chatter as they returned to their desks.

I shut myself into my office and asked Agnes for a cup of coffee, hoping it would help me get over my exhaustion. Aaron's tongue-lashing had cast a pall, robbing me of the will to go back to work. I was tempted, just for an instant, to throw in the towel, to leave it all behind, the damn factory, Levine, my children, even my "trophy wife," and make a break for it. How would it feel to flee this doomed continent like a thief in the night, and to go live the good life somewhere else, on a white sandy beach in some exotic locale among the noble savages?

I took a sip of strong coffee and considered what else remained to be done that morning.

I was about to spring into action when Agnes rang to say the priest was there, demanding to speak to me immediately. Annoyed, I told her to think of some excuse to get rid of him.

"Just make an appointment with him for some time next week," I suggested, and was about to put down the receiver.

"I already tried that, but he says it can't wait," she replied. Then I heard her shout "*No!*" and at the same time my office door flew open. The clergyman, normally so sedate and cautious, burst into my room, slamming the door behind him. His pasty face was flushed bright red, he had a wild look in his eyes, and his black cassock was buttoned askew. He leaned against the shut door, as if hoping to keep out the bogeyman that was on his tail.

"Father," I greeted him, mustering a feeble smile with some difficulty. The last thing I needed right now was a sermon from the padre.

"Mr. De Paauw," he panted, slowly detaching himself from the door and advancing toward my desk, "I must speak to you urgently."

I pointed to the chair in front of my desk and invited him to say what was on his mind, adding that I didn't have much time. Unlike his customary delivery, which entailed beating around the bush for as long as possible, he came straight to the point. "The unspeakable events that took place in this establishment yesterday are the talk of the town."

He drummed his bony fingers together more restlessly than ever. "The town is all abuzz about your brother's brutal attack on that little Jewish girl. People are furious, and are spreading the most horrific stories. They say the girl was grievously harmed, and that she has died of her injuries." As he repeated these rumors, he leaned conspiratorially closer.

"That's nonsense," I replied. "I personally saw her yesterday, at the police station, where she was filing her complaint. She's had a nasty shock, but other than that she's quite unharmed. Don't you know how these stories get spread?"

"Mr. De Paauw, the rumor about the little Jew girl is only one of the stories going around. They're saying this is just the tip of the iceberg." He opened his eyes as wide as saucers to stress the gravity of the situation. "Supposedly there's plenty of other improper cavorting going on here. Not just on the part of your brother, but" —waving his forefinger in the air, he swallowed in his peculiar way— "it's said that you yourself have frequently taken advantage of these young women. I had heard the rumors before but never paid much attention to them, as I told you in our last conversation. I thought it behooved me, however, to inform you of the gossip. Furthermore, the angry mood out there alarms me; I fear that even I may feel the repercussions too."

He paused to give these last words extra weight. So, the truth was coming out at last.

"I therefore thought it advisable," he continued, "to discuss with you how we can put out this fire before it consumes us both."

I looked at him sternly. The padre's knickers were all in a twist, it seemed, because this whole cock-up was threatening to expose his own illicit dilly-dallying with his Catholic flock. And what, he was now expecting *me* to help him get out of trouble?

"Reverend," I said, "am I to understand that you have not always been able to keep your hands to yourself, and are now afraid it may come to light on account of my brother's transgression?"

The man's face grew scarlet; he hung his head and made the sign of the cross as if to ward off my words, which had just hurled his sins out into the universe, and nodded almost imperceptibly.

"So? What do you want from *me*? How am *I* supposed to help you with that?" I steamed.

"Well, we are both in the same boat, aren't we, Mr. De Paauw?" he lisped, glancing up. "I came here so that we might, as it were, join forces."

"In the same boat? You and I?" I asked. "I don't quite see it that way, Father. I gather that you have not been able to control yourself with your parishioners. In my case, however, we're talking about mere rumors. The chief of police himself admitted to me yesterday that there is no evidence to support the accusation of one of my employees, Bertha, also one of your flock, who I'm sure is the source of these rumors insofar as they pertain to me. I do understand that this is an unpleasant situation, but I don't see how I can be of help to you. It seems to me that it would make more sense for you to appeal to the mayor, who may be able to put his influence to good effect."

The padre's face went white as a sheet; he scrunched up his eyes and sucked in his thin lips. His normally beatific expression twisted into a pained grimace.

"You are mistaken, Mr. De Paauw. For years I have been hearing over and over again about quite a goodly number of youngsters in my flock being forced into having sexual intercourse with you, or other carnal practices. Here, in this room, on *that* sofa"—here he pointed accusingly at the Cozy Corner—"all kinds of lewd scenes have played out; my own occasional trespasses pale in comparison. I have always defended you until now, but that can change in a heartbeat," he concluded, trying to muster a threatening scowl. Then he looked at me expectantly, as if he trusted I'd be badly shaken by his words.

"Ha! You come storming in here with some cockamamie story that Rosie was murdered, whereas I can prove to you that she is very much alive and that physically, there doesn't seem to be anything wrong with her. Isn't that evidence enough, Father, that you mustn't believe everything you hear through the grapevine? I have nothing to hide. And I'm not going to atone for anything. My employees know that ugly gossip is not tolerated in our firm. How you deal with it in your parish is *your* problem. And please forgive me, but I am terribly busy right now, as you can surely imagine."

I stood up to show that, as far as I was concerned, the interview was over. The preacher remained slumped in his chair, defeated. I strode up to where he sat, slipped my hand under his arm, and pulled him to his feet. Then I led him to the door. As I showed him out, I said quietly, "Go see the mayor, surely he'll be able to help you hush up those nasty rumors. I wish you the best of luck, reverend Father."

Ignoring my outstretched hand, he turned away brusquely. I quickly shut the door behind him.

29...

The padre's visit had dispelled both my somber mood and my exhaustion. I asked Agnes for Rosie's address and hurried over to her parental home, a ramshackle hut near the tracks. The door-frame was askew and a mezuzah dangled from a loose nail, not to mention the peeling paint on the windowsill; the wood was in an advanced state of decay. The window was so filthy you couldn't see through it, and it was cracked right up the middle. I knocked. A strident voice yelled something unintelligible, and a few moments later the door was yanked open. A frazzled-looking woman appeared, worn down by poverty like so many of the womenfolk in our dreary town. Her thin frame brought to mind Rosie's sinewy slenderness, except that, in the mother's case, all the softness and freshness was missing. She was holding a baby in her large, splayed hands, and I could make out several other children in the dark room.

Seeing me startled her; she took a step back and peered at me suspiciously.

"Good morning," I began, "are you Mrs. Groen? Rosie's mother?"

She nodded with obvious reluctance. "My name is De Paauw, I'm the brother of . . ." I said, rather uncomfortably; "could I have a word with you?"

Grudgingly she moved aside to let me through, and pointed to a chair drawn up to the table in the center of the stuffy room. The children stopped their game and stared at me shyly and wide-eyed as I stepped inside, taking off my hat and unbuttoning my overcoat before sitting down.

"Bram," the mother barked sharply, upon which the oldest boy, a child of around ten, looked up at her questioningly, "take Berel and the little ones out to the shed."

The children scrambled obediently to their feet; the boy took the baby from her and they all disappeared through the back door.

"Is Rosie home?" I asked.

The woman shook her head.

"Do you have any idea where she is?" I inquired carefully.

She shrugged.

"I want to apologize to you, in the name of my brother, for what he did to her. I take it you know what happened?'

The woman laughed scathingly.

"There ain't a dog in this town don't know what happened. News like that spreads faster 'n fire. Folks lap it up, as long as it's not their own kids." She glared at him. "We thought it best for Rosie to go work for you, and not Van der Vlis or Bartelsma. Goyim don't respect the likes of us, and I'd hoped it would be different over at your place."

"I am terribly sorry about what happened, and I want you to know I'll do everything I can to make amends. How is she?"

Again she gave a sullen shrug.

"I would like to speak to her, to apologize to her on my brother's behalf, and to see what we can do for her."

My words had quite a different effect from the one I'd expected.

"You know what you can do, Mr. De Paauw?" she said, standing up and placing her hands on her hips. "You can just stay the hell away, as far away from us as possible. We've got enough troubles without you coming here bothering us with your smut and filth. Isn't all the money we make for you, us and our children, enough? Can't you just be happy being filthy rich? Why do you have to go and drag our kids—the only thing in life we got more of than you—through your scuzzy slime? You've got daughters yourself, don'tcha?"

She strode to the door and yanked it open. "Now get out," she growled. "You've taken my darling, my eldest girl, from me, you and your brother. She was such a happy little thing, the apple of my old man's eye. Now he's kicked her out of the house. Doesn't want people talking. See, that's men for you! And don't ever come back here again. Leave us the hell alone."

Getting to my feet, I pulled my wallet out of my pocket and left a hundred guilders on the table. The woman looked at the money greedily, having probably never laid eyes on such a huge sum. She marched over to the table, snatched up the hundred-guilder bill, and whipped it away into her apron pocket.

"Blood money," she muttered. "You think you can just fix anything, don'tcha, with money. If I didn't have my young 'uns, I'd have you watch me tear it to pieces. But I can't afford to do that. Just don't think this makes up for what you've done to us."

She stepped aside, and I made my escape. The rickety door was slammed shut behind me.

• • •

Back in the office, Agnes handed me the morning editions of *De Telegraaf* and *Volk en Vaderland*, two newspapers that relished any excuse to show the Jewish people in a bad light, turning every smoldering ember into a huge conflagration. Aaron's transgression was front-page news. His "Jew behavior" was described in gory detail. None of it could be verified, of course, simply because no one had witnessed what had really gone on in that room. Rosie was the only one who could have shed light on it, but the papers reported that she could not be found, and reinforced the speculation that she had died of her injuries. The interior pages too featured prominent articles describing our firm's activities. A photograph of the factory gate and of Bertha, the prime witness, ran alongside. The fat bitch reported with relish that not only Aaron but I in particular, as well as the rest of the Jew directors (including that professor from Amsterdam), were all guilty of sexually abusing the factory workers. Interestingly enough, she did not confess to being one of the supposedly injured parties—I guessed because she wasn't sure if such an admission would mark her as a victim or as something worse, and she didn't want to go through the rest of her life branded as the company whore. In the article she claimed she had always resisted my indecent advances, implying that her refusal had led to her dismissal.

What a God-given gift I had handed to our homegrown brownshirts! Inspired by the propaganda of their political brethren across the border, our own extremists were likewise engaged in proving that the Jewish people did not deserve to be called human—a crucial first step in the establishment of a fascist utopia in which there was to be no place for us. After all, getting rid of an inferior species is much easier than going after your own sort. By allowing myself the occasional little indulgence, I had played straight into the scumbag's hands. Crushed, I sat at my desk, cursing the proclivities that had brought me into this fix. In all my fooling around I had never foreseen this scenario. Call me naïve, in view of the tide of hatred that had been sweeping across Europe for some years. What could I do to quell this storm?

As I sat there stewing about what to do, Rafaël called. I'd quite forgotten about him in all the commotion. The daily telephone and telegram traffic between Amsterdam and our factory meant that his lab was already abuzz with yesterday's event. Rafaël grimly insisted on an explanation. When I gave him the story about the dangerous cocktail of drugs, he sounded just as skeptical as the doctor who had sedated Aaron the day before.

"Some months ago you asked me for the name of a doctor who might be able to help an acquaintance of yours with low testosterone symptoms. It occurred to me at the time it might be Aaron you had in mind. What has been going on, Motke? You owe me an explanation."

Unnerved, I couldn't think of what to say. Rafaël went on. "You'd be best advised to tell me the truth. One phone call to Nijmegen will tell me all I need to know. I would very much appreciate hearing from you how it came to this."

"Not over the phone, Rafaël," I responded.

When there's a big brouhaha, switchboard operators tend to forget that their bosses' private affairs are not meant for their ears.

"Can you come here?" I asked him.

It would take a couple of hours for Rafaël to arrive, which should give me some time to concoct a plan. Good God, how was I ever to ride out this storm, what with Rosie nowhere to be found, my brother in the slammer, my dirty laundry hung out to dry, and the colossus from Amsterdam in a steaming rage, on his way to hear my story?

• • •

By the time an obviously agitated Rafaël marched into my room, I had already decided I could not hide the truth from him, not the truth about my brother's testosterone regimen, anyway. Rafaël greeted me curtly and sat down, imperious. He looked even bigger and more imposing than usual. He stared at me with a grim, implacable look, tugging at his mustache, which, unlike his former nationality, he had not yet parted with.

"I am listening," he said, and waited.

I took a deep breath and confessed the truth about my visit to the clinician, stressing that it was concern for my brother that had driven me to it, and that I deeply regretted my foolhardy actions. Rafaël glared at me stone-faced.

"A sorry and dangerous business," he finally decided, looking angrier than I had ever seen him. "Motke, I did not call those hormones soul glands for nothing. Even though we are still in the dark as to how they precisely function, all indications are that the substances we have been extracting don't merely bring about physiological reactions; they also appear to have a strong effect on the psyche. We have no idea how that works. It's a complex problem, a devilish job. In our clinical trials we are exposing patients to processes whose mechanisms we still don't yet really understand. In fact, what we've been doing is dropping the patients into a minefield. We try to contain the danger by being extra prudent, leading them to safer ground with the greatest of caution. That way we are able to expand our knowledge gradually, slowly but surely clearing away the land mines. But *you*—always so arrogant and impatient—you thought nothing of dumping your brother into the middle of that minefield, and letting him run around among all the explosives until he blew himself up. The fact that you so contemptuously disregarded my instructions, thereby not only jeopardizing your brother's health, but also throwing our discovery and my own reputation under the bus, *that*, Motke, is what I cannot forgive."

I said nothing.

"That man will be traumatized for life," Rafaël continued, "and the same goes for that poor girl. How is she?"

I told him I had seen Rosie at the police station, that her father had thrown her out of the house, and that she had been missing ever since.

Rafaël shook his head, incredulous. "Raped and then kicked out of the house by her father? Why?"

I explained that in these parts, it was generally assumed that a rape victim must somehow have asked for it, and that a girl who was no longer a virgin disgraced her whole family. The father wasn't necessarily a monster; he had, as I had seen with my own eyes, a host of other offspring whose miserable chances in this narrow-minded society would only get worse as long as Rosie remained part of the household. In the eyes of the people here, Rosie was now like a rotten head of cabbage in a green-grocer's crate, and the simplest way to make the whole thing go away was to hustle the spoiled vegetable quickly out of sight.

Rafaël lit a cigar and blew a thoughtful ring of smoke into the air. "Poor child," he muttered.

This new turn gave me the courage to give the prof an account of how I had managed to keep both the testosterone and the doctor and myself out of it.

"Your cunning in saving your own skin exceeds by far your insight into your own limitations," Rafaël concluded. "I should like to talk to your brother, to find out what he has gone through these past few months, and how the changes in him manifested themselves. The least we can do is learn from this horrendous experience."

I told him there was little chance of Aaron's agreeing to speak with him.

"First I had better go to Nijmegen," he decided. "I have a bone to pick with that doctor. Let's hope he's been keeping good records."

He was about to get up, but I asked him to remain seated. I showed him the newspapers, which, besides trumpeting the drama of yesterday, also broadly alleged that not only I but Rafaël too was guilty of sexual abuse. Rafaël read the articles with an air of indifference.

"I had heard the rumors concerning you. Whether they are true or not, only you can say. I don't think I even want to know. But the way the supposed misdeeds of a single individual can be shifted onto an entire race, that is something I do know about. I thought moving to this country and becoming Dutch had saved me from that kind of insanity for good. Well, there it is. One cannot escape one's destiny."

He pushed the papers away from him and got to his feet. With his hand on the doorknob, he turned toward me. "There has been a serious breach of trust, Motke. This incident will not improve our relationship, but we are constrained to continue it. I need Farmacom and Farmacom needs me. The situation in Europe makes parting impossible for the time being. I have considered emigrating to North or South America, as far away as possible from the approaching madness." He pointed to the newspapers he had just tossed aside. "But there is a limit to the number of times a man is capable of establishing himself and creating a home in a new place. I don't have the energy to do it again, I fear. I feel old, for the first time in my life."

As he said that, the burly, imposing colossus suddenly seemed vulnerable. Then he nodded and left the room.

30...

Rosie seemed to have vanished off the face of the earth. I did make several attempts to find out what had happened to the girl, but she had left no trace. Even the tabloid rats, who conducted a smear campaign against Aaron, myself, and the entire board for weeks, did not manage to track her down. Where had she gone to escape her father's wrath and the ugly gossip of our town? Had she been given shelter by relatives elsewhere in the country, or was she licking her wounds somewhere all by herself?

The possibility remained that one of my other employees would file a complaint against me, but the danger of that happening began to fade as time went on and nothing happened. My threats of dismissal if any of them so much as breathed a word appeared to have done the trick, and they must have been afraid that in this intolerant hick town, giving evidence against me would backfire on them. Even fat Bertha was keeping remarkably quiet.

The padre seemed to be profiting from the same fear. His offenses did receive some attention in the newspapers, but there was no investigation, let alone a conviction. I went to see the mayor to suss out the situation, and learned the good man was so shocked at the muckraking in the popular press that he was only too eager to agree that the malfeasance ascribed to our firm's leadership was a complete fantasy.

I kept my word to Aaron. I didn't so much as lay a finger on any of the girls, and in fact the horror of what happened did seem to be holding my libido in check. It turns out that fear and guilt are effective antidotes to impetuous passion.

One evening—I had just returned home from England, where I had gone looking for opportunities to transfer part of our operation for safety in case the scumbag next door made good on his promise to invade Czechoslovakia, since the possibility of a war in Europe had to be taken increasingly seriously—Rivka remarked over our after-dinner coffee in the salon, "That catastrophic day has had yet another unexpected consequence, Motke."

I looked at her, alarmed. I had only just begun to relax a bit, and had stopped feeling I had to be on the constant lookout for the next disaster. She smiled, and patted her stomach. "There's an occupant in here again," she said. "You hit another bull's eye, you incorrigible stud." She went up to me and gave me a kiss. Then she said, "What would you think of seeing our harem invaded by a little guy? Wouldn't that be the icing on the cake for our family?"

She looked at me, glowing. Rina, the youngest of our four girls, was now eight years old, and we'd considered our family complete. Each previous pregnancy had led to speculation about a baby boy, and even though after every birth we told each other that a healthy baby was all that counted and we didn't care it wasn't a boy, we did express some regret when the last one again turned out to belong to the weaker sex.

It had never for a moment crossed my mind that our night of love in Aaron's guest room might lead to another pregnancy—as if there was no way it could happen in such an abnormal situation. I didn't know what to think. Of course I congratulated Rivka, but her announcement didn't make me jump for joy, as it had every other time she'd announced she was expecting. The fact that this unplanned baby could only have been conceived during that nightmarish night made me ambivalent, to say the least. The child would be a continual reminder of my culpability, my failings, and my twin brother's downfall. Ezra owed his existence to that whole excruciating fiasco.

• • •

Aaron was moved to the jail in the provincial capital, not far from our sleepy little town. Rivka visited him a few times, always returning home downcast, moved by his terrible remorse, his endless self-reproach, and his great loneliness. She was his only visitor, and even in prison he was deeply despised, reviled by his fellow inmates for being a child molester and a pervert. He never asked after me and did not want to hear her mention my name.

Three months after the disaster it was time for his court date. Thanks to the smear campaign in the papers, the case was still a hot topic and very much in the news. I didn't have the courage to go to the trial, telling myself that Aaron would not want me there. Rivka did go, and I came home from work that night dying to hear what happened. To my surprise, she hadn't come home yet. It was already past seven; the nanny had given the children their dinner and was tucking Rina into bed. My three other daughters were in the salon, in a state of agitation because it wasn't Rivka's wont to come home later than expected. I tried to hide my own consternation from them, absentmindedly ate the food the cook served me, sent the staff home, and then played with the children, something I rarely did—a rollicking game of snakes and ladders. In their enthusiasm they forgot their anxiety. They went up to bed after I assured them there was nothing wrong and that they would see their mother at breakfast.

The hours crept by slowly. I paced up and down the living room, every once in a while going to the front door to peer down the deserted street, and then returning to pacing the parquet until I couldn't stand it anymore and had to go back for another look, hoping for a glimpse of my wife. What could have happened, for cripes' sake?

The telephone rang at ten-thirty. It was Rivka. She informed me in a cold, formal voice that she was at her parents' house in Amsterdam.

"What are you doing there?" I asked, astonished "Didn't you go to the trial? It wasn't canceled, was it?"

"No it wasn't, Mordechai," she said.

I frowned. Rivka only called me by my full name when she was angry with me.

"I was there. It was atrocious; the gallery was chock-full of brownshirts, yelling the most hateful insults at Aaron. The judge had to keep threatening to clear the courtroom. Aaron just sat there motionless, never looking up. He pleaded guilty and said that he deserved his punishment and accepted it. Apart from that he refused to speak. He got twenty-nine months, with credit for time served."

I was stunned. Naturally, the fact that he hadn't tried to defend himself or to deny any of it had made a light sentence most unlikely, but nearly two and a half years behind bars—it was an enormous price to pay for a first-time offense. I sighed.

"How awful," I said. There was silence on the other end. Trying to process the information I'd just been given, I clean forgot how strange it was that Rivka was calling me from Amsterdam.

When I did remember, I asked her why she was at her parents' house.

"I can't and won't go into it right now," she said, still in the same strange, cold tone of voice. "But maybe you'll catch on, Mordechai, when I tell you that the prime witness was present in the courtroom."

"Rosie was there?" I could not hide the shock in my voice.

"Yes, Mordechai, she was there. She was very brave and composed, and told the court exactly what happened that day." Rivka stressed the words *that day*, and I must confess that I was relieved to hear it.

"And then," Rivka went on, "Rosie and I had a nice long chat. About how she's doing, about what happened that terrible day—and about what happened before that day. And you may be interested to know she is pregnant with a child that's about a month older than the one I am carrying. I have some things to arrange here, Mordechai, for her and for myself too. You'll have to look after yourself and the girls for a few days, for a change. You'll be hearing from me in good time." Then she hung up.

All the blood had drained from my face. I felt dizzy and looked around for a chair, but there weren't any in the hallway where the telephone was kept. I replaced the receiver and sank to the ground. Maybe I wept—I don't exactly recall.

31...

That was the night when I was first plagued by the hallucinations that have been haunting me ever since.

Hauling myself up off the floor, I sat down in my leather easy chair, a glass and a bottle of whiskey within reach, roiled by rapidly shifting emotions: remorse, despair, wounded pride, and anger drowning one another out, leaving my mind in utter chaos.

Then came the Furies. They came slithering out from behind the Art Deco geometrics papered over the baroque scenes of romantic idylls that had once upon a time adorned these walls. The three Furies made straight for me; they were dead ringers for Rivka, Rosie, and Bertha. And as they drew closer they were suddenly transformed into gruesome monsters. Their long, shiny locks turned into writhing, hissing snakes flickering their forked tongues at me; their mouths were twisted into contorted grimaces; the claw-like hands ending in long, pointy nails gripped blazing torches that were waved menacingly at me, while their terrifying eyes oozed thick drops of blood that rolled down their cheeks and fell onto the wood floor with soft, dull thuds. The goddesses of vengeance hovered before me, staring at me with their bloody eyes. I mustered all my strength to withstand their gaze, but I couldn't bear the awful sight. I lowered my head and shut my eyes, just as I'd done in the staring contest with Aaron, but it only served to draw screams from their distorted mouths, so that I realized there was no way to get rid of them. Stuffing my fingers in my ears did nothing to keep out the ghastly screeching. I cringed and felt the noise devouring me. It shattered my eardrums and drilled into my brain, setting off an explosion there. I felt the heat of their torches scorching my body as if I were tied to the stake with flames lapping at my feet. I could no longer distinguish my own screams from the harpies' shrieks; it was pandemonium all around.

Until I felt a hand on my shoulder, gently shaking me. "Papa, Papa!" I heard coming from somewhere far away. Slowly the screeching died down. Ruth, my fifteen-year-old firstborn, was standing in front of me, pale in her white nightgown, her long, dark hair tumbling in neat waves over her shoulders, her eyes filled with tears. She was gazing at me anxiously. Dazed, I looked up at her, and then peered around the room to make sure the goddesses of vengeance had really gone. I shuddered violently. Ruth withdrew her hand from my shoulder, cringing as if she thought I was about to attack her.

"What's the matter?" she whispered. "Papa, are you hurt?"

I tried to paste on a reassuring smile.

"No, sweetheart," I said, taking a deep breath. "I was just confused for a moment, but everything's fine again."

My words did not reassure her.

"Is something the matter with Mama?" she went on. "Where is she?"

"In Amsterdam, with Grandpapa and Grandmama," I replied. "She's got something to take care of there, but she's coming home soon, I promise."

"Are you...having a fight?" she asked carefully, afraid of being thought impertinent.

"Your mother is a little upset with me," I admitted. "It's shaken me up a bit, but everything's going to be all right, don't worry."

My soothing words didn't sound all that convincing.

"Does it have something to do with Uncle Aaron?" she pressed on. "With what he did to that girl?"

She was looking down at the floor, choosing her words carefully.

We had never told the children about what had happened to Aaron, explaining his absence by telling them he was on an overseas business trip. I had been operating under the illusion that our girls, in all their childish innocence, had been spared having to know the truth about their uncle.

"Who told you about Uncle Aaron?" I asked, trying to hide my alarm.

"Everybody's talking about it," she said. "In town and at school..." She hesitated, looking at me wide-eyed.

That was how I came to find out about the bullying and name-calling my daughters were being subjected to by their classmates. They were fed all kinds of disgusting stories, not just about the man they had only ever known as a gloomy but kindhearted uncle, but also about their father, who supposedly abused his female employees in the most dastardly way. I had to draw it out of her. She did try changing the subject, but in the end she confessed, sobbing, that it was all they talked about at school, and that my alleged depravity was ascribed to the fact that we belonged to an inferior race. Perversity and criminal behavior were only to be expected from our sort.

Speechless, I stared at my daughter, who, keeping her face averted and with a few last sobs, asked me, "It's only gossip, Papa, none of it's true, is it?"

I tried to reassure her, explaining that her uncle had indeed done a very bad thing, but only because he'd taken the wrong kind of medicine, and that he was terribly sorry for what he had done. And, feeling like the biggest hypocrite in the world, I assured her that *of course* her father would never, ever indulge in the obscene sort of behavior being whispered about in the schoolyard.

Somewhat mollified, she let me send her back to bed. I poured myself another large whiskey, but I couldn't shake a deep sense of shame and dull despair.

32...

My body is growing more sensitive by the day. It's as if my nerve endings have lost the ability to distinguish one stimulus from the next, so that everything gets chalked up to excruciating pain.

Mizie caresses my cheek, and it's as if her fingers are wrapped in barbed wire, scoring deep grooves into my skin. The young thing rubs the pink washcloth dipped in lukewarm, soapy water all over my body, and it feels as if I'm being scraped with burning-hot sandpaper. Their tender palliative care is just plain torture to me.

They don't take my screams seriously. Mizie croons at me, making the shushing sounds of a mother comforting her baby, and I can't seem to get it through to her that my oversensitivity isn't all in my head. Both this physical torment and the harrowing memories are making this futile extension of my life—ha, "life," is that what this is called?—a veritable season in hell.

Today Mizie has called in a doctor to back up her dearly held conviction that keeping me alive is still the right thing to do. The young man, who calls himself a geriatrician, is the "expert" when it comes to life-and-death decisions. Getting saddled with this jerk must be my comeuppance for all the medical concoctions I unleashed on the world in my lifetime. All those miracle drugs that were fought tooth and nail by the Catholic Church because we had renounced the humility expected of man and taken on ourselves the mantle of creator.

So now the quack is working his depressor like a surgical blade between my clenched lips, forcing them to open wide so that he can determine whether my tonsils are free of infection, and that my wizened tongue has yet to take on the appearance of terminal morbidity. Next he digs his icy stethoscope into my rib cage and avers that, despite my loud screams, he can hear my heart, that piece of creaky junk, still beating strong as an ox, and that my lungs, despite some evidence of fluid, which explains why I sometimes produce a rattling sound when I exhale, still have the wherewithal to pump the required air in and out. Palpating the abdomen, tapping on the kidneys, this whole cursed examination apparently persuades the quack that I am not yet qualified to die. When Mizie, still not completely reassured, asks him why even the slightest touch has me screaming like a banshee, he replies—peeling off the slippery gloves that protect him from getting infected by my vital dribble—oh, she mustn't worry about it too much. Old people are hypersensitive, that's all; it's not to be confused with physical pain. It's more like the screams of a toddler being made to submit to something it doesn't like. God, how I wish a long drawn-out deathbed on this subscriber to *Car and Driver* and *Arthritis Today*, so that he'll get to see for himself that even overqualified geriatricians can get it horribly wrong. A specialist is just a guy who's spent a lot of money drawing out his studies for as long as he could. It doesn't mean the twit's any smarter.

This state of pain and wretchedness propels me back to that time of utter despair when both my brother and Rivka were lost to me for good. The misery I felt then was like nothing else that's ever happened to me in my life. And that deep depression, which I did in the end find the willpower to overcome and never allow to take hold of me again, has begun gnawing through the wall I erected between myself and the pain. The poison is working its way in again, like a mole tunneling underneath the mightiest fortress and causing it to crumble to dust.

"Release me from the poison in my head!" was Hercules' cry of despair to Zeus. "I can endure any death, but please end this now." Like the king of the ancient gods, however, the almighty muck-a-muck up there refuses to hear my prayer.

• • •

It was the only time in fifty years of doing business that I called in sick. I told Agnes that I did not want to be disturbed. I couldn't seem to lift myself out of my funk. It took all I had the morning after Aaron's trial to face the children and give instructions to the domestic help. I explained that something had come up and Rivka wouldn't be coming home for a few days, and asked them to look to the children and the household; I wished to be left alone. I locked myself in my study and did not eat for days. I did sip a little water from time to time, but mostly I drank whiskey, leaving me in a permanent state of delirium. I'd sit staring into space for hours on end like a sack of potatoes, or I'd stretch out on the couch only to tumble into some horrible nightmare and wake up again in a sweat. I lost all sense of day or night and received constant visitations from the screeching Furies, who gave me a pounding headache, alternating with the specter of Aaron silently staring me down. Even Levine would appear every so often to chew me out for messing with my brother's soul glands and exposing him to a minefield of dangers. I was trapped in a cocoon of disconsolate gloom, the despair that had taken possession of me sapping all the strength I'd once possessed.

• • •

I had no idea how many days and nights had gone by when I heard someone trying to get into my room. An incessant knocking gradually roused me from my stupor. The knocking turned into banging, which stopped when I shouted at whoever it was to fuck off and leave me alone.

"I don't think so, Mordechai," I heard Rivka say evenly on the other side of the door. "Open this door at once."

Startled, I sat up and looked around my usually spotless study, which was in a sorry state. Empty whiskey bottles were scattered all over the floor, along with my shoes, waistcoat, tie, and jacket. An overflowing ashtray sat on the coffee table, surrounded by even more strewn cigarette butts. A glance in the mirror confirmed my worst suspicion: I looked awful, with my crumpled shirt untucked and my belt unbuckled; my hair was a tangled, dirty mop, and my eyes were bloodshot. I looked like my brother had on that terrible day that had been the start of our undoing. Rivka began hammering on the door again and I felt I had no choice but to open it and face my wife in that sorry state.

There she stood, the only woman who had ever really meant anything to me in my life—that was what had been dawning on me over the past few days. It's one of those cruel jokes fate likes to play: not until you've lost something do you understand how precious it is. I had taken Rivka's presence at my side for granted, as something that was mine by right, but it wasn't until I found myself imprisoned in that gray cocoon that the bitter truth came to me. I was certain that I had lost her forever. Like Orpheus, I was condemned to wander through the rest of my life mourning her. I cursed my blasted sex drive and infernal impatience, the root causes of all our misfortunes.

My wife stood in the doorway, shoulders squared, as if to steel herself for an encounter with the enemy. The troubles of the past days did not seem to have left their mark on her; she looked as beautiful as ever. Her sad, slightly bitter expression was that of a lovely, sorrowing Virgin Mary. Her long, dark curls were held in place by two simple combs, she wore dark-red lipstick, and her hands rested on the slight bulge of her stomach. When she saw me she raised her eyebrows.

"Is this how you look after the children?" she said coolly, averting her face as if I were a putrid rat. "You stink, Mordechai, go get washed, make yourself presentable, and then I'd like to speak with you."

I sidled past my wife with my head down, unable to look her in the eye, and mumbled that I'd be back as soon as I could.

33...

Bathed, scrubbed, and wearing a fresh suit, I appeared before Rivka. I had cleaned myself up as best I could, but I couldn't wash away my pallor or bleariness.

She was sitting in her armchair in the living room as I walked in, and gazed up at me critically. There was a pot of coffee on the table, which she picked up in order to pour a cup. I reached to take it, but she put it down in front of her, showing no intention of pouring me one. I looked at her, surprised, but she just launched into her monologue, staring straight ahead. It seemed that over the past few days she had zealously mapped out a future for both Rosie and herself. She spoke in a loud monotone, as if the only way she could get through what she had to say was by keeping all emotion at bay.

"I'll tell you what happened, and what I have decided to do. At the end of the trial, Aaron was immediately led away; I never got a chance to speak to him. He left the courtroom without a glance at the public gallery. Rosie, however, was quite startled to see me there, which wasn't at all surprising in light of the story she told me later, after I'd persuaded her to have a bite to eat with me. Her father had thrown her out of the house, and an aunt and uncle in the city had taken her in. At the time of Aaron's assault, she had already been pretty sure that she was with child. *Your child, Mordechai. You* had long been taking advantage of her; you had molested her over and over again. How *could* you?"

I could find nothing to say. She stared at me coldly for a while, and then went on with her story. "She hasn't told anyone. Not about what you did to her, and as little as she could get away with about her ordeal at the hands of Aaron. 'As long as you don't put it into words, you can pretend it never happened,' was her motto. 'I've never wanted to talk about it with anyone,' she said, 'because talking about it makes it real. As long as I'd only had to go through it inside that posh room—I'd never been in such a fancy place in my life!—and as long as it was my little secret, I could tell myself it wasn't real. I pretended it was just a bad dream, you know, the kind that keeps coming back night after night and you're helpless to stop it, you just have to wait it out until you wake up.'

"She told me she had found a way to endure your unwanted advances. Whenever you pulled her close, untied her apron, tugged down her undies, put her hand on your prick and then made her move it up and down, when you made her put it in her mouth or you put it inside her"—Rivka spat out the words in a voice containing nothing but revulsion—"she'd pretend she was drifting up and away, that she wasn't down there on that disgusting sofa. She was looking down from above, feeling absolutely nothing, watching you taking her, devouring her, as if she were looking at some man and some girl who had nothing to do with her. And once you'd pulled your *schlong* out of her, she'd go to the bathroom and vomit until nothing came up but bile. And then she'd return to her workstation and go back to filling pill bottles, ignoring the glances from the other girls, who were all smart enough to know what was going on, and trying not to think about it anymore."

It had never even occurred to me that the girls I lured to my sofa might not appreciate my advances, even though Aaron did try to warn me. I'd just taken his rebuke as yet another sign of his troubled soul; I thought he was envious of my easy conquests. I was, after all, an attractive, successful man. I sincerely believed that if the girl did show some resistance at first, it was only out of a sense of propriety, and that deep in her heart she had to be flattered by my attentions. I did not recognize myself in Rivka's description of me: a vile brute forcing innocent victims to pretend they were somewhere else in order to endure a horrific rape. I was just floored. I wanted to tell Rivka that, I wanted to explain to her how it had looked to me, but she didn't give me that chance.

"When her aunt found out she was pregnant, she ordered Rosie to get rid of it, even though by that time she was already showing, and so pretty far along. She was told that with a baby on the way she couldn't stay in her aunt's house. Rosie refused to submit to a back-alley abortion, which led to a terrible fight. One night her uncle threw her down the attic stairs in hopes of making her miscarry. She still has the scars from her fall on her face and arms. Another time her aunt gave her a big mug of coffee to drink, brewed with a good helping of sulfur from matchstick heads. When Rosie realized it was poison, she refused to drink it, but the uncle and aunt forced it down her throat. But the child in her belly is a stubborn one; it's determined to survive, welcome or not. Rosie couldn't really tell me why she was so keen on protecting the fetus, when having the baby would only create even more problems for her.

" 'It's not the baby's fault, is it, that I got myself knocked up?' she said to me. 'The day before my uncle pushed me down the stairs I felt it move for the first time. After all I've been through, am I supposed to spend the rest of my life feeling guilty for murdering my baby as well?'

"After that, her aunt and uncle told her she couldn't stay. She begged and pleaded with them not to throw her out until the day of the trial, and they agreed on the condition that she wear a baggy coat when she went out. Whenever there were visitors, she had to go sit in the attic; they didn't want her to be seen by anyone. The day of the trial was the first time she had appeared in public. The judge had asked her who the father of the baby was, but she'd refused to say. Leaving the courtroom, she'd had no idea where to go. That was why she agreed to come with me, and told me the whole story."

"So—did you take her to your parents' house?" I asked. My wife and my employee, both of them pregnant by me, in my in-laws' house—I couldn't think of a worse scenario.

"She did come with me, on the condition that I wouldn't tell anyone who the father was. She wanted to get as far away as possible from our town, from the factory, from her family, and especially from Aaron and you. We've done quite a bit of talking these past few days, and I have found a place for her in Amsterdam. She'll be safe there for the time being; the people there are helping her to look for work, and then we'll see. I'm going to keep in touch with her and have promised her she doesn't have to worry about money."

I nodded.

"And as far as the two of us go," Rivka went on, "I've been giving that a lot of thought too. The moment I realized what you'd been up to with Rosie and God only knows how many others, something inside me just died. I cannot and will not love a wicked man, even if he *is* the father of my four girls and the unborn child I am carrying.

"I dread the day it is born. What will I do if it turns out to be a boy? I wish I believed in God. I'd have fallen to my knees and begged him to give me another girl. How can I be a good mother to a child who later in life may be capable of doing to others what you have done?

"I seriously considered taking the children to live with my parents for a while. But if I were to tell my father and the rest of the world what you have done—what sort of future would my children have? Your reputation for depravity would rub off on them. If the world weren't such a terrifyingly dangerous place right now, I do think I'd have the guts to leave you. But with a child on the way, and that lunatic next door drooling about his Thousand-Year Reich, I don't dare. So I'm staying put for the time being. Our marriage is merely a business deal from now on, for the sake of the children. If someday I change my mind, or if the political situation changes, I'm out of here. With the children. You can take one of the guest rooms, and I'd appreciate it if you would be gone as often as you can. Just immerse yourself in your work; isn't that what you really want to do anyway? And if I ever catch you so much as touching one of the factory girls again, if you turn out to be a hopeless case and can't make yourself stop, I'm taking the story straight to *Volk en Vaderland*. Let those brownshirts go to town on you; see if I care."

I opened my mouth to respond, but she stood up and walked to the door. "Mordechai, I'm not interested in what you have to say. You've been pulling the wool over my eyes for far too long. Don't you remember the time I told you that I felt you were out on an iceberg somewhere, and there was a wild and savage sea between us? I've lost the will to swim over to your side. I'm giving you permission to float away, as far away from me as possible, in fact. As long as you make sure that for the children nothing changes. It's for their sake that I am staying, to give them as happy a childhood as possible."

She shut the door quietly, and the clacking sound of her heels on the floor tiles faded gradually away.

34...

I longed for my wife the way the Israelites once longed for the fleshpots of Egypt, but her rejection of me was so final that I had to accept her proposal of a marriage on ice, and believe me, it was agony, a festering wound.

At first I assumed that I would be able to win her back. So I tiptoed through the house, was on my very best behavior, and took great care not to upset the apple cart. I paid ample attention to the children, treated them more affectionately than was my wont, and did everything in my power to please my wronged wife in the hope of melting her iceberg, though she seemed set on remaining in a permanent state of war with me. Consoling myself with the thought that the birth of our baby would surely move her to forgive me, I waited, more patiently than ever before, for that day to arrive.

• • •

At Farmacom my return was greeted with relief, and I was immediately up to my ears in work obligations. It was urgent that we hammer out a deal with the German firm that had taken over our subsidiary in order to contain the harm done by the loss of our important Austrian market. The brutal annexation of Austria had taken a big bite out of our European sales territory, a serious hemorrhage from our bottom line.

The vacant office space left by my brother's abrupt departure was temporarily taken over by one of our staff, but in view of the increasingly complex, multifaceted nature of our business, it was important to find a heavy hitter, someone to strengthen and energize our management team. Even though Aaron had never been a very dynamic executive, I couldn't help noticing that his absence left a big hole, not only on account of his foreign connections, but also at home, since he had always had a better rapport with our employees than I did.

We had to hire more people for our chemical-pharmaceutical division, and right away, for new synthetic substitutes were being invented all around the world at an ever-accelerating pace. This meant new opportunities for us, but also fresh pitfalls. What to make of the British breakthrough that now made it possible to fabricate the female hormone synthetically, in the lab—so much simpler than our method of processing the urine of pregnant mares, which involved a huge capital outlay? A synthetic version of our testosterone hormone also already existed. It was the start of a great sea change for our industry: our line of work had become an exploration of substances imitating the effects of the naturally occurring hormones, often yielding superior results. A wild new horserace had begun worldwide, and we were going to need a great deal more manpower to keep up.

Furthermore, the precarious political situation compelled us to take steps to safeguard our business in case of an invasion. The Munich Agreement, in which the charlatan Neville Chamberlain, the bloody fool, had simply handed Sudetenland over to the great power-hungry bully in return for the worthless guarantee that the pig would leave the rest of Czechoslovakia and Europe alone, wasn't exactly reassuring.

"Peace for our time," Chamberlain declared once he was back on British soil after shamefully haggling out this deal like any low-down huckster. The idea that the prime minister of the nation that had become our most important export market (now that we could no longer sell our products to the den of thieves next door) could have let himself be hoodwinked by that brute filled me with rage. Not only did he hand Sudetenland to the ogre on a silver platter, but he also signed a non-aggression pact with that archfiend from hell! Still, there was nothing for it but to make the necessary preparations in case an invasion of our country obliged us to hightail it over to Chamberlain's stomping ground. A cousin of mine, Simcha de Paauw, ran the English branch of the De Paauw Slaughterhouse and Meatpacking Co. I had turned the shares of our foreign subsidiaries over to him in the form of a collateral loan. The deal was that in the case of an invasion, these would become property of the English branch.

I deposited duplicates of all the manufacturing instructions of our medical preparations in a London bank, and we converted our subsidiary, which we had set up in the early thirties, into a British limited company: Farmacom Laboratories Ltd., transferring the clients, brand names, and other rights. In this way we were able to honor any past deals with our competitors. We were bound by various hormone-consortium agreements, but the way we had structured those agreements gave us leeway to sell our products to our English partner without violating our commitments, although our rivals can't have been very happy to find their hands tied through such legal ruses.

It also allowed us to honor our existing commitment to Levine, giving him (in my opinion, much too great) a say in various aspects of the business: hiring and firing, product launch, quality control, publicity materials and advertising campaigns, as well as third-party agreements. No matter how much Levine's need to crack the whip rankled with me—his thirst for power invariably reminded me of the proclivities of his identically mustachioed countryman—I could not afford, in these uncertain times, to alienate him even more than I already had with my tomfoolery. We were still in the process of renegotiating Levine's contract; the old one was about to expire, and we were bogged down in haggling over his excessively stringent demands. For the time being, therefore, he had an equal stake in the British firm. Even with all my gloomy forebodings about the situation in Europe, however, I could not have predicted back then that his role in Farmacom would shortly be curtailed. I had no problem picturing that piece of fascist gallows-scum next door as our soon-to-be dictator, but the notion that I'd ever be rid of Levine's tyranny wasn't even a pipe dream yet, let alone a reality I could count on.

• • •

In October 1938, our annus horribilis, Rivka coldly informed me that Rosie had been delivered of a daughter. The young mother had named her Chana. That name, Hebrew for "mercy," moved me more than I dared to admit. The baby appeared to have weathered the attempts on her life while still inside the womb and had come through with flying colors. She seemed healthy, and Rosie, according to Rivka's curt report, was philosophical about the unsavory way she'd been saddled with an offspring, and did not seem to hold it against the baby. Mother and child were to remain at the Amsterdam shelter for the first couple of months, and once Rosie was used to motherhood, she would be moved into a place of her own. Rivka saw to it that she had everything she needed. I'd have liked to visit her but was explicitly forbidden to contact her, and besides, exacerbating Rivka's ire was the last thing in the world I wanted.

Babies don't give a damn about the circumstances of their birth. I wished I could have told my youngest offspring just to stay inside that warm womb of Rivka's for the time being; he'd never get a better deal outside. But my innocent boy was deaf to my quiet plea to postpone his arrival in these glacial times. On a freezing cold day in December, one month after Kristallnacht, when the brownshirted murderers across the border had given the world a foretaste of what they had in store for our people, I received a phone call from Marieke, our housekeeper, informing me that my wife was in labor and had just been driven to the hospital in the city. Rivka had not sent for me, but my loyal Marieke thought it unfair to keep me in the dark about the baby's imminent arrival. I raced over to the clinic, which happened to be located not far from the prison where my brother had been serving his sentence for the past nine months. Since I wasn't any different from any other father sitting around waiting helplessly for his child to be born, I was asked to sit outside the delivery room. Never is the true uselessness of the male species more evident than when our wives are in labor, huffing and puffing, screaming, raving, bellowing, and bearing down. Giving birth is a cruel, excruciating ordeal that just goes on and on until the exhausted mother is finally dilated enough to spew the baby out into the world—a rude ending to the kid's peaceful sojourn deep inside that warm body. Maybe all our male philandering can be traced back to this: that we're made to feel so utterly dispensable at the one moment of human existence that really counts.

I took a seat on a metal chair in the maternity clinic's icy corridor, cringing at every scream that reached my ears from behind the closed door. From time to time the door would open to let out a nurse who would push me back down onto my chair with a reassuring gesture and explain that my wife was having a hard time, and that it was a difficult labor, which was why it was taking her a long time to dilate—quite surprising, actually, in light of the fact that she'd had four previous straightforward deliveries—but that I should on no account be worried and just stay calm and wait. I waited but was far from calm. For, unlike the nurse, I did have an inkling as to why this birth was so much harder than the previous ones. I was sure it was Rivka's apprehension that was making it difficult for her to open up, which had been a breeze for her with the girls. But how to explain that to the nurse? And anyway, what difference did it make? So I waited, racked with fear that my wife would not survive this arduous labor, and yet pumped with the secret hope that, in spite of Rivka's apprehension, the child would be a boy.

I sat there until deep in the night. At one point there had been a shift change, when the obstetrician going off duty had tried to assuage me with some more evasive reassurances before hurrying home. I must even have nodded off for a bit on my rickety chair, because when I was startled awake, I saw that an hour had gone by. It was close to six a.m. and a drizzly day was dawning when the delivery room door swung open and an exhausted-looking nurse walked over to me.

"Congratulations," she said, smiling, "you are the father of a healthy boy."

I felt a rush of joy before anxiety about what the announcement had left out took over.

"And how is my wife?" I asked.

"She is very tired," said the nurse, "but that's no surprise; it was an unusually tough delivery and has left her quite drained. So drained that she didn't have it in her to take the child in her arms after it was born. But that's bound to change once she's had a good rest," she concluded. She said she'd let me go in briefly, even though my wife had indicated she wanted to be left alone. "But," she said, nodding kindly, "that's not unusual, and then they're only too delighted to show off the baby to the papa. Go ahead, go have a look, but don't stay long."

I knew perfectly well that Rivka's despair at having given birth to a boy wouldn't change to delight when she saw me, but I couldn't resist the temptation of seeing with my own two eyes how she was, and to have a glimpse of my first son.

She was lying prone on the metal hospital bed, the crib at her side. Her face was averted from the bassinet, and when I entered she did not react. Approaching the bed cautiously, I whispered her name, placing a tentative hand on her hair. She shook her head free.

"You've had a hard time of it, haven't you, my love," I said carefully, "but I hear you were a trooper."

Slowly she turned her face toward me, opening her eyes. "Don't take advantage of the situation, Mordechai," she said, sounding terse and weary. Her eyes filled with tears, which she swabbed away angrily. "Have a look at your son and then go, leave me alone. Tell the girls not to come yet."

A sob escaped her, and she turned her back to show that as far as she was concerned the conversation was closed.

"What about a name?" I asked. "We haven't discussed it yet, but he needs a name, I need a name for his birth certificate."

"I'll let you know in three days," she said, indicating she couldn't bear my presence any longer with a wave of her hand.

I glanced at my vulnerable, unnamed son, who, after such an arduous journey, had to do without his mother's love in these first hours of life. I stroked his soft little face, sniffed the distinctive smell of a newborn, pressed a kiss on his forehead, and left the room with a heavy tread.

35...

Two days later Ruth had permission from her mother to visit her new little brother, and on returning home she gave her sisters and me an enthusiastic report, saying what a cute little fellow he was, that she'd been allowed to hold him in her arms, and that he'd refused to let go of her pinkie. She also informed me that Rivka had said my son's name was Ezra.

Although religion played no part in our lives, we had given all the children Jewish first names. We had no wish to hide who we were, and the more the hatred and bigotry intensified, the more important it seemed to stand up for our right to exist in the choice of names for our children. To name a child is to give it its identity and set it on a certain path in life. In the name Rivka had chosen for my son, it wasn't hard to read her wish that he be guided not by his father and his foul behavior, but by that righteous priest of old.

Seven days later I was allowed to go pick up Rivka and my son. We were greeted at the door by the girls, who had planned a lavish welcome for their mother and their little brother. The front door was decorated with a large cardboard stork carrying a blue baby bundle in its beak; the crib in the nursery was beautifully made up with a sheet the older girls had embroidered; a tray of baby-blue sugar treats was set out in the living room, and a long garland of their cheerful, colorful drawings spanned the lofty hallway. Their excitement over their mother's homecoming and the addition of a little boy to their mostly female household was boundless; their enthusiasm seemed to make Rivka relax a bit. In the car she had been silent, aloof and preoccupied, holding the baby a little away from her body, as if trying to avoid physical contact with the little fellow. Feeling her daughters' elation, watching the girls smothering their brother with kisses and caresses, her face softened somewhat, and she had to agree with the girls when they declared that this was the sweetest, cutest, loveliest little baby the world had ever seen.

Thanks to the hospital nursing staff's persistence and cajoling, Rivka had in the end overcome her initial resistance to breast-feeding, and her milk had come in. She'd resigned herself to nursing him, since she felt she should not deprive her son of breast milk. But after a few weeks the kid developed an unnaturally voracious appetite. He clamped onto his mother's breast with aggressive force, biting her nipples until they were bruised and sore. And it was that very fierceness, that hunger for love, that only pushed her away further, so that I had no choice in the end but to hire Alie Mosterd from packaging to provide him with purchased breast milk — motherly warmth for a price.

• • •

My secret hope that Rivka's coldness toward me would thaw once she had had her baby was dashed. If in that last month of 1938 or during the next year she had shown some understanding, if she had been willing to give me one more chance, had trusted me again, I might have found the strength to change. Like a snake sloughing off its skin to rid itself of parasites, I might very well have been able to shed my bad habits to be reborn a virtuous man. I imagined that with my wife at my side, supported and encouraged by her love, I might have done it. But then our company would in all probability not have grown into the thriving multinational it is today. Putting empathy and altruism above all other considerations won't make you come out on top; for a business to be truly lucrative, there needs to be at least a little skullduggery. For Rivka, I'd have been prepared to give up my dream of building a major company; it would have been worth it. Her silent hostility, however, the constant unspoken recriminations goosing my sense of shame and guilt, were just too much to bear.

As the world prepared itself for the greatest cataclysm of all time, I began to let go of my wounded ego. When it finally became clear I would never win back my wife's love—the second-greatest blow in my otherwise sensationally successful life; the first, of course, was the symbolic mark of Cain on my forehead—I proceeded to shrug off those distressing feelings, the unbearable hurt. From that moment on, my conscience ceased to bother me—I put a lid on it and sealed it shut.

It is only now—after the rust has eaten through my self-protective armor and reduced it to dust—that those unbearable feelings have flared up again, just like the electrical fire that once very nearly reduced our new lab to ashes. Thanks to the quick intervention of our in-house firefighting team, we were spared that calamity. But here, inside my cocoon of decrepitude, there is no one to put out the blaze.

36...

This evening the young thing turned on the television for me. Very softly, so that it won't disturb Mizie, who's out cold one floor down after taking a strong sleeping pill. She is determined to shield me from any direct confrontation with my poor martyred son. Is she worried the excitement will deal me the deathblow I so dearly desire?

But the sound is up just high enough for me to hear the voice of my blood, my dearest spawn, the ravenous whiz kid, as he tries to deflect the questions of the foreign journalists, the hungry European gentlemen of the press who can smell a good, lucrative story here, a story that will keep them on the air for days, weeks even, who swarm around him as he walks from the car to the courthouse. He's holding his head high, his eyes are tired, his face drawn, but proud as ever, his bearing resolute.

The upshot is that he is to be released on bail, set at a million dollars. Provided he surrenders his passport, to prevent him from fleeing the country. So, wearing an electronic ankle bracelet like some lab animal awaiting a lethal injection, he is now permitted to hole up in his apartment and spend his days looking out at the Hudson River or down at the pack of paparazzi bloodhounds stationed outside his building. How I'd like to call him on the phone, to give him some encouragement, to support him as a father should, and tell him to steel himself, to be a man at this critical moment—his Waterloo, with the vultures circling, intent on getting rid of him and sending the whole business down the tubes. My son, at the very pinnacle of his career; my son, a driven man, a dynamo bursting with ambition who clawed his way to the top step by step, until, at the crowning point of his career, he was made chief executive officer of the giant multinational that began as a precarious little division of our meatpacking factories. Don't let him hang his head, he has to fight back; a sturdy anvil does not fear the hammer. Let those lawyers of his—they must be costing him an arm and a leg—get the alleged victim to withdraw her complaint. How hard can that be? The papers say the charges are a jumble of inconsistencies. It had to be entrapment, some clever plot cooked up by those cannibals who if we don't watch out are going to gobble up all our life's work.

He was too open, too ready to show his hand; my warnings fell on deaf ears. Traitors never sleep, I told him over and over again, but he'd just laugh and insist on doing it *his* way, always so damn cocksure of himself, that boy! But what do you expect—a child of affluence, with no firsthand experience of how evil or dangerous those sharks can be. Born into the lap of luxury, could have anything his heart desired, grew up in a normal family— well, *normal*, I mean, what's normal? Normal doesn't exist. Normal is a Russian pogrom, normal is Christ on the cross, normal is a whore in a brothel. To Ezra, normal was a mother who never loved him and who was irked by his indisputably boyish behavior. His spunk, his aggressiveness, his competitive streak, and, young as he was, his determination to get the better of his sisters; all that unruly behavior annoyed the hell out of her. She never tried to hide it, and the enthusiasm and pleasure she took in raising our daughters was totally missing in Ezra's case. Was it just my genes, or was Rivka's attitude somehow also responsible for turning him into this testosterone-driven man, addicted to the chase, the attention of women, the overwhelming need to be seen, to be known, to be *felt*?

In the many interviews he has given, he likes to confess with a certain measure of pride what his three weak spots are: his love of money, his fondness for women, and his Jewish birth. And every time I tried warning him not to put himself in the spotlight, he would pat me on the back, laughing, saying the times were different now, that xenophobia and petty-bourgeois notions about sex were no longer relevant. "Thanks to the Pill— the one *you* created a worldwide demand for!" he said, to stroke my ego, "anyway, thanks to the Pill, times have changed, Father, and I thank you from the bottom of my heart for it. In your heyday you had to be on your guard; woman trouble could ruin your reputation. But nowadays showing off your weaknesses is a perfectly good strategy." That was the kind of naïve swagger I'd hear from him when, on one of his visits over from the land of the brave, he made time to have lunch with me. "All you need to make it to the top is a slick presentation; a thorough grasp of the facts couched in short, easy sound bites, never too complex or involved; a healthy dose of humor; and a knack for showing your human side." And then a pitying smile for his old father, so sadly behind the times.

Living it up, overconfident and at the top of his game, thinking himself invulnerable, he blazed his own trail through the world of international power brokers.

The fact that death has not yet come for me, forcing me to be an impotent witness to this, to watch my son fall into the very same trap I once narrowly escaped, is the ultimate cruelty. And as if that weren't enough, I have no way to communicate with him. Neither my personal Florence Nightingale nor the cute young thing has any notion that I am still compos mentis; that it's only my tongue and the other motor skills that don't work, like a stubborn horse balking at taking another step.

The young thing leans over me, telling me three times that the man on the screen is Ezra, my son. As if I can't fucking see that for myself. She interprets the garbled sounds coming out of my trap as a sign that I don't know what's going on. She explains to me that my boy is in New York and, sadly, can't come visit me. I fling my head wildly from side to side to make her understand I want to speak to him, but she doesn't get it, and when my eyes start leaking—not out of sentimentality, dammit, but because my body tends to weep from every orifice, not just the stupid dribble from the tip of my beast—she takes a tissue to dab at the tears on my face. She does it gently, but it feels like a scouring pad lacerating my thin skin and I let out a scream of pain, of impotent rage, of my terrible yearning for one last exchange with Ezra, my son, my Benjamin, my Achilles' heel.

37...

Even before our country was overrun by the jackbooted hench-men of the great jackass, I had known that if the worst hap-pened, I would have to hustle big-time to save my own neck. Not only was my religious background a lethal liability, but so were my government connections and my business, which the Kraut vultures would no doubt have their beady eyes on. I had done everything I could to ensure the firm would keep going in the event of war, but now it was time to take steps to save myself and my family in case our country fell.

Toward the end of April 1940 I met with Levine, who had a ticket to sail to America, where he was scheduled to give a series of lectures.

Over the past few years he had been much in demand as a speaker abroad. Thanks to his reputation as head of one of the most highly respected laboratories in the world, his discovery of testosterone, his knack for cranking out promotional arti-cles for top scientific journals, as well as the worldwide pro-fessional network he had built up over the years, he received untold invitations to attend conferences, to give lectures, or to join advisory boards around the globe (the only exception being the ever-expanding nation next door). He liked to accept these invitations, doubtless flattered by all the attention and respect. They also allowed him to bask in the unencumbered mood of those faraway places, reminiscent of the rosy, carefree times our own part of the world had enjoyed in the roaring twenties. The somber, oppressive damper the brownshirts had cast over our continent had yet to reach those other shores, so it was a joy to go there. Besides, by traveling abroad he could get away from the strain that had come between the two of us. We never seemed to see eye to eye these days, whether it was about a board meeting, some transaction involving doctors or pharmacists, or even a simple phone conversation about his damn contract renewal, on which we had yet to come to terms. Too many cooks spoil the broth, as they say, and the heady partnership of the early days had turned into a never-ending power struggle. Coming as we did from such different perspectives, we were constantly at each other's throats. We pecked at each other like two angry fowl in a cockfight—he, the venerated professor and great man of science, facing off against me, the royal merchant attempting to steer our firm safely through the greatest crisis the world had ever known. Our once mutually beneficial accord was now all rivalry and strife, each of us convinced he was right.

As I walked into Levine's office, he told me he was calling off his planned trip. "I expect all of Europe will be at war soon, therefore I'm not going," he said somberly.

The brownshirts had invaded Denmark and Norway earlier that month, and there were persistent rumors that the great shithead's troops were amassing on our borders, and although our government kept putting out unfounded bulletins claiming there was nothing to fear, there weren't too many suckers out there still allowing themselves to be lulled to sleep. Anyone with a grain of common sense knew that the *Gröfaz* (the Greatest

General of All Time) would not rest until he had the entire continent under his thumb, with Great Britain thrown in for good
measure.

"But Rafaël," I replied, "you have just given me the exact reason you *should* get out of here while you still can. You are in the
fortunate position of possessing both a ticket and a visa; I don't
know a soul who wouldn't envy you. Why don't you just go?
You'll never have a better opportunity."

He looked at me haughtily. "Do you really mean to say that
I ought to save my own skin, even if it means leaving my family
behind, my institute, and my employees? Do you really think
that's the right thing to do? Don't I have an obligation to do
everything in my power to protect the people who are dependent on me in this time of crisis? Shouldn't I at least *try*, come
what may?"

They were rhetorical questions only. He was implying that
the very *thought* of saving himself and leaving the people he
lived and worked with to their fate was quite reprehensible and,
as far as he was concerned, not even worthy of consideration.

"If there's anyone who will be capable of helping them when
Hitler starts running the show around here, it is me. My name,
my connections, my money—I'll use everything I've got to
protect them. I shall try, anyway. I could never look at myself
in the mirror again if I fled now, leaving everyone who's dear
to me in the lurch. If I did that, how could I ever call myself a
mensch again?"

There he went once more, rubbing his moral superiority in
my face, putting me in my place. If I'd had a ticket and a visa,
I'd have jumped at the chance to get out of there. On reaching
safety, I'd have made every attempt to bring my family over.
Although calling it "family" was a stretch these days—it implied

an intimacy that for the past two years had been lacking in our household.

Once out of the country, Levine could have pulled out all the stops to have the Dauphine and his children, now nearly all adults, join him. But his scathing attitude would have made any objection sound ignoble, so I just shrugged, muttered that it was too bad we had to miss such a great opportunity to promote our latest products, and then coolly changed the subject to other orders of business.

That short meeting at his lab was the last time I was to see him before the shit hit the fan. We met again five years later in the exact same place. By then the once so respectable laboratory had been trashed. Barely a stick of furniture was left, the windows had been stripped of their wooden frames, and the doors were gone, all used for fuel during the Hunger Winter of 1945. But the damage done to the laboratory was nothing compared with the estrangement between us after five years. In fact, the dressing-down Levine gave me on that day just before war broke out would be the last he'd ever give me. Or, rather, the last I ever allowed him to give me. By the time I was back, after the war, I no longer gave a flying fig about his so-called moral superiority and simply forged ahead, ignoring him. The moment the brownshirts were finally licked, I made sure that Mordechai de Paauw, Royal Merchant, Purveyor to Her Majesty the Queen, would from now on be the sole potentate ruling over the Farmacom empire.

38...

I was startled awake by the roar of aircraft engines overhead. I thought for an instant I must be dreaming, and then realized what was going on. *"Too late!"* everything inside me was screaming. "You've missed the boat!" Oh, sure, I *had* transferred our subsidiaries' shares to London for safekeeping, had neatly deposited all our manufacturing secrets there as well, had locked away the purest samples of insulin and other preparations in a vault, and set up an emergency facility in another part of the country; but in the end, there I was, asleep in the fucking guest room as the scumbag was crossing our borders with his overwhelming military force, and twelve thousand *Übermenschen* were parachuting down on us, having brought neither myself nor my family to safety. I hadn't even taken the first concrete steps to arrange our departure. Maybe I'd had too much on my plate with everyday concerns, or perhaps, like so many others, I'd been counting on the odds that, despite all the portents, it wouldn't happen all that soon, and we needn't be in a rush to leave our comfortable life at home just yet. I had been sticking my head in the sand so that I wouldn't have to venture out into the unknown, so that I wouldn't have to rouse myself from the stupor of familiar habit. In acting like an ostrich I certainly had lots of company, but Christ, how I kicked myself, lying there in that solitary guest bed, hearing the engine drone overhead—the noise of a cataclysmic flood that would very shortly swallow up all the land.

I got out of bed, threw on some clothes, hastened downstairs, and turned on the radio to hear confirmed what I'd already suspected: our country was at war. I rushed into the hall to try to reach one of my government contacts on the phone, and there I ran into Rivka in her nightgown, her hair in disarray and a worried look on her face, surrounded by the girls, gathered on the stairs like a bunch of white ghosts.

"It's war," I announced. "I think we should try to get away."

"Away?" Rivka exclaimed, frowning. As if she hadn't heard the part about being at war. "What do you mean, away, where should we go?"

I explained that our little town lay not far from the Dutch army's outermost, and probably very weak, line of defense, and that we'd have to try to make our way north, across the so-called Holland water line, where the big cities were. The closer we could get to The Hague, the better. Preferably The Hague itself, since, as the seat of our government, I assumed it must be the safest spot in the country right now; the royal family, the cabinet, and parliament would certainly be defended to the last. Once there, I would be able to call on my highly placed connections to help us escape from the country, should that be necessary.

"Escape from the country?" asked Rivka. "Where would we go, then?"

I sent the children upstairs, telling them to get dressed and pack a suitcase. The girls, led by Ruth, quietly tiptoed back up the stairs.

I explained to Rivka that the firm and I were prime targets for the brownshirts, but that she and the children weren't any safer, since seizing a large and profitable business would mean getting rid of inconvenient heirs. Rivka, apparently, had never thought of her own situation in those terms.

"But what about Aaron?" she said, visibly reluctant, "and my parents? And Rafaël, and Sari, Rosie, and...?" She began naming others one by one. It was impossible for her, it seemed, to cut and run, leaving the whole *mishpocha,* everyone she cared for, behind.

Aaron. I hadn't thought of him at all. He was serving the last month of his sentence; in a couple of weeks he would be a free man. From time to time I'd hear news about him from Rivka, invariably along the lines that, unhappy and guilt-stricken, he was just sitting out his tedious incarceration and refused to give any thought to his future. Surely it ought to be possible in these extreme circumstances to spring him from prison—some kind of bribe might do it—so that he'd be able to leave with us.

"We may be able to take Aaron," I said. "I can certainly try. But your parents and Rosie live in Amsterdam; I don't see how we'd get them out. It's already going to be a hellish feat getting ourselves to The Hague. It's every man for himself now. It's unfortunate, but true."

Rivka looked at me coldly. "It has always been every man for himself as far as you are concerned, that's nothing new. But what makes you think I'll want to go with you? Why should I leave everyone I love behind, and follow you?"

Something inside me snapped; I just lost it. "Because I'm not going to let you risk our children's lives because of your pigheaded anger at me," I shouted. "Do you think I'd allow you to put them in harm's way just because you like to play the offended, betrayed spouse? You and your saintly airs and your stubborn lack of forgiveness! Okay, so you've been bearing a grudge against me all these years. But are you really prepared to drag your children into God knows what misery, maybe even death? I'm not giving you the chance. What you decide to do yourself is your business, but the children are coming with me."

The blood drained from Rivka's face. She had never seen me like this. Nor, for that matter, had I; it felt like a huge relief to finally blow my top. But then I heard a sound above me. I turned and saw Ruth, holding Ezra's little hand, staring at us wide-eyed with worry from the top of the staircase. "If we're leaving, we're all going together, aren't we, Mama?" Ruth asked anxiously. "Otherwise I'm staying here, with you."

Rivka gazed up at her; her cheeks were now flushed bright red. She glanced at me, then back at Ruth, and sighed. "All right, fine," she said, pursing her lips. She started up the stairs, the slap of her feet on the bare wooden treads unnaturally loud, shouting with forced cheerfulness, "Come on, Ruth, we've got to start packing."

"Rivka," I said.

Stopping halfway up the stairs, she turned around.

"Thank you. Why don't you call your parents; perhaps they can find some way to get to The Hague. I'll run over to the factory, and then I'll see about getting Aaron released."

She nodded and continued up the stairs.

• • •

It wasn't yet eight a.m., but those members of our staff who lived locally were already at their desks, wan from lack of sleep and all in a tizzy about what was happening. We held a short meeting and decided the team being dispatched to man the emergency facility up north should leave as soon as possible. A pickup truck leased from a shipping company was to ferry this group, twelve girls and two supervisors, on their perilous journey. Many of them had never been away from home, but all had declared themselves ready and willing to give it their best shot. A great many of the young men in our employ were volunteering for the front; we decided to pay the entire workforce half a month's salary. As the morning went on we heard that all German nationals were forbidden to go out, so several employees had to be sent home immediately. I ordered all manufacturing blueprints and other important documents to be destroyed; as it turned out, this was never done, because an employee with Nazi sympathies countermanded my directions. I also spoke to Levine on the phone, to inform him I was planning to leave. He was quiet for a moment and then said, "I hope, Motke, that it turns out you are jumping the gun, and that we'll see each other again very soon." Then he quoted two lines from Schiller's "The Invincible Fleet":

Gott der Allmächt'ge blies
Und die Armada flog nach allen Winden.

God the Almighty blew
And the Armada flew to every wind.

"I'm afraid, Rafaël," I replied, "that the Schiller is not applicable here. Farewell, and good luck. Please say goodbye to the Dauphine for me."

I took leave of the staff and walked out of the new building, which we had inaugurated to such fanfare just a few months earlier.

• • •

I drove through the bright, early-spring morning to the house of corrections, where I found the warden very resistant at first, until I pushed some bills into his hands, persuading him to at least permit me to speak with Aaron, which was very much against the rules. I waited in a bare, airless room for my brother to be brought to me. The moment he entered the room and caught sight of me he froze, gazing at me stone-faced. There was nothing left of the stocky build, the full cheeks, or the paunch that had defined him after years of excessive alcohol consumption. His ashen face was gaunt, with protruding cheekbones; his emaciated limbs were lost inside the baggy prison overalls; his eyes were hollow, sunk deep in their sockets. He looked drawn and exhausted, as glum as ever. The guard at his back prodded him to go in and ordered him to sit down in the chair across from me. Evidently accustomed to following orders, he did as he was told. The corrections officer stationed himself by the door, and Aaron gazed at me, showing no emotion. His expression did not change when I explained the situation we were in—namely, war—and told him I was going to try to get across the Holland water line with my family, and wanted to take him too. It wasn't until I mentioned the last part that his eyes flew wide open. With unreasonable ferocity he declared, exactly as he had two years earlier when I'd offered to find him a good lawyer, "Out of the question. What *you* do is your affair. It's got nothing to do with me. We are no longer brothers, Motke, and no war, no dictator, will ever change that."

"Aaron," I said emphatically, "now is not the time to stand on your principles. In a few days, a few weeks at most, they'll be the ones in charge here. Our army is a joke, hopelessly outnumbered, they'll never hold out against that horde. Right this minute, thousands of Huns armed to the teeth are busy hacking our amateurish troops to pieces. By the end of today they'll have barged through our outer defenses. We've got to get ourselves out of here, as far away as we can. I don't know if you're aware of what they've been doing to our people in Germany. I, for my part, have been reading the papers all these years, listening to the refugees' stories. I even tried plowing through that asshole's book, because you have to know your enemy. I can get you out of here. Once we're out of that motherfucker's reach, you can go wherever you want, you won't have to have anything to do with me ever again. Just give me a chance to get you to safety."

It came out sounding more pleading than I had intended.

He gave me a look of contempt. "You haven't changed one bit," he said coldly. "Still busy saving your own skin, as usual. Have you spared even a single thought for all the people you're leaving behind? What about all your employees, what about the young girls and their families? You think it's okay to just make a run for it, do you? Is what happens to them suddenly not your business?"

He hadn't changed one bit either.

"Staying here waiting to be slaughtered won't do my employees much good either. There's much more I can do for them once I'm ensconced somewhere safe."

He laughed scathingly. "You go ahead, Motke," he said, "but leave me out of it. I'm going to finish serving my time in here. And after that, I may still be able to be of some service to someone. Times like these call for people who no longer have any illusions. Being able to do something to offset my guilt—now that's something that appeals to me. There are plenty of people who are far more deserving of life than me." He stood up. "Give Rivka my love," he said. "She's the best thing that ever happened to you. For her sake I'm glad you're getting out of here. Take good care of her."

Then he gave the guard a nod to show he was ready to return to his cell. I got up and, once outside, lit a cigarette to try to shake the feeling that I had just been in a brawl—and lost.

39...

When I got home I found the whole house in an uproar. In spite of the general panic, most of the household staff had faithfully shown up for work and were busy packing our suitcases under the supervision of Rivka and our housekeeper, Marieke. The radio was blaring the news of the war throughout the house, lauding the brave resistance of our heroic troops with immoderate optimism, from which one might conclude the enemy must be sustaining heavy losses. It did make me start second-guessing myself, wondering if we weren't being a bit precipitous about leaving; maybe it would make more sense to wait calmly at home until the invaders were defeated. Besides, the government was telling everyone to stay home, to prevent noncombatants from getting in the way of the fighting. A quick phone call to the government official who was my crony, however, was enough to confirm my worst fears: the situation was dire. He urged me to try to cross the Hollands Diep estuary to our north as soon as possible, in case the final showdown wound up taking place there.

I informed Rivka that Aaron had refused to be sprung from prison. She shook her head and sighed. Then she told me, in a meeker voice than I was used to hearing from her, about her phone conversation with her parents. They were not going to try to get away.

"We have been on the run too often, sweetheart," her father had said. "We are old, they'll leave us alone. Why would they bother with a pair of old fogeys?" He had tried to sound unconcerned, but Rivka knew her father well enough to know it was his way of making it easier for her to say goodbye.

"I asked them to look after Rosie and Chana, and they promised they would. And we vowed that we'd see each other again, alive." She said it grimly, to conceal her obvious despair. She gave a helpless shrug.

I emptied the safe in my study, which I'd been stacking over the past several months with cash, checks, and some of the rarer ingredients needed for our most important products, and stuffed the lot into my briefcase. We loaded the car with as much as it could carry, and said goodbye to Marieke and the rest of the staff. I gave them each a few months' pay on the condition that they look after the house. Then we drove off, Rivka next to me in the passenger seat, the girls and their squirmy little brother squished into the back. Tense with apprehension and excitement, we drove for the last time through the streets of our little town—the place I'd kvetched about all my life, but which I was now leaving with a deep sense of nostalgia. The girls made little Ezra wave at all the familiar sights as we passed: "Bye-bye church and ding-dong-bells, bye-bye baker's-wife, bye-bye milk cow, bye-bye school..." and so on. Hearing their enthusiastic exclamations, you'd think we were on an innocent outing. Ruth was the only one who seemed to be aware of our true predicament, but she gamely played along as her little brother's caretaker.

We weren't the only ones on the move; the road was a sea of humanity—in cars, on heavily laden bicycles, and in horse-and-wagons packed to the brim with household goods. We saw whole families loaded onto handcarts, on motorbikes, or on foot, all eager to get as far away from the front as possible. The trip took ages, and we kept getting caught in endless traffic jams, having to stop to make way for the columns of grim-faced soldiers bound for the front or, far more worrisome, returning from the opposite direction with panicked looks on their faces.

It was night by the time we crossed the Hollands Diep, on a ferry without running lights, praying the boat wouldn't hit one of the mines that had almost certainly been planted there by our army to stop the enemy from getting across the wide estuary of the Rhine and the Meuse rivers. But, despite fearing the worst, we came through unscathed.

We were forced to abandon the car outside The Hague and make our way through the Scheveningen Woods on foot; the outskirts of the city had become a battlefield, where the last brave Dutch troops—those who hadn't yet run off with their tails between their legs—were slugging it out with squads of ferocious German parachutists.

My contacts turned out to be either unreachable or else unprepared to help. All of my supposedly great connections in the Dutch government, the top brass who used to come to me for advice on the meat industry or on hormonal issues, were all too busy saving their own skins. By the time the Netherlands capitulated, they were already nicely settled across the North Sea, safe and sound in the only country that was still bravely putting up a fight: Great Britain.

Bitterly disappointed, we jumped into a cab and rushed over to the port of Ijmuiden, where we managed to get on board a ship. Here I wasn't the royal merchant, here I was just one of the clamoring horde of rich men prepared to part with huge sums of cash in the hope of persuading a captain to get us out of our doomed land. After spending an endless, chilly night huddled together on an overcrowded foredeck, we found out that the ship wasn't seaworthy and that the crooked skipper had absconded with our money. There was nothing for it but to return, a few thousand guilders poorer, to The Hague, where we were finally offered shelter by the Uruguayan ambassador, the only one of my many connections who came through for me in the end. We camped out in the elegant town house for several months, Rivka quiet and withdrawn; the four cooperative girls, timid and sweet, trying their best not to get in anyone's way; and a fidgety Ezra, who drove everyone crazy with his temper tantrums and ear-splitting howls. The North Sea, our ticket to the free world, was just a stone's throw away, but tantalizingly out of reach. The days and weeks crept by as we waited anxiously, cooped up among the metal filing cabinets, with consular officials darting around us trying to save what was still salvageable.

Uruguay was a fairly important export market for us, and Christobal Carballo, the envoy of that South American nation, had made it his mission to hustle me and my family out of the country. Once Seyss-Inquart was installed as Reich commissioner of the Netherlands, Carballo seized his chance. Since the royal family and practically the entire cabinet had fled right after the invasion—they were now sitting pretty in London—there was nothing to stop the brownshirts from taking over our country and turning it into a branch of the Third Reich. There was no one in authority left to object. The day our nation ceased to exist, the continued presence of foreign embassies or consulates on Dutch soil was no longer required, and so all foreign diplomats were to be expelled: nosy aliens no longer welcome! And that is how I, Mordechai de Paauw, who never finished school and didn't speak a word of Spanish, came to receive the title of consul of Uruguay. This adventitious appointment meant that we were hastily issued diplomatic passports, with exit visas authorized by Berlin.

On July 16, 1940, a train left The Hague's Hollands Spoor Station jam-packed with foreign diplomats and persons pretending to be such. A representative of Joachim von Ribbentrop, Reich minister of foreign affairs in Berlin, came in person to see us off. I took great pleasure in shaking the man's hand in my diplomatic role and, once inside the compartment, bestowed my most charming smile on the sour-faced bureaucrat through the closed window while wishing him, using the crudest profanities I could come up with, a speedy demise courtesy of some British bomb.

It still gives me a thrill to look back on the moment, weeks later, when we finally crossed over into Portugal. The first part of our journey had taken us to Estoril, a lovely seaside resort just outside Lisbon. There we had time to restore ourselves a bit before setting out for England, arriving on September 24, 1940.

40...

Our little family found a safe haven in the picturesque Berkshire village of Wargrave. There were good schools for the girls, who adapted amazingly well and, in no time at all, picked up their lives right where they'd left off, soon becoming fluent in English, making new friends, and, in the case of Ruth, having her first experiences with boys. Summertime swimming idylls along the river, horseback riding in the Berkshire hills; they didn't waste any time thinking about what they had left behind. Rivka, on the other hand, spent most of her time at home brooding about her relatives and all the other people she cared about, from whom she was now totally cut off. As more and more ghastly rumors reached her ears about what was happening on the Continent, stories so horrific that people simply refused to believe them, her anguish grew. In England Rivka lost her previously merry, optimistic disposition, growing dispirited and morose. She hated the long days stuck at home with Ezra, who was turning into a temperamental toddler: demanding, impatient, noisy, and, in Rivka's eyes, taking up altogether too much room. My youngest was growing into a little macho prince, an obstinate, ornery troublemaker and, young as he was, not only slippery as a tadpole but stiff-necked as a mule. Seeing the never-ending struggle between him and his increasingly estranged mother, we decided to hire a nanny to deal with the boy. Rivka had as little to do with him as possible after that. She frequently went for walks in the rolling hills, pored over the newspapers, and listened to the radio for hours on end to follow the progress of the war. To Rivka, those five years in Wargrave were five years of heartache, five years of time standing still as she waited for life to resume, which would not happen until she was reunited with all the people dear to her. I, of course, no longer fit that description.

She was just as intolerant of me as she was of Ezra, and there came a time when I'd finally had enough. I refused to be hurt by her rejection any longer. I felt that her behavior was the childish reaction of a spoiled princess who didn't know how to make the best of the cards she'd been dealt. She had to count herself lucky that I left her so well provided for when I finally turned my back on her and dove head over heels into my work.

In London I had found office space for Farmacom in a large residential building with a great view of the river and Waterloo Bridge; we also installed a manufacturing facility just outside the city. I spent most of my time in London, which was getting the full brunt of the Blitz, especially in that first year. The air raid sirens heralding bombs raining down became a daily routine to which, strange to say, we soon grew accustomed. The first few weeks we'd run to the bomb shelters as fast as we were able, but as time went on we became more blasé; I would keep working when the sirens started going off. Not until I could actually hear the bombs falling close by would I grab the folder with my most important papers, kept always within reach, and dive into the corridor to get as far away as possible from the windows in case of shattered glass. It happened only once, toward the end of the war, that a bomb actually hit a building right next to ours. The building shook on its foundations, and we watched in astonishment as the entire façade collapsed. It was a hallucinatory experience.

That constant walking of the fine line between life and death tends to bring out the most delicious sense of abandon in people. I frequently spent the night in the city, and seldom spent it alone. The daily threat of death seemed to unleash a devil-may-care promiscuity calling for instant gratification. It was as if the bombs were blanketing the city with testosterone, infecting everyone, women and men alike. Ah, sweet days and nights, when I could again indulge myself completely and without guilt; since my wife had more or less banished me from her sight, I didn't consider it cheating. And besides, I was no longer alone in being a slave to my urges, but was surrounded by women unabashedly on the prowl for male companionship, while men like me were driven more than ever before by unquenchable cravings, as if our lust could keep death at bay.

But mostly I was working, working. I had to pull out all the stops to keep both Farmacom and the De Paauw Slaughterhouse and Meatpacking Co. afloat, and do everything I could to prevent the Nazis from getting their hands on our company, our patents, and our licenses. I transferred our assets to an offshore corporation in Curaçao, out of reach of the fiend who was planning to loot every Jewish business he could get his hands on—now conveniently dubbed "enemy property." I added a clause to the bylaws preventing any member of our board living in the occupied Netherlands from having a say over any current transaction, thus tying the hands of the directors who had been left behind. Any director who either chose to collaborate with the enemy or was forced to do his bidding no longer had any say over our foreign subsidiaries. Meanwhile, we were able to strengthen our ties with the North and South American firms already allied with us, forging ahead as best we could with research and production in order to keep the business going in the absence of the parent company. I had a hell of a time trying to keep the various companies supplied with the raw materials they needed; communication was an extremely tough task at best, and most of the time near impossible. I did miss Aaron, who'd had such a good rapport with our partners, the Argentines in particular. At this difficult time my brother could have played an important part in keeping our foreign divisions going. He would have been our point man overseas, where he'd have helped the local management teams navigate an increasingly complex business climate—a minefield of potential pitfalls. Production was being held up by a shortage of raw materials, exacerbated by the fact that the ships transporting the necessary commodities were regularly blasted to a watery grave by the U-boats deployed by that hound from hell.

I realized the Nazis were plotting to take over the Dutch parent company with some stratagem that would guarantee acceptance of their grab abroad, in order to keep the overseas assets from splitting off from those falling into German hands. Levine doubtlessly had an important role to play there, since he was the only shareholder left in the Netherlands. Fortunately, our bylaws stipulated that no one could sell their shares without offering them to the other shareholders first.

At one point I did find out that Levine had apparently been negotiating with Berlin about trading his shares in return for permission to emigrate to America with his family. As if he was entitled to change the rules as he saw fit! It galled me to think the prof was prepared to ride roughshod over our corporate rules in order to save his own skin, so I did the only thing I could: I forbade the foreign subsidiaries from doing business with the parent firm. The thought of the great scumbag getting his dirty paws on all our hard-won patents and licenses made me shudder. As long as that double-crossing bastard was running the show over there, our little backwater would be off-limits, verboten, and, in case the Nazis managed to wrangle Levine's shares away from him, we severed all our branches from the parent company that was once so dear to my heart.

Partnering with my cousin Simcha proved to have been an inspired decision. He became a loyal and helpful comrade in our British soul-hormone enterprise; with him I never had to worry about the kind of strife that had arisen between Levine and me. Simcha was much too accommodating and compliant for that to happen. And so Farmacom did after all become the family business I had so much wanted to share with my brother. When Simcha and I put our heads together, there was no dissension. I knew that even after the war was over I'd want to continue our partnership, which would bring us even greater global reach.

Our prime minister, Pieter Gerbrandy, invited me to join the Advisory Board of the Dutch Government in Exile in London. My ideas for restoring our country's economy once the war was inevitably won, and becoming a prominent trading partner in the global marketplace, were enthusiastically received. I also became a welcome guest at the lavish parties organized by Bernhard, the prince consort.

As the Allied troops stormed the beaches of Normandy, Simcha and I came up with a blueprint for modernizing our company. It was a grandiose plan that called for some radical housecleaning; we would have to hack through the Gordian knot that had caused so many problems at Farmacom. It would be one of my first tasks once peace was at hand.

41...

Early in the morning of Tuesday, May 8, 1945, that joyful day when the self-proclaimed *Übermenschen* finally capitulated, I returned to the Netherlands. A military airplane full of self-important government officials had flown me across the North Sea, and an army jeep had given me a ride home. There I stood, staring up at the large, impressive house, my parents' pride and joy, which, to my own surprise, I had so often longed for the past five years. It isn't until you have had the rug pulled out from under you that you discover man isn't all that different from a plant: pluck him from his roots, and he'll wilt.

I removed the house key from my wallet; in London I had kept it in the top drawer of my desk and, though I'm normally the least sentimental of men, took it out and cupped it in my hand at least once a day. With some trepidation I inserted it into the lock. It turned effortlessly. I pushed the heavy door open, stepped inside the stately hall, and put down my suitcase. I stood in the very spot where I had stopped to hang up my coat since I was a child. The chrome modernist coatrack Rivka had bought to replace the antique wooden stand that had graced the entry before she arrived on the scene was empty, and when I hung it up, my overcoat was a lonely, incongruous sight. I shivered in the chill of the lifeless, deserted building.

Wandering through the rooms, I saw that the house was outwardly unchanged. The basic structure was intact, all the different components were still there, and yet it was not the same. It was life that was missing, the life manifest in the murmur of voices, in laughter, in a Duke Ellington recording coming from behind the closed doors of the living room, the smell of cooking tickling your nostrils and making you realize you were famished, the sight of a spinning top trailing in the hall, a stuffed animal on the stairs, a bunch of tulips on the sideboard. My house was still all in one piece, but it was as desolate as the frozen wastelands of Stalingrad after the Krauts had their asses kicked out there.

My footsteps echoed in the empty rooms and the doors I opened made an ominous creaking sound. My home was in immaculate condition; I knew it must be the work of our loyal servants. But where were they? I crossed the living room in a daze, picking up an object here and there and turning it over in my hands, staring at it as if to remind myself what it meant to me. The chrome Bakelite ashtray; the picture the children had made for Rivka's birthday; the red roses porcelain dish, which Rivka used for offering guests chocolates or cookies; the copper Winkelman clock on the mantelpiece, its silver face showing the hour of our departure five years ago; the empty silver cigarette case that still held the scent of tobacco—a roomful of objects that had witnessed a life that was now a thing of the past.

When I heard the front door open I hurried back to the hall to see my faithful old Marieke standing there. The war years had changed the unflappable custodian of our household into a frail old woman. Her body seemed to have shrunk, you could see the pale skin of her scalp through her sparse graying hair, and her bony frame was dwarfed by her threadbare summer coat. Startled, she stared at me, blinking, then cried, "Mr. Motke, is that you?" As she began walking stiffly toward me, I met her halfway, and—quite unheard-of for us—we fell into each other's arms like a mother and son reunited after a long separation. Then she held me at arm's length, looked me up and down critically, and finally exclaimed, "You are well, thank God!"

"Yes," I replied, "quite well, and you, how have you fared?"

"Oh, you know, an old rat knows how to avoid the trap, I'm just happy it's over. What about your wife and the children? They must be so big now, how will I recognize them? I'm *so* looking forward to seeing them again!"

"They are all fine and in good health, but they'll be staying in England for now," I answered.

"That's wise," she agreed, "there's so little to be had here yet, they're better off waiting for things to get back to normal a bit. Everything's still rationed, so . . ."

"No," I corrected her, "Rivka and the children are not coming back. Well, possibly for a holiday sometimes, but my wife and I—we are separating."

The old woman's hand flew to her mouth. "Oh dear," she said, and, after a long pause, added, "Troubles can tear people apart, but they can also bring people closer sometimes. What a shame, what a shame." She shook her head.

The problems between Rivka and myself had not escaped the servants' notice, and apparently hadn't been forgotten, even after years of war and occupation.

"Ah well," I replied, "my wife has decided she no longer wishes to be with me, much to my regret."

I was surprised at myself for blurting out that Rivka had left me. I'd been planning to save face in public. Marieke shook her head again and said firmly, "Well, then we'll just have to take extra good care of you, Mr. Motke. Would you like a cup of coffee? It isn't real, of course, it's fake, but nice and hot anyway, I always say."

"Yes please," I said, "I'll come into the kitchen and sit with you, and then you can tell me what happened here."

After drinking my ersatz coffee with Marieke and receiving a quick briefing from her on what had transpired here over the past five years, I walked over to the factory. It was with some emotion that I walked through the gate and into the yard. Just inside the entryway yawned a huge bomb crater; not a single window of the main building was still intact, the broken panes a patchwork of cardboard. Our factory hadn't gotten off scot-free, but the damage wasn't all that bad from the looks of it. I walked into the administration building, where I found my dear Agnes—not half as pretty as before, but as loyal as ever—still sitting behind her tidy desk, as if for five long years she had never left her post. She looked up when she heard the door open and, greeting me with a cry of joy, jumped up and flew into my arms.

"Mr. Motke, you're back!" she cried, hugging me as if she'd never let me go.

"Yes," I said, gazing at her, "I am back and you are still here, I'm so pleased to see."

The Allies had liberated our corner of the country half a year before the war was officially over, so during the past several months I'd been able to correspond with our various managers, giving me a good idea how the factory had weathered the war.

Now, back on home ground, I was keen to swing into action and put together a new and revitalized organization, a modern conglomerate of companies from around the world, bringing the De Paauw Slaughterhouse and Meatpacking Co., Farmacom,

Farmacom Ltd., and our American subsidiary all under one umbrella. I envisaged a cutting-edge multinational that would have an important role to play in the development of drugs discovered or improved upon over the past few years despite the war's intrusion, just waiting to be readied for distribution. Penicillin, DDT, vitamins, steroids, synthetic variants of the soul hormones—an enormous world market was there for the taking. We had already lost so much time. To catch up, I wanted a team of people I could implicitly rely on, people without even a whiff of collaboration stench about them. Our brand-new firm had to be swept clean, purged of anyone suspected of collusion with that washed-up gang of swindlers.

At my request, the entire workforce of both the slaughterhouse and Farmacom was ordered to gather in the canteen just before lunch. The people thronged inside with much excitement, and there was a festive mood in the air—elation, even. Peace had been declared that day, the peace so ardently longed for, and the fact that it coincided with the boss's return brought out fervent expressions of emotion. There was a good deal of back-slapping, handshaking, hat-doffing, curtseying, congratulating, and embracing; many a tear was shed, wiped away with handkerchiefs extracted from sleeves or overalls, and, yes, even one or two demure pecks on the cheek, although I was careful not to be the one initiating this. A new beginning, a completely fresh start, was the wish filling each and every heart, the thought reverberating through every head, there in that overcrowded canteen. It was a wonderful moment in which we all keenly felt that the lengthy separation had not broken our team spirit.

I gave a short speech saying how happy I was that the terror that had gripped our country and the whole Continent was now behind us. I asked for a minute of silence for all the relatives, friends, and strangers who had fallen for our fatherland, and whose sacrifice had made it possible for us to breathe the air of freedom again. I also said we should not forget those whose fate was still unknown, and that I wanted us all to stay strong and keep hoping for their safe return. I was thinking of Aaron, of course; though I had not yet had any news of him, I was almost certain he was dead.

(On a cold morning in January 1944, I had sat up in bed, awoken not by the air raid sirens, not by the roar of bombers overhead or by the screech of falling bombs, but by the feeling of being stabbed in the gut. It felt as if some force was slashing open my torso and ripping out part of me, the way a butcher cuts through the blood vessels attached to a calf's heart in stripping the dead animal of that vital organ. I tried to lie quietly and not give in to the urge to roll up into a ball from the excruciating pain. And then suddenly the image of Aaron came to me, the way he had sat facing me the last time I'd seen him, emaciated and glum. The pain began slowly to seep out of my body, and a feeling of emptiness, a dead zone, seemed to have taken root inside me ever since. I can't explain it, but from that moment on I was convinced my twin brother, Aaron, was no longer alive.)

I ended my speech by expressing my profound gratitude to everyone who had tried to resist or sabotage the fiend, no matter how humble or highly placed; anyone who'd had the guts to act heroically and refused to give in to fear. I assured them that each and every lowdown traitor or collaborator would get what was coming to him. Then we all sang the national anthem, and there wasn't a dry eye in the house—the sound of sniffling nearly drowned out the bracing words. With that, the assembly came to an end.

At my meeting with the skeleton executive staff that afternoon, I asked about those who were missing. No one was able to give me any information about my brother. No one had seen him, and nothing was known about his fate. There was plenty of information about Levine, however. It turned out that he was one of the very few Jews who had survived the war in Amsterdam, in his own home, and neither he, his wife, nor their one daughter still living at home had even had to wear the Jewish star. How that was possible nobody knew, but there was plenty of speculation that he must have taken advantage of his many important connections, and that he could only have saved his neck by collaborating with the enemy. I remembered the rumors that had reached me about Levine's attempting to trade his shares in the company for an exit permit. That ploy had apparently not worked, but he still seemed to have managed to pull some strings. He who spits into the wind spits in his own face. Naturally, the other executives, the ones who had stayed at their post during the occupation, had cooperated with the German authorities by keeping the factory churning out our products at the scumbags' behest; I had to take their word for it that they'd only done what was best for the company. By staying on the job, they had tried to forestall a total takeover by the Hun so that the firm's precious secrets wouldn't fall into enemy hands. They assured me that in their dealings they'd always had my best interest in mind, finessing it the way they thought I would have done wherever possible. Although I had resolved to give every collaborator the boot, I now realized that a certain opportunistic expediency had been unavoidable. I could hardly get rid of the entire administrative staff, even though some had cooperated rather enthusiastically with the occupying forces. Having to run a severely truncated operation just when it was going to take a gigantic effort to make up for lost time would be most inopportune. I therefore decided to sack only the true turncoats, or those tangentially implicated on account of their background or some other connection with the crooked mob. I was by no means the only one to take that position. Our compatriots' antipathy to anything that smacked of our neighbors to the east in those months right after liberation found an outlet in widespread harassment and abuse, fanatical hatred, and harsh reprisals against anyone of Teutonic origin, making no distinction between the criminals who'd been licking the brownshirts' asses, and the assholes' victims.

Nuance is a luxury no one has time for in the midst of war, and that goes for the aftermath as well, when people are trying to put the war's abominations behind them. I have to confess that I too found it a great consolation to let myself loathe all that was German.

42...

When, several weeks later, I was finally able to get to Amsterdam, I found it in a deplorable state. It was with growing dismay that I toured the great city, once so proud, now a drab, impoverished, bare, dilapidated urban desert with no electrical power and very few trees. No buses or trams were running, and many of the houses were in ruins, stripped of anything for which the desperate citizens might have had any use. Some shop windows displayed the official portrait of the queen, as if her likeness could make up for the lack of merchandise. As I walked through the former Jewish quarter, now practically razed to the ground, the ominous silence chilled me to the bone. That teeming anthill of shouting and yelling, laughing and singing humanity that had once tried to eke out a living here in abject poverty had vanished. Those proud, distinctive folks with their singular brand of humor, Amsterdam's heart and soul, had been eradicated like a plague of rats.

I had gone to the capital to try to find out what had happened to my brother and Rivka's parents, and also to see Rafaël Levine. I had to have the talk with him that would clear the way for the new enterprise.

With a suitcase full of provisions from our rural town, which for once was far better off than poor, plundered Amsterdam, I trudged through the gray streets to the house of my former in-laws. I was scared of what I might find, worried I would find them gone, but just as afraid of the unlikely chance that I'd encounter them at home and have to tell them Rivka and I had split up.

I halted in front of the house that for twenty years had been a warm substitute for my own childhood home. The building looked run-down, but it was not in ruins. At the second-floor windows I could see the curtains that had hung there since Rivka's childhood. I thought I saw some movement inside. Could it be my parents-in-law? Had they survived? Lugging my heavy suitcase, I climbed the front steps and rang the doorbell. The shrill noise reverberated inside the house. A few moments later I heard a voice calling from the window, "Who's there?"

I stepped back out onto the sidewalk and looked up. A blonde with a bouffant hairdo waving on top of her head like a proud cockscomb was leaning nonchalantly out the window. She wore a flowered apron and had a dust rag in her hand.

"I'm looking for Mr. and Mrs. Salomons, are they home?" I asked.

"No idea," the woman answered in a surly voice, "why don't you ask them? They don't live here, anyways."

"But they used to live here," I called up to her. "Will you let me come up?"

"Why should I?" the woman yelled back. "*We* live here now, we've been here two years and we ain't got nothin' to do with no Salomons. They left, and now it's ours. Good day, mister." She slammed the window shut.

I sighed, considered ringing the bell again and making a pest of myself until the broad let me in, or even kicking in the front door, but decided instead to go see Levine first; perhaps he'd have some more information.

Crossing the Amstel River, smooth and indifferent as ever, as if the most harrowing scenes had never taken place on her banks, I made my way to the Levines' house, which looked untouched except for the peeling paint on the window frames. The electric bell didn't work, but after quite a bit of knocking I heard footsteps, and the Dauphine threw open the door. There wasn't much left of her once portly girth. Her old-fashioned, matronly dress hung loosely around her emaciated frame, her face was wan, and her double chin, which had once billowed majestically over her tight collar, was now a deflated jumble of empty skin drooping over the lace jabot like a quivering turkey wattle.

"Motke," she exclaimed in surprise, looking me up and down, "do come in!"

She gave me a hug, and I followed her up the stairs. The familiar living room looked emptier and more austere than before. She served me a cup of ersatz coffee and told me that Rafaël had gone to his lab for the very first time that day. But before letting me go after him, she said, she wanted me to tell her what had happened to us.

I told her that Rivka would be staying in England with the children for the time being, and that we had decided to separate. I also said Rivka was anxious for some news of her parents, and that I'd promised to try to find out what had happened to them. I hoped the Dauphine might be able to enlighten me.

Enlighten me she did, and gladly. She rattled off her story at top speed, about their terrible suffering during the Hunger Winter of that year, and their anxiety about the two daughters who, with their husbands and children, had been deported to the east and whose fate was still unknown. About all that Rafaël had done in trying to save as many of the hunted and persecuted as he could. And about Aaron, who, I was surprised to hear, had once paid a visit to them in their canal house.

It seemed that one day in 1943 Levine and my brother had bumped into each other in the crowded corridors of the Jewish Council, where Rafaël spent most of his time in a never-ending quest to obtain the coveted *bis auf weiteres* reprieve for every desperate soul turning to him for help. If you were lucky enough to have that stamp in your identity papers, it meant the feared "transport to the east" was temporarily deferred in your case. There, in the nerve center of the deportation industry, the building where despicable officials—conniving with assiduous civil, police, and railway authorities—had facilitated a smooth and flawless transport operation, Levine and Aaron suddenly found themselves standing face-to-face. They had not seen each other since the 1938 debacle and, in light of the extraordinary times, were able to put aside their onetime antipathy. When Levine invited Aaron to go home with him, my brother accepted. Sitting in the very chair I was now occupying, he had given the Dauphine and the professor an account of how he was surviving.

He was living in a poky little room in the Jewish quarter, which was crowded with Jews from all over the country who'd all been ordered by the occupiers to move into that sector of Amsterdam. When members of the "inferior race" were instructed to hand over their valuables, he had managed to hide some money from those crooks. What was left of his capital was going into helping people postpone deportation. Like Levine, he had been arranging reprieves and helping with medical deferments; he also seemed to have underground connections, although he was very vague about those. It was clear, however, that he was involved with acquiring forged identity papers and arranging hiding addresses.

"You wouldn't have recognized him, Motke," the Dauphine said with a smile. "There was nothing left of his old apathy. There was a dogged intensity I had never seen in him before, an acute restlessness that seemed to be driving him on. He would not stay for dinner, although he probably hadn't had a good meal in quite a while—he looked pale and exhausted—but he said he had to go. He was in a fever to do what he could to save what could be saved."

Some months later, in September 1943, Levine saw him one last time. This had been at the railway station. The last Jews still remaining in the city had been rounded up and were being packed into trains bound for the Westerbork transit camp, including Levine's daughters and their families. The professor had run to the station in a last, desperate attempt to rescue them; a fruitless mission, for the German officer in charge would not relent. Levine was running along the platform looking for his daughters to say goodbye, and spotted Aaron in the doorway of one of the crowded railcars.

"Levine!" Aaron had shouted. "Have you come to wave us off? We're traveling in style, just like our pigs on their way to the slaughterhouse." He gestured at the packed cattle car at his back. Just then Levine was ordered off the platform, and the freight car doors were slammed shut. He had failed to find his daughters. The sounds of the doors screeching shut and the clang of bolts sliding home went on ringing in his ears for a very long time.

"Rafaël returned from that mission a broken man," the Dauphine continued. "His health has been going downhill ever since. He started having heart trouble. But he never gave up trying to stop our children or his friends and colleagues in the transit camp from being sent on to Poland. He just kept going day and night with the same single-mindedness that he'd applied to running his institute, doing as much as he could for them, largely in vain. When the children were finally sent on, we tried to console ourselves with the thought that the special stamps in their ID cards would land them in a camp in Germany, and not in Poland; that they'd be sent to what was called a 'preferential treatment camp.' But now we hear that in those last few months, the German camp was actually the worst of all, an inconceivable hell, with prisoners dying by the thousands from hunger, exhaustion, and typhoid. We still refuse to give up all hope, but we haven't yet heard a word." She sighed, staring bleakly into space.

I was silent. I was dying to ask her how far, exactly, Rafaël had taken the role of savior; what he had done with his shares, whether his hands were dirty or clean, and how they were still living scot-free in their own unscathed house, when elsewhere there were no Jews left, except for the lucky few who had come out of hiding. But asking about it now seemed inappropriate. Besides, the Dauphine was not yet finished. She jabbered on, as if putting the horrors of the past five years into words would lessen their sting.

"As for Aaron," she continued, "we heard he was very quickly sent on to Poland."

The gaping hole in my chest began to ache. "And the Salomons?"

"For the Salomons too, Rafaël left no stone unturned. But then they asked him to stop. They weren't afraid of dying. 'We've had our time,' they said. They explained they'd rather Rafaël spend his money and efforts on saving the young people. They were sent on almost immediately. Old people didn't stand a chance."

We sat there for a while in silence, the only fitting response to the Dauphine's harrowing tale. No, that's wrong—the only suitable answer to her story would have been a visceral scream, an animal cry like the howl of a jackal, growing louder and louder as it passed from person to person, from nation to nation, from continent to continent, until the whole world was one great sound wave of anguish, a cacophony of cries, a pandemonium of pain, a symphony of despair, culminating in a frenzied finale of agonized screams. And then, silence.

43...

I left the suitcase of food with the Dauphine, who thanked me profusely; she was going to use the ingredients for a rare feast. I turned down her invitation to join them for the meal, since my primary errand in Amsterdam was to have a rather painful conversation with Levine, and once he'd heard me out, I didn't expect that he'd be very keen to have me at his table.

Getting up from a rickety desk in his ransacked laboratory to greet me, Levine appeared fragile. The august dinosaur of yore had lost much of his former imposing looks. He too had grown thin, and he seemed shrunken. The little mustache, however, with its now infamous association, had managed to survive these five years, although it was no longer jet-black, but gray. He greeted me warmly; I was more reserved.

I told him in broad strokes how we had fared, and that the Dauphine had already updated me on their bitter news. He seemed relieved to hear it.

"Good," he said, "then we can get on with discussing how to get the business back on its feet. We have no time to waste. It seems there have been incredible new breakthroughs in the development of steroids and synthetic preparations, which I am only just now finding out about. We have quite a bit of catching up to do! Who knows if we'll ever be able to make up for lost time. Especially since so many of our esteemed colleagues are not likely to have survived, although I haven't given up hope that many of them will still show up someday. If they wound up somewhere on the Russian side it could take some time for them to reach the Western sector. And as for you, Motke, I understand that you have been working diligently on expanding the firm. I applaud you for that."

This was Levine all over. His laboratory had been verboten to him for all this time, and now he was eager to get back to work as soon as possible, all systems go and full speed ahead, to catch up and recover his preeminent position as a trailblazer in the pharmaceutical field. He looked frail, but far from defeated. For an instant I was tempted to take up again with my old partner where we had left off. The Dauphine's sad tale had softened my stance on Levine's wartime choices; the day's emotional turmoil had aroused some compassion in me. I sorely wanted to give in to that sense of sympathy, but I could not ignore what my cousin and I had decided: I was here to settle an important issue. In our blueprint for the multinational we had been working on while Levine was putting all his efforts into keeping himself from deportation, there simply was no place for the former colossus. He was too old, too stubborn and set in his ways, too passé, and, worst of all, too German.

So I said, "Rafaël, before we go any further, I'd like to clear up a few things. I'm not going to beat around the bush. People say that you were the only Jew to have kept your privileged position throughout the occupation. How did you manage that? What did you have to do? Who did you have to pay, and what price?"

Levine shut his eyes. Then he smiled. "Aha," he said, and the derision in his voice did not escape me, "do I hear a judgmental undertone in these questions by my dear colleague, the chairman of Farmacom, who turned and ran as soon as he had the chance? Is he sorry that I managed to keep myself, my family, and a few of my friends out of the gas chambers?" he asked, tapping his pen angrily on the mangled desktop.

"I am very happy that you have survived," I replied, "and to find you in such good health. And as far as my flight goes, I left because I had received information from my contacts in government that the brownshirts were keen to get their hands on the company, and that I was a prime target of theirs. I got out of here for the sake of our firm."

Levine laughed scathingly. "They were keen on getting their hands on Farmacom, you are correct about that. They couldn't get over how you managed to escape. They were furious that you outfoxed them with that diplomatic train ploy, and they were crushed to think they might be missing out on the income from our foreign patents and licenses. They were also afraid you'd cut the foreign branches off from the Dutch concern. It was that fear that caused them to treat me with kid gloves at first. Which, in turn, gave me the opportunity to help many people obtain those exorbitantly expensive, ultimately worthless deferment stamps—they fleeced us blind! I did manage to help finance a hiding place for some—including for one of your workers, in fact: the Salomons' protégée and her child. That one cost us a pretty penny. Even over there in your luxury exile you must have heard that going into hiding often meant having to pay through the nose. If they were going to stick their necks out for a stranger, most of the Dutch weren't all that keen on being made worse off by it; they much preferred being made richer. A mercenary lot down to their very bones they are, these compatriots of ours who are now celebrating like mad, piously pretending they were all resisters. As if there weren't a single enthusiastic Nazi flunky or Jew hunter among them. I can't say they've left me with a very favorable impression, all those good folks who are now the first to sing the national anthem, and the loudest. Hypocrites wrapping themselves in the red, white, and blue—I've seen too many of them with their arms stretched out in the Nazi salute."

"You helped Rosie find a hiding place?" This was the first time I'd had any news of her.

"I did," Levine answered. "At the Salomons' urgent request. But I heard later that she was picked up anyway. Betrayed, I believe, by the very people who'd been hiding her, because she hadn't been able come up with any more money than the amount I had already shelled out. Which only goes to show that evil isn't limited to just one nation."

I swallowed, and steeled myself. I had to stick with what I had come to do; our company's future depended on it, and my cousin back in London was waiting to hear the outcome of this meeting. "I think I'll save my opinion of the Dutch for later, Rafaël. That isn't what I've come to discuss right now. First can you explain to me how it is that you were spared? What did you have to do to make that happen?" I asked, fixing him with a haughty stare.

"I shall answer your questions, my good Motke," said Levine, "since I gather you are curious to know if my conscience is bothering me. Well, I can tell you this much: I torment myself day in, day out, wondering if I did enough, if I could have done more, if I should have gotten my hands even dirtier. I still don't know if my children and grandchildren are alive, and every night I torture myself trying to imagine the horrors they may have gone through and, should they still be alive, the state they'll be in when they finally do return from that hell. I weigh all that I did, and especially all that I did *not* do, on a calibrated scale, and then ask myself—did I do enough? Every hour I spent asleep or col-lapsed on the sofa, every meal I ate, every time I hesitated to go back to pestering my vile contacts with yet another request, or was too exhausted either to write one more letter or to return to that horrible building to debase myself with yet another desper-ate spiel—so many occasions when I failed to do what I might have done. These war years may have turned me into a barrel of self-reproach, but that barrel is not filled with the poison you are talking about. Yes, Motke, I did use my connections. I did try to trade my Farmacom shares for exit papers for my family, and for nearly two long years I truly believed that we would be given permission to leave. I filled out truckloads of forms, I wheedled and fawned and licked their boots. I reminded a top general in the Führer's own inner circle about the good old days when we served together in Flanders."

He gave a bitter laugh and went on. "I even tried to convince that scumbag Rajakowitch—Eichmann's right-hand man, the one responsible for practically every Dutch deportation—of my international prominence and my economic value to the Aryan nation. I got Willem Mengelberg, the conductor of the Amster-dam Concertgebouw Orchestra, whom the Dauphine's love of music had brought into our circle of friends but who was also popular with the brownshirts, to intercede for me. I bragged that in the First World War I had voluntarily returned to Ger-many to serve my fatherland. I waved the Iron Cross I'd earned for my devotion to the German cause in their faces, and I even reminded them that I had kept my German nationality until 1932. Reprehensible conduct on my part, Motke, to be sure. It wasn't pretty; it won't win me any accolades. I am not proud of it. But all that haggling did result in our being granted deferments, and dispensation from having to wear that revolting yellow star. I don't know if it will comfort you to know that in the end, we too were called up. That all the trouble I'd gone through, and all the groveling I'd done, had been for nothing. We were to report to the transit camp for deportation. Only the summons came just as the trains stopped running and the enemy was as good as beaten. If D-Day had happened just one month later, you wouldn't be sitting here putting me through the wringer; you'd be writing my obituary instead. But perhaps you'd have preferred that outcome, rather than having to confront me now. So there you have it: my scandalous conduct."

He'd been slowly twirling his fountain pen in his hands. Now he put it down and looked up. "Just for the record, I now have a question for you, Motke. I understand that when you boarded that diplomatic train you were seen off by the deputy of Minister Von Ribbentrop himself. I should like you to tell me how you feel about that rather remarkable circumstance. Is your conscience quite clear about Von Ribbentrop's signature permitting you to run out on everything and everyone? Was it fine, in your view, to take advantage of that powerful crook's scrawl, while my desperate scramble to keep myself and my fellow man out of a living hell was a disgrace? How do you justify *that*, in your kingdom of self-righteousness? Let me guess. I think that from your comfortable ivory tower in London it was easy to look down your nose at your friends' last-ditch struggles to stay alive. It's like putting a bunch of rats in a steep-sided box, topped with a mesh roof to make sure they can't escape, filling it with water, and then watching the rats panic, run out of steam, and drop dead one by one. That's how you looked on from a safe distance. How easy, then, to pass judgment on what went on over here.

"I'll give you one assurance, Motke, and that is that on this continent, there is no one alive who has kept his hands clean. Some hands may be dirtier than others, some may never come clean again, but all are contaminated. Yours are no exception."

"Alas, Rafaël," I said, getting to my feet and walking over to the window, which overlooked a deserted courtyard strewn with piles of garbage, "this is no time for niceties. I am prepared to accept that your hands are not that much dirtier than my own or those of many others, but it's the perception that counts. For the sake of our company's future, you must understand that I have to clean house."

I turned and saw Levine slap his right hand over his fist. "Rafaël," I said in a gentler voice, "I thank you from the bottom of my heart for your efforts over all these years; for your excellent discoveries, and for having trained so many scientists here in this lab, who have become such stellar researchers thanks to you. You have passed your consummate knowledge on to the next generation; you are therefore no longer needed. It is time for you to start enjoying a peaceful retirement."

Levine punched his left fist into his right hand. "Are you giving me the boot?" he shouted indignantly. "Right this minute? For five long years I've been kept out of my lab, for five years I was prevented from doing research, for five years all I did was run around taking care of the most ridiculous nonsense, having to prove how many Jewish grandparents this one or that one had, licking the boots of all those anti-Semitic dolts in uniform, humoring them, rushing from pillar to post, wasting five precious years on futile inanities. And now, now that I can finally get back to the lab again, you have the gall to kick me out of the company that has thrived largely thanks to my work?" He banged his fist on the table.

Turning away from the window, I made my way through the ravaged laboratory, picked up a distilling flask lying in the corner of a shelf, put it down again, and pressed on with what I had come to say. "I know this sounds harsh, Rafaël, but in our company, in its new incarnation"—I hesitated briefly—"there is no room for Germans."

The profanity Levine let out echoed throughout the bare space. "This is totally absurd, Motke," he thundered, jumping to his feet and starting to pace back and forth behind the desk like a caged tiger, his steps furious. "For five years I've had my nose rubbed in the fact that, no matter how German I may have felt all my life, I was not a German but an *Untermensch*, a contemptible Jew. And no sooner have those brownshirts turned tail than you show up here accusing me of being more German than Jew! Don't you remember I told you that long ago I had myself baptized, because I thought it would give me a chance to prosper in my former fatherland, a nation that has always been of the opinion that some people have more rights than others? And have you forgotten that I became a Dutch citizen because I felt that after almost twenty years in this country, it was time to show my affection for the nation that had given me such great opportunities, a country that professes that everyone starts out on an equal footing? Apparently none of it makes any difference. In the end, the individual has no say over the identity he gets saddled with. I may be Prussian, an ex-soldier, scientist, laboratory chief, father, grandfather, spouse, author, pianist, idealist, Jew, Christian, pharmacologist, and physician; I may *think* those are the distinguishing traits that make me who I am, but in the end it's other people who decide. Pinning a label on the individual—that's the trick used to isolate the other, to rob him of his humanity, in order to rub him out. And the fact that the Nazis aren't the only ones to employ that method is proved right here and now by you." Shaking his head somberly, Levine sank back onto his chair.

I felt very uncomfortable and experienced a rush of pity on seeing my former mentor slumped behind his desk, looking so crushed and defeated. But then I steeled myself. Not happily; on the contrary, I was loath to do it, but he who wants the rose must deal with the thorn. So I responded, "I don't really feel like having a philosophical discussion on identity right now, Rafaël. No matter how unfortunate it may be, you are, and will always be, German, regardless of how many other selves you may have. And right now there is no room in this country for people from the same background as the brutes who ran this place into the ground. Farmacom's future depends on our ridding ourselves of anything that reeks of the brownshirts and their ilk."

Levine took a deep breath and squared his shoulders. "Of course there is distaste for anything German in this country, I am only too aware of that; it's understandable. But the Dutch, surely I don't have to tell you this, are a mercantile folk first and foremost. This country's existence depends on export, on international trade, and these anti-Teutonic sentiments will very soon be history; it won't be long before the Dutch come to realize that they need the Krauts to get the economy rolling again. Take it from me, Motke, trade and profit-making are worshipped here, over and above any other principle. Within a year the merchant mentality will win out over anti-German sentiment."

"That could be, Rafaël, but even so, your recent conduct has at the very least set tongues wagging. I can only go forward from here on with people who are squeaky clean and unimpeachable. You will never regain your spotless reputation; therefore, your involvement is a stain on Farmacom's good name. And that is something we can't afford right now. I'm sorry, but that's the way the cookie crumbles. I aim to do the right thing by you, however; the honorable thing. You are turning sixty-five this year, and you deserve, after these terrible times, to enjoy your golden years with no financial worries."

The volume of Levine's voice rose again. "Me, not squeaky clean? Squeaky clean! Your insinuation stinks to high heaven, it's more putrid than any rotten thing I encountered in these past years. It's the pot calling the kettle blacker than black. It's filthier than the grubby brownshirts goose-stepping up and down our streets. Maybe you've conveniently forgotten how you yourself are besmirched all over! Has your stay abroad affected your memory? Who's the one who messed around with your brother's testosterone dosage, despite every warning not to? Who's the one who took advantage of his position and sexually harassed, abused, and raped his workers? Who's the one who cadged a signature out of Von Ribbentrop, of all people, then turned and ran without giving the factory or the people he was leaving in the lurch another thought? Who's the one who, while *we* were trying to save lives, was concerned only with expanding the business, and never even lifted a finger to prod those quaking cowards of our government-in-exile or that useless lump of flesh who calls herself queen into doing something, anything, to stop the murder of millions on this continent? Who, Motke?" He paused, glaring at me. Then he went on. "And yet you want to give *me* the boot, because *I* am supposedly the one who's setting people's tongues wagging? If you pursue this course, I shall see you in court. I'll do everything in my power to take you for everything you've got, and create a colossal scandal for the firm."

His last words came out as a shout. His cheeks had turned a fiery red and his eyes glittered with a fierceness I had never seen in him before.

"Rafaël," I tried one last time, "of course I won't let you go empty-handed. An honorable retirement is what I am offering you. The times are changing, and we need young people. The synthetic hormone field has been advancing at an extraordinary pace. You'll never catch up now. Just accept that your time is past, and enjoy the years you still have living in peace and comfort with your Dauphine."

He pushed back his chair angrily, stomped over to the door, and savagely yanked it open. "Out!" he raged. "I'm giving you a week to come back to me with a different offer; if not, you'll be hearing from my lawyer."

In the doorway I turned and looked at him. "I hope, Rafaël," I said, "that you will use that week to get used to the idea that for everyone there comes a time to bow out. If this fucking war had never happened, you might have stepped aside years ago."

His crimson cheeks grew even darker. He was having trouble breathing. "All this time, I felt able to cope with the racial hatred engulfing us," he said with visible difficulty. "I refused to be debased by it. For all that time I was able to steel myself against the mudslinging and contempt. But after all that, to be stabbed in the back by you, my friend, my partner, *that* is more than I can take. Get out, I can't stand the sight of you a moment longer."

He slammed the door shut with a deafening crash behind me.

44...

Levine and I both stuck by our positions. Stubborn as a mule, he was. In that regard, the world war hadn't changed him one bit.

It was of the utmost importance to get started straightaway on our firm's makeover—we needed a clean break from everything that had been holding us back from participating in the huge strides being made in the medical and pharmaceutical fields, and were ready to deploy an eager, partly brand-new team chomping at the bit to win the synthetic-hormone battle. Time stands still for no one. It was to be a firm with just one clear leader at its head, for too many cooks spoil the broth. A leader with a squeaky-clean (yes!) image, who knew how to command trust and respect all over the world—an esteemed royal merchant. Farmacom, a consummately Dutch concern, was to go international without a single principal or employee under even a speck of a cloud. It was the only way our firm could hope to become a major player, eventually growing into the mega-conglomerate for which my cousin and I had been laying the groundwork. I could not and would not turn back now. If you want to make an omelet, you have to be willing to break a few eggs. I have never been one to dodge my responsibilities.

• • •

In those early postwar years I spent a great deal of time in London getting the ball rolling. In the war-ravaged Netherlands, conditions were primitive; you simply had to jump through too many hoops to get anything done.

In July 1945, as I was getting ready to return to the U.K., Agnes announced that the Dauphine was at the door, demanding to see me. This was unheard-of. Never before had she visited me at the office, and on the rare occasion when she deigned to leave the city, always in the company of her husband, it had been for some exceptional, usually festive occasion, such as Rivka's twenty-fifth birthday, or Farmacom's tenth anniversary. The rest of the time the Dauphine was kept busy spinning her artistic web inside her Amsterdam canal house, forever running up and down the stairs, barking out orders at children and servants, and then retiring to her leather armchair, where she devoured books like a spider guzzling houseflies, or settling down on her minuscule rickety piano stool to play her antique pianoforte and bring back to life the bygone baroque world of an as-yet undefiled fatherland.

The fact that she had now undertaken an exhausting trip into the hinterlands was bound to have something to do with my conversation with Rafaël. I squared my shoulders before opening the door, and greeted her with a fair amount of trepidation. She sailed into my office like a panzer tank storming an enemy position. Her multiple turkey-wattle chins quivered with bottled-up indignation. She was dressed in a long and baggy dark coat and sported a broad-rimmed black hat with a large silver hatpin impaled in it that made me think of the bayonet affixed to a rifle. Like a little Napoleon, some indomitable general, she stood in front of me drawn up to her full height, clutching her black patent leather handbag with the gold clasp in her balled fists as if she were hiding a murder weapon in there. She pointedly ignored my outstretched hand and the invitation to take a seat on my tried-and-true Cozy Corner.

"Motke," she said, coming straight to the point, "you are making an unforgivable mistake. Revoke that scandalous plan of yours. It's just criminal, and makes you guilty of patricide— nothing less! Farmacom is just as much his creation as yours. You cannot do this to him, not after all that has happened." She glowered at me like Miss Marple confronting the murderer with the evidence of his guilt.

I tried to placate her. "Sari, do please sit down and let me offer you something to drink. It's lucky you caught me, I was about to leave for England."

"I don't want anything to drink, and I prefer to stand." She clutched the handle of her pocketbook to her chest as if to underscore her resolve. "I want you to promise me you'll take back what you said to Rafaël."

I sat down on my desk.

"Sari, you're wrong. Both of you are making a huge drama out of something that's standard policy everywhere. Rafaël is sixty-five, an age at which it's only normal to slow down a bit, if one can afford to. Why make such a fuss about it?"

The Dauphine's voice was starting to sound less and less composed. "Because it isn't his choice. Because it's being forced on him on spurious grounds. Because you are accusing him of *collaborating*, and of being German-born, because *that's* what's really behind all this. That's what is so intolerable." She paused for a moment, then went on in a choked-up voice. "Yesterday we heard that our daughters and their husbands have not survived. All four died of typhoid, after liberation. Our grandchildren are now orphans."

She clicked open her bag, took out an embroidered handkerchief, and dabbed at her eyes.

"I'm so sorry, Sari, that is dreadful news."

Over the past several weeks we had been hearing almost daily of the tragic fate of this or that one who, euphemistically put, "had not returned." And each time, whether it was my twin brother, a friend, employee, or passing acquaintance, I would feel a stab of grief. But as the bad tidings kept coming, I became increasingly adept at tucking away the sadness as quickly as possible. It was the only way not to give in to despair. Just as today they bury the spent uranium in layer upon layer of concrete in hopes that the lethal sludge will never seep out, so I salted away my anguish, allowing me to focus instead on the stuff I could actually do something about.

The Dauphine rattled on. "Work is the only thing that can save Rafaël. It is imperative that he be free to immerse himself in his research and in the business once again, so as not to succumb to his terrible guilt over having allowed their deportation to happen. Over not having been able to prevent it. If there's even a crumb of humanity left inside you, Motke, then with all my heart I beg of you to change your mind and let him decide for himself when is the right time to stop. By kicking him out this way you are robbing him of his last scrap of dignity and integrity, and to Rafaël, that is the most important thing there is, and the only thing remaining to him now."

Ah yes, Levine and his confounded sense of integrity; as if that hadn't thrown a wrench in the works often enough! As if there didn't come a time for every man to step aside. I tried pointing out to the Dauphine that most people, when they grow old, find it difficult to say goodbye to a career that has been a lifelong fulfillment, but later laugh at themselves for their initial reluctance and are only too happy to enjoy the freedom of their retirement. And didn't my offer give the Levines the opportunity to look after their orphaned grandchildren?

The Dauphine gave me a withering look. "*Judas*," she snarled at me. "You are no better than the traitor Judas. Remorse, Motke, often comes too late. If this does turn out to be the death of him, it will be on your conscience. Never forget that."

Then she turned and marched out of the room.

Over the course of my life, as all the kvetching about my supposed hardheartedness grew louder, my sensitivity to it lessened. Just as I had been learning to steel myself against emotional hurt, I became increasingly adept at shrugging off the spiteful accusations. Most people aren't able to see beyond their own reality, their own perspective. Rafaël was no exception. I was prepared to give him an honorable send-off with a generous payout, a pocket full of company shares, and a grand retirement party. But Rafaël and the Dauphine remained stubbornly stuck in their rancor, and I held fast to my decision.

A few weeks later I received a lengthy epistle from some pricey lawyer in which Rafaël's demands were laid out. These included, among other things, over fifty percent of all company assets. A rather ugly legal tussle ensued, but before it ever made it into court, news reached me of Rafaël's sudden death. He had been on vacation, staying in a Swiss hotel somewhere in the Alps, trying to regain his strength after the years of deprivation. One day, sitting in the lounge, he was startled by a loud noise. An automobile had missed the hairpin bend in front of the hotel and had crashed into the steep rock face. Levine, still a medical doctor through and through, had jumped up to help. As he raced outside faster than was advisable in his precarious condition, he'd had a massive heart attack and keeled over, dead on the spot. The colossus was slain performing his cherished calling: saving human lives. At least he went out with his boots on—a blessed Tommy Cooper death, one might say.

His passing was world news. Elaborate obituaries appeared in every established newspaper around the globe, unanimously commemorating him as one of the most important scientists of the century, a congenial fellow, and a great inspiration to younger talents. Most of the articles also mentioned his significant role in our company. Fortunately, our recent dispute had not yet become public; the court case was still at a preliminary stage, and the matter could now be put to rest, thank God.

• • •

On the death announcement, scribbled in the Dauphine's handwriting, I read the following:

Judas Iscariot, you will understand that your attendance at the funeral is not required. You are the one who broke his heart.

After five years of chaos and war, Rafaël was the first person we knew to receive a proper burial. The fact that my presence at his send-off was unwelcome hurt my feelings more than I liked to admit. I posted a death notice in the newspapers on behalf of Farmacom, and arranged with the finance department a— to my mind—very generous widow's pension for the Dauphine in the form of cash and shares; I later heard she found it most inadequate.

A month after his death a memorial service was organized for him at the Amsterdam Concertgebouw. That time I *did* go and pay my respects, was haughtily ignored by the Dauphine and her remaining offspring, and sat through the ceremony in one of the back rows. There, listening to the tributes and musical interludes, I was suddenly overcome with appreciation and gratitude. I remembered the early years of our inspiring collaboration, when we had stimulated each other and worked side by side to launch the business—the innovative partnership that had given birth to the prize venture it was today.

Of course, he should have been granted a few more peaceful years with his Dauphine, but I can't deny that I did feel a certain measure of relief when I realized that with his death, all the head-butting, the incessant stream of rebukes about all my alleged transgressions, had finally come to an end. His passing gave me free rein to run Farmacom the way I chose to. I was the royal merchant, an honorary professor at the University of Utrecht, the prince consort's bosom buddy, an indisputable captain of industry, and a leading light in postwar Holland's economy. Not bad for a kid who never finished high school.

The death of Rafaël Levine, the Prussian fossil from Amsterdam, underscored the fact that a new era was at hand.

45...

With a conspiratorial wink, the young thing has turned on the television for me, with the sound down so as not to wake Cerberus-Mizie from her beauty sleep.

Tonight the poor abused slut has shown up for a press conference. There she stands, the sacrificial lamb, the pathetic victim, claiming that my Ezra forced her to submit to his filthy fumbling in his New York office just hours before the board was to announce its dastardly bid to take the company public. *Our* company, in which my son is chief executive officer. He has a veto, and was surely planning to use it to stop this IPO. And rightly so: Ezra represents the firm's history, he stands for over seventy years of a family firm stoutly rooted in the Netherlands' sandy soil, watered by my own blood, sweat, and tears, eventually sprouting into the huge multinational it is today. Could this have happened if I hadn't been prepared to make so many sacrifices, breaking out of my comfort zone time and time again? Would the business have become such an international success story if I hadn't felt fine from the start about getting my hands dirty? If I hadn't always put the firm first, might Aaron and Levine not have lived longer? Did I not sacrifice my marriage to Rivka to it? Isn't my life a bit like the story of the patriarch Abraham, who climbed the mountain with his son Isaac, prepared to cast his dearest child onto the pyre in his zeal to obey a higher power? Those are questions you tend not to ask yourself as long as you're whirling through the maelstrom of life. It's only now that they come to me, here in my metal cage, flashing like lightning bolts through my fevered brain. My mind is on fire, as Abraham's must have been when he was climbing that mountain with a heavy tread. He must have asked himself why he was being made to commit such an unspeakable act. But when you're in the thick of it, it doesn't seem possible to do otherwise. You see only what's in front of you, like a blinkered horse on a treadmill.

I wish I didn't have to deal with those questions, and I don't want to be a witness to my son's downfall; the fact that he got caught in this trap means he'll soon be given the old heave-ho. A CEO accused of rape is no longer able to serve the interests of his company. What they're out to do, in fact, is hijack our life's work and toss it into the greedy maw of the money-grubbers on the U.S. Stock Exchange. They're not doing it for the good of the firm; no, there's no reason other than the needs of the pitiless shareholders, the vultures of the modern age, who don't care a fig about any company they're invested in, but are just out to make a quick buck, even if it's at the expense of an entire business, an entire country, a continent. Farmacom will be fodder for those deadbeats, the slick operators in their expensive Italian suits who'll put the whole place up for sale in a heartbeat. What do those thieves know about the importance of research, of the interdependence of science and commerce, of the countless sacrifices that were made just so they could fatten their portfolios?

Is it a coincidence that it is now, in these final hours before the crucial vote, that my Ezra gets booked by a posse of grim-looking cops, all on account of this sleazy tart's allegation that he raped her when she came to clean his office? Ha—just look at her standing there in a respectable little dress; it hurts my eyes, and not just because of the blinding camera flashes of the paparazzi, the hacks who will milk this scandal for all it's worth. Just as sewer rats splashing through the muck ingest the plague's deadly germs, so the press hounds slake their thirst on the obscene slander of this she-wolf in her prim and proper sheep's clothing.

You can't fool me: the little trollop the whole circus is focused on, that pious little saint, isn't a hair better than that other hayseed I once had to deal with, fat Bertha.

Is Ezra upset he can't come and see me? Is he as sick as I am about the fact that I can't just pick up the phone and call him? I'd so very much like one last opportunity to talk to him, to strategize how to deal with this sneak attack! I long so terribly for my son that it makes me scream. It comes out sounding like the raspy croak of a frog at sundown. The pain of losing our family business is just unbearable. Enough! For God's sake let me get back to a time when life was all triumphs and accolades.

46...

If you want to be a winner in the struggle for success, you must always know for certain what others dare only guess.

That advertising slogan of the postwar period became my motto. Those years of reconstruction were, in a sense, reminiscent of Farmacom's earliest days. Despite the rapidly growing political tensions between East and West, the world was bubbling with energy, and the survivors were chomping at the bit to set the Continent back on its feet as quickly as possible and get to work on creating a new society.

We certainly did our fair share, restructuring the De Paauw–Farmacom Co. by setting up a central board as the chief operating body, at the head of which I, as chairman, ruled the roost. For, as they say, he who pays the piper calls the tune. Not even a year went by before we were able to open new factories in Scotland and Belgium; the next year it was Sweden.

We seized any opportunity we could get to capitalize on the needs of a convalescent Continent. We added the recently developed insecticide DDT to our industrial output, and it turned out to be a golden goose, for lice were rampant throughout Europe, a downright plague. During the war years those itchy, irritating little parasites had infested the camps with their foul pestilence, attacking the already weakened prisoners with lethal diseases like the dreaded typhoid. Even when the war was over it took years for hygienic conditions to improve. Many concentration camps in the East were still crowded with refugees, the homeless and the displaced. Conditions in those warehouses of human misery remained alarmingly unsanitary.

One of our colleagues had read about the wonder chemical DDT, which had famously stopped the 1943 Naples typhoid outbreak in its tracks. That epidemic had been brought under control within three weeks, and thousands of lives were spared. As Europe began getting back on its feet, I decided we should jump on the bandwagon and market the stuff under our own trademark. It would cultivate goodwill and help us get name recognition, besides bringing in a tidy profit to boot. We began distributing the chemical in powder form in late 1945, and by the following year the demand for DDT was such that it had overtaken even insulin, heretofore our most reliable cash cow. My hunch was proved right: even without our grand mastermind, Rafaël Levine, at the helm, Farmacom was chugging full speed ahead.

Not long after the success of DDT, we began manufacturing vitamin A and vitamin B_{12} from liver extract, and had another hit on our hands. With four outside partners, we signed a licensing deal for cortisone drugs derived from the adrenal glands, which proved to have a spectacular effect on rheumatoid arthritis; we also made the switch to synthetic production of estradiol, a female hormone, which freed us from the enormously labor-intensive and smelly job of distilling the stuff from horse urine. No longer at the mercy of the local farmers' foolish superstitions, we were now able to manufacture the chemical version year-round, not just during the short window when pregnant mares produced enough of the stuff.

Our business was booming; we were forging new partner-
ships and making acquisitions all around the world. Clinching
our success was the most famous product of all, the mother lode
of pharmaceuticals: the birth-control pill. The Pill was made from
lynestrenol, the most important steroid our firm ever developed.
Some other, more tentative brands of the Pill had already come
on the market in Belgium and America, but we were the first to
mass-produce it on a larger scale. It wasn't until many months
after we'd begun manufacturing it, however, that we discovered how strong its effects could be—that even just handling
the stuff was enough to cause distinct physical changes. Slowly,
in dribs and drabs, we started hearing from stammering male
employees, blushing furiously and hanging their heads, that
they seemed to be growing female breasts, and as if that weren't
bad enough, their male parts weren't working properly either.
Shame had kept many of them from coming forward for far too
long, aggravating the problem considerably.

Ah yes, the Pill—the hostility it aroused was not just because
our men were suddenly turning into ladies. It was the clergy,
those pricks, the pastors and priests in this backward and God-
fearing region, who were stirring up the workers against a drug
that freed women from the fear of pregnancy. But did I ever
have the last laugh! We wound up sending the euphemistic
"menstruation-regulating drug" to a number of the convents in
the area. There the pills were packaged and readied for shipment
by the industrious Catholic nuns, in blissful ignorance of the blasphemous nature of the product they were so efficiently handling.

• • •

There was one aspect of the war I did miss afterward: the dis-
sipation and loose morals of wartime London. That was a time

when we were like moths around the flame, when respectability went flying out the window, when everybody seemed to be on the make, when lust became a communal sport and I suddenly wasn't the only one driven by those uncontrollable urges. Since everything might be wiped out in the German Blitz at any moment, the debauchery brooked no delay. People threw caution to the wind and cavorted unashamedly everywhere you could think of—in beds, on carpets, on kitchen floors, on lawns, in toilet stalls, in doorways, in broom closets, and in taxis; you name it.

It wasn't long before that wild promiscuity was squelched by the priggishness of the nineteen-fifties. Just as the Jews had had to go underground during the Spanish Inquisition, so free love just seemed to fizzle out, and many a sexy nympho suddenly turned into an uptight mademoiselle, queen of decorum, prissy paragon of virtue; the lady-is-a-tramp resurrected as the primmest of vestal virgins. Suddenly their voluptuous bodies became impregnable fortresses, their saucy behavior hidden beneath strict corsets of propriety. A dramatic turnabout, occurring just when I was finally no longer tied down by the marriage vows I'd never wholly embraced in the first place. Ever since my divorce from Rivka had gone through, I was spending more and more of my time at conferences, universities, receptions, corporate headquarters, embassies, and in hotel lobbies, where it was important to be assured of some company, some arm candy, some tasty piece of ass. I refused to pay for it, ever. Not because I'm cheap, mind, but because I consider myself too good a catch. After fat Bertha, who probably came closest to what you might call a whore, I swore never again to get involved with any hussy interested in being with me only to make a buck. I was still a good-looking fellow, and well-endowed young women fortunately tend to go for guys like me, even if we're a bit older. As long as you're a winner, and they smell the sweet sweat of success on you.

• • •

I kept my distance from the factory girls; I had learned my lesson, but even in the new puritan atmosphere there were plenty of attractive, available women. I found them at conferences and conventions, on business trips, and at the many parties to which I was invited. There were the secretaries of various colleagues who enjoyed my attentions, or the medical technicians only too glad to be wined and dined in fancy restaurants and to be spoiled with delicacies. If I invited them to come up to my hotel suite for a nightcap after an elaborate dinner, I was nearly always taken up on the offer. Some felt honored to be asked into the luxurious private lair of the legendary Mordechai de Paauw. Others might hesitate, but they usually caved in the end; after all, they had allowed themselves to be shamelessly pampered, and since in the fifties it was assumed that you got nothing for free, if a girl said yes to an expensive dinner, she couldn't exactly turn down what came next.

My need for such one-night stands began to lessen when, in the mid-nineteen-fifties, I met Diane Drabble in New York. She was one of the rare female chemists at the time and worked in our U.S. lab. She was an intelligent, fine-looking woman and had nothing in common with the prim little misses mincing through the fifties in their coy wasp-waisted dresses, their nylons and garter belts, the immaculate white collars, the veiled little hats, the silk gloves, the clicking stiletto heels and prissy pocketbook in which, in a kind of courtship ritual, they were constantly fumbling to pull out a powder compact, a lipstick, an embroidered handkerchief or chrome cigarette case.

Diane was one tough broad, accustomed to being the only female among men. Having apparently decided to become one of the guys, she had succeeded admirably. She could drink anyone under the table, told the dirtiest jokes, and laughed at them louder than anyone else. She wore her hair cropped short and was usually dressed in tight pants and a form-fitting turtleneck that showed off her curves to perfection. People who jump to superficial conclusions would call her butch—big mistake. She was blessed with a fiery sensuality and exercised it with unblushing abandon. Besides Rivka, she was probably the woman I was fondest of in all my life. I once blurted out that she was a female version of myself, since we both suffered from the kind of libido that's so insistent it can't stand delay; often we'd start tearing our clothes off and fall on each other half-dressed in the most unlikely places.

"Me, a version of you?" she grinned, giving my balls a friendly squeeze. "What a sexist monkey you are, Motke. I'd say, instead, that you are a male version of me..." Pulling me by the hair, she pushed me back onto the bed for another round.

She was a fanatic researcher; if she was on to something, she could spend day and night at the lab without eating, keeping herself going with short naps, which she took curled up on a blanket under a lab bench, only to return to work refreshed and ready for action. She was one of a group of biochemists who'd discovered a potent new compound that turned out to be effective in combating tuberculosis. That invention, and the speed with which we were able to rush the resulting drug to market, meant that by the end of the fifties the TB sanatoria began running out of patients and could be put to other uses.

If Diane permitted herself a lunch break, she'd go to her favorite dining spot, Horn & Hardart, a dirt-cheap automat, where after choosing an item from one of the chrome self-serve compartments, she'd gobble down her Salisbury steak in the company of longshoremen and textile workers. At night she liked to hang out in one of the jazz clubs in the Village and listen to John Coltrane, Miles Davis, or Dizzy Gillespie, sipping whiskey at the bar while waiting for one of the little front-row tables to open up so she could watch the stars from up close and egg them on with encouraging wisecracks. Sometimes I'd find her at the Savoy Ballroom, a Harlem dive, working up a sweat boogying until deep into the night, one of the only white faces in a sea of black dancers. She'd be back in the lab early the next day with no visible ill effects from alcohol or lack of sleep, intent on her work once more. Diane Drabble was vivacious proof positive that a scientist didn't have to be dull or insipid. And she was one of those rare women who indulge wholeheartedly in all forms of sexual pleasure; she wasn't shy about initiating sex, and was indefatigable, unembarrassed, and quite uninterested in commitment or getting tied down. That was another thing we had in common.

For several years we saw each other regularly, but only when I happened to be in New York for my work. She refused to make any arrangements ahead of time, and never wanted to know when I was going to be in the Big Apple.

"Surprise me," she said, "because if it gets routine, it'll become a drag, and then, I'm warning you, we're through."

So I would catch her unawares at her lab, or show up late at night in the Five Spot or one of the other clubs she liked to frequent, sneaking up on her from behind, grabbing her tits, squeezing her tight, and mouthing something lascivious in her ear. Our encounters usually ended up in her tousled bed on the top floor of a tenement building. She was stubborn in her refusal to come back with me to my posh hotel room, because she claimed that the swanky atmosphere would ruin her mood.

"In a bogus setting like that, what's authentic and true becomes vulgar and sleazy." So went one of her pet peeves. "I love being a shameless tramp, but I don't want to be looked down on by people who put on airs thinking they're better than everyone else just because they're rich. How you, Motke, with your magnificently depraved ways, can stand such a phony world is beyond me."

The truth was that I did come from that world, the one she loathed from the very bottom of her heart. Being with her allowed me to escape, however briefly, a life where status and outward appearances were the only things that counted, and to dip my toe in the liberated waters of her bohemian world—short detours into a life governed by a wholly different set of rules. A life where I was an outsider, where nothing was expected of me except to provide my Drabble with the sexual satisfaction she craved, and where I could indulge myself to my heart's content. I would not admit it to anyone, but I couldn't wait for the moment when I could throw myself on Diane Drabble, my wild gypsy temptress, again.

47...

Rivka and Diane were the real women in my life. All the others were just extras, walk-ons who did give my life some color and pizzazz, but were otherwise interchangeable and expendable. Mizie? Ah well, you could call her my caretaker in old age, and in that sense she does mean more to me, I suppose, than some chick who just happened to cross my path.

The women I truly loved were Diane and Rivka—well, the younger version, anyway, the feisty, happy-go-lucky girl who was such a good sport about following me out to the provincial boondocks. But that Rivka was gone for good; the disastrous events of 1938 and the long war years that followed had turned her into—I can't put it any other way—a bitter old sourpuss.

Rivka blamed the Dutch for delivering her family and friends to the henchmen, and she was only too happy never to have to return to our hick town. I left her and the kids well taken care of; she lacked for nothing financially. The only contact I had with my ex in those postwar years was over the phone, when there were important money matters to be decided. At first I did make an effort to see my girls whenever I was in London, but their mother was always coming up with reasons why it was inconvenient. My invitations to have my daughters come and spend their vacations with me were likewise rejected again and again, until one day Rivka told me point-blank that I should stop bothering them. It seemed my daughters wanted nothing to do with me, and from then on Rivka wouldn't stand for them to be left alone with me.

"But why not?" I'd asked her, astonished. "Why can't my daughters be with me?" There was such a long silence that for an instant I thought the connection had been broken. Then it dawned on me what her silence meant to suggest.

"Rosie was younger than Rachel is now..." she snapped. "I don't think we need to go into it any further." She hung up.

Rivka had poisoned our daughters against me. I didn't know what to do about it and just hoped that one day they would grow curious about their dad. As the years went by, I was sometimes asked to attend events where a parent's presence is indispensable, such as graduations and, later, weddings. Then I would play the role of father to the girls whom I was forbidden to see otherwise; none of them ever made any attempt to get to know me better.

Only Ezra, my youngest, was left to me, and the bond I was able to build with him made up for a lot. When he was eight years old, his uncaring mother sent him to an exclusive boarding school, as is the custom in England, freeing up her time so that she was able to obtain a degree; eventually she worked her way up to become the head of an international antipoverty organization. The life she thus made for herself went counter to anything that could possibly smack of her marriage to the worst capitalist on earth. Except for the generous alimony, naturally, which she continued to accept for the rest of her life with neither a squeak of protest nor a token of gratitude.

Ezra spent most of his vacations with me. I took him along on business trips all over Europe, and he drank it all in with an avidity I loved to see—the fast life of airplanes and limousines, of having the red carpet rolled out for us everywhere we went. He loved staying in fancy hotels, where the staff indulged his every whim. His toddler tantrums had been redirected into buoyant energy and an almost irrepressible curiosity. He'd cruise the corridors of Farmacom, peppering everyone he met with questions, and loved to visit the lab animals in their pens. There he'd pet the monkeys, dogs, and rabbits, explaining to each animal in detail what had been done to it to make it cringe, shaking and whimpering, in a corner of its cage, and then he'd insist on giving the researchers his observations, whether they wanted to hear them or not. Sometimes they'd let him peer through the microscopes or assist the technicians with simple experiments. He was adept at attracting attention and charmed people with his curiosity and his bluster, his quick mind and intelligent questions; he was a real joker too, which made him a hit everywhere he went.

At night, his energy all used up, he would allow old Marieke to mollycoddle him. Before being sent up to bed, he liked to climb onto her lap as if she were his granny and snuggle his head against her chest, his restless hands playing with her lace collar as she read to him from books that were still kept in the dismantled children's bedrooms, silent remnants of a forgotten life.

I think I must have spoiled him rotten. I loved seeing his rapturous delight, the raucous cries of joy, the dancing around the room and exuberant hugs smothering me half to death that greeted every gift—every Erector Set he received, every bike, every watch, every ski vacation, and, later on, the cars and houses. The enthusiasm of that boy filled me with warmth; it was worth every penny.

Ezra hardly ever mentioned his mother, whom he seldom saw, and when he did refer to her, it was with some bitterness. He never asked me about our failed marriage or about the time when we'd still lived together as a family, which he barely remembered.

48...

One fine day—it was sometime in 1958—I flew to New York for a working visit to our U.S. subsidiary to discuss with the executive team several new developments, including the discovery of a new category of pharmaceuticals to alleviate psychological complaints. Levine had been the one to come up with the name "soul hormones" for our discoveries after observing time and again that these substances affected not only the patient's physical condition, but the psychological as well. Our firm's newest offshoot, therefore, would focus on the human soul; specifically, on a remedy that had originated in the Himalayan mountains, where for centuries the inhabitants had been using the roots of a certain shrub as an antidote for snakebites. It was found that this "snakeroot" not only lowered high blood pressure, but also had a salutary effect on patients with mental disorders. At roughly the same time, a new synthetic compound was developed that was capable of calming down frenzied mental patients, while at another lab, certain antihistamines were found to be effective against depression. Taken together, these developments demanded a quick response in what came to be called the psychopharmaceutical field. It was to pay off for us in a big way.

I had checked into the Waldorf Astoria, that crown jewel of the Art Deco era and one of my favorite places to stay, not just on account of the luxurious accommodations, but also because of the draw of its famous Peacock Alley. I liked to think that this lovely space, this ebony-paneled, marble-pillared gem of refined elegance, was named after me (*pauw* means "peacock" in Dutch)—a piece of forgivable indulgence on my part. But what I really liked about that lobby was that, positioned at regular intervals among the palm trees lining the many seating nooks, there were ornamental display cases exhibiting the most up-to-date gadgets and inventions—the best new products on the domestic American market. There one could admire the cream of the crop, America's splendid merchandise, exemplifying a nation that was fast becoming the world's greatest commercial success story. To my mind, these exhibits perfectly embodied the successful merger of art and commerce.

One of these coveted items, only recently launched but already on the verge of conquering the world, was a can of hairspray. This aerosol product finally promised to give the ladies some guarantee that their beehive hairdos would stay firmly in place. Before this clever invention, women had had to make do with natural materials like gum resin or clay to tame their unruly hair into some kind of style. Here, for the first time, was an effective alternative. The pink cans, with their brightly contrasting caps, were lined up triumphantly inside the stylish cases. The cheerful slogan gushed, *Go Gay Girls are discovered first!* I decided right then and there to buy a few cans to take home with me, as gifts for some of my women friends. I dreamed of seeing our own pharmaceutical wares promoted in this illustrious hall someday, but the fact that we were a Dutch company precluded that possibility for now. In my imagination, however,

I furnished one of the cases with that menstruation-regulating pill our lab was so feverishly working on. Or would the hotel rule such a product too controversial and ban it from the hallowed hall of fame?

It was late afternoon; I had just arrived and was looking forward to surprising Diane. It had been a while since we'd seen each other, for I hadn't been there in almost a year. I was savoring a whiskey in Peacock Alley as I lazily opened the letter the reception desk had handed me when I checked in.

My dear Motke, it said in Diane's recognizable scrawl. My heart leaped, as did my beast. But then I noticed the letter was dated some weeks back.

By the time you read this I'll be dead. I have breast cancer and it's metastasized, so I've decided to take my fate into my own hands. A sorry decline and drawn-out suffering—you know that's not me. I've been storing up a bunch of pills, and tonight I'm going to wash them down with a bottle of whiskey. I've bought the latest Coltrane, Stardust—the title suits my last voyage, don't you think? I'll let the sounds of the master carry me off, and I don't expect it to be all that bad, dying. My only regret is that I can't finish my work on the female hormone; it does appear to be capable of preventing pregnancy. But as you know, I'm not the only one working on it, and it'll definitely be a go, with or without me. I have no doubt you'll turn it into gold. It may even set off a revolution! I hope that it does. I hope it helps all those uptight prigs break out of their shells.

I'm sorry there's no time left for one last night with you. The pain is getting worse. I don't want to be trapped by the doctors who'll want to keep me alive at all costs; I'm getting

*out of here while I still can. So you'll just have to go to the Five
Spot without me. Please go there and have a drink on me.*

*I don't know if I was ever in love with you, but I do want to
thank you for the fun we had together, and for being the one
man who never felt the need to own me.*

Be well, and don't ever let yourself be tied down!

Love, Diane

Slowly I unglued my eyes from the sheet of paper with the
tightly packed script and became aware once more of the women
tottering in their high heels, the swaggering men, the painted
walls and the intricate carpet. It was as if I were suddenly seeing
the splendor around me through a scrim of gray. An infinite feeling of grief washed over me. Diane had been the light of my life,
although I had never had the courage to admit it to her, knowing
I'd be roundly mocked if she ever got wind of it. Her refusal to
be tied down was far more deeply held than my own vaunted
independence. Her aversion to any kind of commitment sometimes made me wonder what deeply ingrained fear might be at
the bottom of it. But we never spoke about it. I certainly never
asked. I'd had no idea that she was ill. Diane had always been
evasive about anything personal, and seemed determined to live
only in the here and now.

Although it was business that drew me to New York, the nights
spent in the company of my wild Drabble had always given my
stays a special luster. Now, for the first time, I felt like a fish out
of water in my prized Peacock Alley. I was overcome with almost
sickening revulsion as I gazed at the well-to-do, the spoiled prin-
cesses and trust-fund babies strutting around this hushed sanc-
tuary of sham glitz and feigned glamour. I was disgusted by the
fine airs of the extravagantly dressed, hustling beau monde,

pretending to be engrossed in one another but painfully aware of being in a place where they came to see and be seen. They all seemed to be trying to present themselves in the most flattering light, scanning the room like animals on the prowl, intent on not letting any famous quarry get away. A white-gloved waiter standing next to my yellow leather chair leaned across the table to pick up the empty whiskey tumbler and, depositing it on the elegant silver tray, asked in a hushed voice if he could bring me anything else. I shook my head and got to my feet; I couldn't wait to get out of there. Peacock Alley suddenly felt like enemy territory to me, an insult to Diane Drabble's memory.

I took a taxi down to the Village, intending to stroll around the neighborhood my Drabble had been so fond of. I couldn't make myself head straight to the Five Spot; the thought of Diane's absence there was unbearable. I drifted aimlessly through the winding streets, dodging the pipe-chewing men in shabby secondhand jackets and girls in boyish haircuts and tight black turtlenecks hanging out on street corners or packed into one of the crowded bars from which escaped the occasional plaintive blare of a trumpet or saxophone. I felt out of place in my suit and tie; the royal merchant had no business being there without his wild bohemian chick at his side, the girl who'd been his ticket for entry into this world.

I ended up in a sleazy dive, bleak and dreary, where a young, badly dressed female bartender was kept busy supplying a lonely drunk at one end of the bar with shots of rum. I hoisted myself up onto a rickety barstool, as far away as possible from the wino, and got the skinny, drab-looking barmaid to pour me a double whiskey. She stared at me, and I could tell from her expression that I was an unusual apparition in a place like this. Behind her was a drinks cabinet filled with a mishmash of bottles with faded labels carelessly arranged on chipped, peeling shelves, backed by a filthy, greasy mirror that wasn't inclined to reflect anything. The girl held her arms crossed in front of her chest, her dark eyes fixed gloomily on the floor. The minutes ticked by as we lolled there, three lost souls, each in our own separate world. Every once in a while the silence was broken by some unintelligible outburst from the drunkard, upon which a snarled *"Shut up, Toby!"* from the girl would send him back into his blurry alcoholic haze, like a dog kicked back into its kennel. Now and again, at a sign from the intoxicated Toby or from me, the girl would refill our glasses, until finally the barfly hauled himself laboriously off his stool and, with much writhing and squirming, pulled a wad of dollars out of his back pocket and slapped it down onto the counter before making his exit, staggering and muttering to himself. In the doorway he turned and yelled at the top of his voice, for the first time quite distinctly, "Beware, beware, the Ides of March!" He shook his fist in the air like some ancient prophet in a B-movie before hobbling out into the night, lunging at the walls for support.

The tootsie gave a shy, apologetic smile as she walked over to the far end of the bar to clear away his glass.

"Regular customer?" I asked.

"Yeah," she said, "he always comes in here. His is the only kind we ever get in this shithole." Glancing at me as she walked to the slop sink to wash the glass, she asked, "What's a fancy gent like you doing in a place like this, are you lost or something?"

I smiled. "You might say that," I said. "What about you, why are you working in such a dump?"

She shrugged. "Oh, to support myself. I'd had it with my mother nagging me all the time. And, yeah, sure, I'd heard cool stories about the Village, but the stories make it sound better than it really is." She grinned a bit sheepishly.

"Isn't that the truth," I said. "Here, let me have one last drink, make it a double, and one for yourself as well."

She poured me a glass and another one for herself. Then she pulled out a stool from under the counter and sat down across from me. "Cheers," she said, "to the stories."

"To the stories." I raised my glass.

"Where are you from?" she asked, the question that always seems to come first from Americans.

"The Netherlands," I said, "a small, insignificant country that's mostly below sea level."

Her eyes lit up briefly before clouding over again. "I know," she said. "Holland, that's where my family's from too."

"What a coincidence," I said. "Do you speak any Dutch?"

She shrugged. "Nah."

"Too bad," I said.

"Why?" she said. "Shitty country, horrible people."

"Thanks for the compliment," I laughed, and raised my glass again. "To the horrible people and the shitty country! Have you ever been there?"

She gave a scornful laugh. "If I had the moolah to travel, I'd go somewhere completely different. You bet!" she added indignantly.

When her face lost its sullen expression, she wasn't bad-looking. She had nice hair, dark and wavy; she was skinny, but her skin was smooth and fresh.

"What's your name?" I asked.

"Hannah," she said.

I had an idea.

"Hannah," I asked, "have you ever been to the Five Spot? Do you like jazz?"

"Yeah, I guess," she said. "But going to a club by myself stinks. I did go into one of those joints once," she went on, "but I hated it. I was just standing there, like, all by myself, looking like a dope, and I sneaked out as soon as I could. I'm kind of, like, a wimp, when it comes right down to it." She said it with a sad grin.

"Hannah, will you do something for me?" I asked. "I need to go to the Five Spot. It was the favorite hangout of a close friend of mine who just died. Her last wish was for me to go there and have a drink on her, but I can't seem to make myself, not on my own. I'm a wimp too as far as that's concerned. Will you go with me?"

She hesitated for a moment, as if trying to figure out whether I might be dangerous. Apparently I wasn't, because after establishing with a glance at the clock on the wall that she could close up the joint, she nodded, and together we strolled over to the Five Spot. I ordered some drinks at the bar, and we drank a toast to Diane Drabble, my delightful drinking-buddy diva. The crowd around the bar jostled us against each other, and I put an arm around her. Gently swaying to the mellow sounds of the jazz quartet, I drew her in closer until I had her in a tight clinch. I could feel her heart pounding. The heaviness that had taken possession of me ever since reading Diane's letter was gradually pushed out by a building excitement. My beast, which had been limp and lifeless, was starting to wake up. I felt it rising, and cautiously pressed myself against the girl's flat stomach while making a few tentative dance moves with her on the slice of floor left to us by the young people ordering drinks around us. I caressed her soft brown hair, and then gently kissed her ear, and she reacted by resting her head on my shoulder. I brushed her cheek with my lips, and finally sought her mouth.

We stood there for a while gently swaying to the music, my hand exploring her body, her small but firm breasts, her bony back, her muscular arms and firm buttocks, and finally her mound of Venus, which I pressed firmly against me to tweak my beast.

When I judged it was time, I steered her out of the crush at the bar and suggested going somewhere where we could be alone. She nodded shyly. With my arm around her narrow waist, I led my barmaid out of the joint, thinking that this was the best possible way to remember Drabble: to end my commemorative visit to the Five Spot with a nice little roll in the hay, which, although bound to be a poor substitute for my wild nights with Diane, would nevertheless serve as a fitting memento of our so dearly cherished freedom.

Once outside, I quickly formulated a plan. I kissed her and suggested that we spend the night together, a proposal that received a similarly resigned, rather lukewarm assent. Taking the girl to my luxury suite wasn't an option—there are some worlds that just don't mix—and so I dragged her into the first fleabag hotel we happened to pass, paying for a room in cash. On shutting the door, I gave my conquest no time to change her mind. She stood there giggling nervously. I pushed her down on the creaky bed, pulled the scruffy dress up over her head, and, still kissing her, in short order yanked off her bra and panties, wriggled out of my own clothes like a veritable Houdini, and forged a way into her pussy with my fingers. But after the obligatory round of finger play, as I started pushing my beast inside her, she stopped me.

"You can't get me pregnant," she said uncertainly.

"That's not going to happen," I reassured her. "I'll pull out before I come, I promise, all right?"

Before she could answer, I covered her mouth with mine and thrust my tongue and my beast simultaneously inside her. I made sure she came before I did, pulling out perhaps a fraction too late, but most of the semen ended up on her thigh, so that was all right. I kissed her and, rolling off her, asked, "Did you like that?"

She shrugged. "It's nice not to, like, be alone, I guess," she said. We stared at each other, and there was an awkward silence. Shyly she closed her eyes, lying on her back and not moving. I looked around the shabby room. The faded flowered wallpaper was torn, the wardrobe in the corner listed to one side, and the stained linens on the sagging mattress hinted that the management wasn't too finicky about changing the sheets. I gazed at the pale little face with its rather crestfallen expression, and guessed her to be about twenty. Suddenly I felt a wave of revulsion. Why was I still compelled to do my beast's bidding, now that my hair was going gray at the temples? It was that cursed libido of mine that had led me to wind up in this dreary room, shooting my wad into this dirt-poor wench only to feel desperate to get the hell out of there as soon as it was over. To forget the whole sordid episode ever happened.

I got up and started collecting my scattered clothes.

She opened her eyes and sat up. "What's the matter, are you leaving?"

"Yeah," I replied, leaning across her to retrieve my pants, which had slipped down behind the bed. It wasn't until I was dressed and had my hand on the doorknob that I looked at her and said, "All right then, Hannah, best of luck." Her eyelids quivered, the corners of her lips started trembling; shit, she was about to cry. I walked back to the bed; she pulled the sheet up to her chin, like a little kid who believes that hiding under a sheet makes you invisible. I patted her on the head a bit and said, "So, now that you've been to the Five Spot, you can go there by yourself, as my girlfriend used to do. No more being a wimp, all right? Okay then, goodbye." Avoiding her gaze, I hurried out of the room, pulling the door shut behind me.

I left the hotel like a thief in the night, slinking past the sleepy doorman, who asked with a smirk if everything had been to my liking.

I wandered aimlessly through the deserted streets. I walked over to the river, past the piers of the Meatpacking District, where the stench of rotting meat made me think of our factory long ago. A kind of homecoming, just as I seemed to have lost my way. Overhead were the train tracks of the High Line; the warehouses loomed in the darkness, silent and gloomy. I sat down on one of the piers, stared into the dark water of the Hudson River, and asked myself if there would ever come a time when I'd be master over my beast. Why did I need to expose my health and my good name to dangerous or joyless escapades such as the one I had just endured? I so badly wanted to be free of them, those tyrannical urges of mine! I thought of Aaron, and how disgusted he had been with me, and I felt his disgust bubbling up inside me. If only Diane were still alive! For just an instant I had to fight the ridiculous, romantic urge to jump into the black water of the Hudson and let myself sink to the bottom. To renounce a life in which I had to contend not only with the jealousies of all the people who resented my success and the malice of my competitors, but also with the grief of losing Diane, the only one who'd ever helped me cope with this everlasting struggle with my baser instincts.

But when morning broke and the workmen in their bloody aprons began showing up outside the warehouses as the loaded cattle cars came rattling in overhead, I left the dock and returned to the gracious splendor of the Waldorf Astoria. There I showered and shaved, then put on a clean suit before proceeding to make a grand entrance at our branch office, where I was received with all due deference. Work is work, after all—and a great way to drown out unpleasant thoughts.

49...

As Ezra grew into a handsome teenager keenly interested in girls, he also grew more interested in the economic aspects of the business. Occasionally I'd let him sit in on a meeting, and then afterward go over it with him in detail—enjoyable father-son sessions in which, prompted by his insatiable curiosity, he peppered me with questions about what had just gone on. I could see that he already possessed a finely honed business instinct.

As time went on I became more and more convinced that my son had the talent and gumption the firm needed for its growth. He was destined for a glorious career in the future global behemoth Farmacom. Knowing that my life's work would someday be in my son's hands was an enormous incentive for me, enhancing the pleasure of seeing our company thrive.

He read economics at Oxford, and before joining the firm he went on to Nyenrode Business School in the Netherlands, where he was groomed for the life of an international businessman. He was an excellent student, and I made it clear to our managers that when he graduated, I expected him to be offered a position in the executive suite. I wanted to groom him for the global side of the business; that way I'd have someone I could depend on across the pond. I needed a trusted partner over there to represent the interests of the parent firm, since the Americans had been starting to throw their weight around, trying to gain more influence in the company.

"The most important thing I learned in business school," he often told me, "is that in all that you do, you have to work with others, so you must always try to find common ground." It was from this starting point that he became determined to tear down the wall that still separated the commercial and ivory-tower sides of our business and to end the tug of war between those conflicting interests. Mindful of the stories I had told him about the clashes I'd had with Levine, he felt it as a thorn in his side that in all these years nothing had changed; once he was in charge, therefore, he instituted a "strategy unit" to implement his ideas and outlook, so that everyone at Farmacom would henceforth start off on the same page.

It was in 1965 that Rivka and I finally met again, at Ezra's graduation from business school at Nyenrode Castle. After the speeches and diploma ceremony, we walked into the garden together. There she told me sourly, chain-smoking one Caballero cigarette after another, that she had finally succeeded in tracking down Rosie after years of searching for her name on the lists of the dead provided by the Red Cross.

As it turned out, both mother and daughter had survived the war and had emigrated to the States shortly afterward. Rivka had visited them in Brooklyn, where the two women lived together in a miserable tenement. Rosie and Rivka had greeted each other like long-lost sisters. Rosie gave her a quick rundown of what had happened to her: after being flushed out of hiding, she was sent to three different concentration camps. She'd been liberated in the nick of time, more dead than alive.

Once back in the Netherlands, she had gone to pick up Chana, who'd been hidden on a farm, but the little girl hadn't recognized her mother, and her foster parents had refused to give her up. Rosie had finally managed to pry the recalcitrant child away from them. Their life in America was hard and lonely; mother and daughter didn't seem to get on very well. Chana moved out and lived by herself for a while, but had been forced to return home upon being saddled with a kid after a one-night stand with some random guy. Just as Rosie had always refused to reveal to her daughter or anyone else the identity of the girl's father, so Chana too was determined to keep quiet about the prick who had done this to her, but Rosie's big, splayed hands had managed to beat some information out of her anyway. She had gathered that, God forbid, it had been a guy on a business trip to the Land of the Brave who'd gotten her daughter pregnant—a story not all that different from her own experience on the Cozy Corner sofa.

Rivka's voice grew more and more indignant. It reminded me of when she used to fling the refugees' stories in my face, insinuating that the persecution and indignities they'd suffered were all my fault. "It's as if the whole world is getting poisoned by perverts like you," she exclaimed, angrily puffing on her Caballero. "They ought to lock you up, the lot of you."

"Rivka," I said carefully, "isn't it going a bit far, to blame me for something that happened to Rosie's daughter? Aren't you getting just a tad carried away?"

"Do you have the gall to tell me you've changed?" Her anger with me seemed to have been rekindled by seeing Rosie again.

I thought about my little affairs and was silent.

"Why don't you people invent something that will squelch that cursed libido of yours? So that our daughters will be safe?

You're so goddamn brilliant at marketing a pill that prevents pregnancy; you know how to pump men full of testosterone; why, then, can't you come up with some way to rid yourselves of that vile male lust? *That* would be doing womankind a service!"

She turned, tossed back her shoulder-length hair, and walked up to a group of guests a bit farther on. I saw her angry expression change into an effusive smile as she joined the conversation; she proceeded to ignore me for the rest of the event.

It was the last time I ever saw Rivka. One year later, I heard from Ezra that his mother was suffering from the emperor of all maladies, as Diane had, and that after several months of chemotherapy, it had been pronounced terminal. He also told me that Rosie had flown in from New York to nurse her.

I wrote Rivka a letter asking for permission to visit her one last time. It would have meant a lot to me, to be allowed to make peace with the woman who for almost twenty years had played such an important role in my life. I received a short scribble in reply:

You will never deserve peace until you learn to control that monstrous schlong of yours. I suggest castration. Rivka.

I wrote back tersely:

You seem to be more attached to your anger than to living. Forgiveness, Rivka, is an important part of love, and I recall that you once said love was the "greatest power" of mankind. I'm sorry that in this life you seem to have lost the capacity to forgive.
Your Motke.

She sent me one last note:

Forgiveness is something one earns, by being prepared to learn one's lesson. You are incorrigible. Leave me be. I won't embitter my last days thinking of you, the worst mistake of my life. R.

She died with Rosie and our girls at her bedside; they let me know that I would not be welcome at the funeral. Rivka was buried in the village of Wargrave, the English hamlet with the very apt name where years earlier, in the war, our marriage had been laid to rest.

50...

Ezra was the ultimate sybarite. He loved to consume great quantities of food and drink, he was exceptionally curious and interested in every subject he encountered, and he was, like his father, incapable of resisting the profusion of feminine beauty the world had to offer. It was very hard for him to resist the urge to grab, caress, or touch anything female, soft, or alluring when the situation called for restraint. The times were on his side, of course, since thanks to the Pill, the miracle drug we had given the world, puritanism had given way to the sexual revolution, and so it had become much easier and less risky to let off a bit of steam. Even so, Ezra still had a tendency to go too far, blatantly feeling up an employee, a reporter, or some other tootsie who might not appreciate it; these gals, unlike the ones back in my time, refuse to keep their traps shut about it. Until now his charm had always helped get him out of the tightest spots. People adored him and tended to turn a blind eye when his behavior crossed the line, behavior that would have meant ruin for anyone less well-liked.

As he climbed the corporate ladder, taking on an increasingly important role first in the Netherlands and later in the U.S. branch, his intemperance and devil-may-care attitude began to grow more worrisome. Not only was I kept apprised of his exploits through company gossip and the tabloids when he was seen squiring some actress, TV personality, or football player's wife about town, but I also heard about it from the man himself, since Ezra liked to regale me with reports of his latest conquests.

Watching from the sidelines, I began to be afraid, more afraid than I had ever been before in my life, even when I was the one playing with fire. My fear started stalking me like some cowardly assassin. A blanket of foreboding threatened to suffocate me; I just couldn't seem to shake it off. And as old age began sneaking up on me, it ruined any remaining moments of triumph and joy. It was as if the cesspool of my forgotten misdeeds had gradually become clogged up, and Ezra's philandering was the last straw that caused it to back up and overflow. Everything I had been so good at sweeping under the rug was coming up to the surface in the form of a crushing dread that one fine day, all my transgressions and failings would be made public. I was consumed with the thought that someone was going to out me and reveal how the royal merchant, recipient of an honorary doctorate from a highly respected university, proud bearer of the title of commander in the Order of Orange-Nassau, had wronged his female employees, his brother, and his mentor. A fear like some invasive weed overtook me that I or, even worse, my son would be found out, our life's work snatched out of our hands by heartless assholes and greedy pigs with no idea what it means to sacrifice yourself and your loved ones for a higher purpose.

Now that I have one foot in the grave, that fear has turned into harsh, bitter reality. Ah, the agony, that I am alive to see this! The papers here are running triumphant headlines like *"PRIDE OF THE PEACOCKS MUST HAVE A FALL!"* Our country's yellow press is drooling over my son's disgrace just as they did twenty-five years ago when my brother, my poor brother, got it in the neck. There on the front page is my Ezra, my son, lured into a trap by the vultures wanting to destroy him. That too is a replay of Aaron's plight: Ezra isn't just being punished for his own offense, his own peccadillo. What else can it mean but that Death has decided not to take me before making sure that I get it; that with this arrest, Ezra, my Achilles' heel, is also being punished for his father's sins?

Meanwhile, the television keeps on spewing its venomous pictures. It's showing the young woman, the martyred victim, behind a forest of microphones, being bombarded with questions.

I can't seem to make heads or tails of it; it's all mumbo jumbo, and the subtitles are too small for me to read. The press mob is peppering her with rapid-fire questions, like circus knife-throwers hurling daggers at a target. The little tart is dolled up for the occasion in a demure little dress, but a high neckline and below-the-knee skirt can't disguise what a slut she really is. I'm still perfectly capable of gauging what's underneath, or in this case what's behind that forest of microphones. I just *know* the lying bitch was hired by those American bastards, the ones who are set on having the public offering go through and therefore can't wait to kick Ezra out on his ass.

Just look at her flaunting her primly clothed chassis, as if that nylon *schmatta* she's wearing conceals a bastion of puritan prudery, instead of a sexy bod with pointy, provocative tits no man can avoid staring at, with curves just begging to be stroked, pinched, or sucked, and a pussy hiding under that skirt demanding to be plugged. Those dark eyes with their come-hither look belie the sob story she's reciting; no doubt she was thoroughly coached by those shyster lawyers. The inviting eyes, the nervous pout, the chewed lip, the tip of the tongue emerging every once in a while to lick the modestly painted mouth, the awkward and rather jerky gestures of the fingers, as if to underscore and confirm what she is saying—the way she's standing there, she looks just like the tootsie I once picked up in that Greenwich Village bar twenty-odd years ago. Only this time she's playing the role of a lifetime; it's her one shot at preening in the spotlight, pretending to be an innocent, abused, downtrodden, and dishonored Madonna.

Actually, she's also very like—yes, come to think of it, she is remarkably like Rosie was, with her wavy black hair, the sinewy body, the jiggly fingers I so often saw performing their singular hand dance back in my office. Wait—how long ago was that?

Could it be that my son, my blood, my youngest, has fallen into a trap that was set in order to punish his father?

A trap set, for instance, by the three Furies, those harpies Rivka, Rosie, and fat Bertha, who continue to torment me as I lie on this jailhouse cot with their heart-wrenching screams, their eyes dripping blood, and their cries for revenge? Or else there's Aaron—the image I have of him looking at me with such hatred and despair, the ghostly picture that's forever scored into my brain; a stabbing, aching wound constantly reminding me how terribly much I miss my twin. And finally, Levine and his Dauphine, the old tart whispering *Judas Iscariot!* while the professor stares at me in outrage.

No, no, no! There's no such thing as coincidence! This viper isn't just some random sexpot coming out of nowhere to be accidentally violated by my son; no, my Ezra was tricked into it, and just as he was about to stop our firm's being stolen from us too! But it wasn't only those greedy grab artists who set the snare; surely this is also a booby trap carefully planned and executed by three generations of bitter women. This is an act of vengeance, payback for the wham-bang-thank-you-ma'am that may have resulted in two little girl-bastards, and it's come after decades of silence, a calm that had lulled me into a false sense of security. I thought that by now all the old wounds were healed, including those of my alleged victims.

I want to shout at my boy, "They're out to wring your neck! It's not just those American vultures who've set this phony-innocent slut on you; her mother and grandmother must have something to do with it too. The sanctimonious bitches have used her as the sacrificial lamb to lure you to the stake; it's their way of venting the bitter grudge they've been harboring for years. They're exacting their vengeance by wounding me in my weakest spot. They've found the way to stab me in the heart—by crushing, squeezing, destroying my son, my Achilles' heel. And in doing so they're sending our company down the tubes to boot."

I must tell the young thing, so that she can warn my son. He must be allowed to establish his innocence by exposing the malicious intent of that little cunt. I've got to tell her, if it's the last thing I do in this goddamn world.

My roar makes the young thing nearly fall off her sentry chair next to my jailhouse bed. She leans over me making shushing sounds, talks to me in soothing tones, and turns off the television.

Oh sweet tarnation, grant me just one last coherent sentence so that I can save my son from his imminent doom. But the attempt to twist my old geezer's tongue into the right groove makes me gag. A coughing fit leaves me breathless, squeaking, rattling, gasping for air. "Not yet, not yet," I scream, I have to get that sentence out, but the massive coughing fit is choking me. The young thing hovers over me, helpless. She pulls me up to a sitting position in an attempt to let me recover my breath.

I can't get any air; I grab at my throat and hear a weird squeaking sound coming out of my mouth. The young thing starts whacking me on the back as if to wallop the life back into me. I hear a rattling sound, and then my body slumps in her arms. She lowers me carefully back onto the mattress.

Then she walks out of the room to wake up Mizie.

afterword

I grew up in a family buzzing with unspoken stories. My Jewish father survived the concentration camp Bergen Belsen; many members of his family never "returned." The fate of the murdered relatives was a touchy subject, one we knew was best to avoid, as was my father's concentration camp experience, which was never mentioned. Yet my father sprinkled almost every conversation with words, phrases, and expressions alluding to the horrors he had suffered. From a very young age we learned that words such as "family," "brother," "father," "cousin," "grandfather," "pain," "anger," "hunger," "turnip," "sickness," "weakness," and "war" were a minefield to be avoided at all costs, although they were also very much a frame of reference. Everything we felt, experienced, or thought paled in comparison with the horrors of the camps and the ordeals to which my father and his family had been subjected. Growing up in that kind of atmosphere leaves its mark on you.

It took me more than fifty years to find the courage to research my family's history and to probe what kind of influence that history and my father's concentration camp stay had on me. That inquiry resulted in my first book, the nonfiction *Obliged to Be Happy: A Portrait of a Family* (Amsterdam: Cossee,

2011). My research took me to the NIOD (Netherlands Institute for War, Holocaust and Genocide Studies). There I came across the file of Professor Laqueur, a famous pharmacologist and clinician, one of the founders of the pharmaceutical company Organon and the man who discovered testosterone. More important, he also happened to be my father's first father-in-law. In 1941 my father had married Renate Laqueur, the professor's flamboyant daughter, who was responsible for saving my father's life in the camps, scavenging for food and taking care of him when he grew too weak to walk or even lift an arm. Renate and my father divorced in 1950—"Marriage isn't made to withstand hell," was how Renate explained their breakup.

My father always talked about his former father-in-law with deep respect; he admired Laqueur's erudition, his refinement, and his intelligence. So I was intrigued to come across the following article in a German journal:

> In March a report appeared in the local paper regarding Organon in the town of Oss concerning the director, Mr. van Zwanenberg in particular, who has apparently been abusing the girls working in his factory for years. That fact has been known in Oss for quite a while, but nobody has heretofore dared to lodge a complaint, since almost everyone who lives in Oss either works for the firm or depends on it for his income.

The article goes on for four pages, citing reports in the Nazi press and implicating other directors of the firm, alleging, at the very least, that they were aware of the abuse, or were guilty of it themselves. Professor Laqueur was also named. Although the tone of the article was clearly anti-Semitic, it nonetheless roused my interest and made me wonder to what extent these accusations had a basis in truth.

Organon was founded at an exciting time. The great hormone search was in full swing; there was a race on to be the first to produce and market the new miracle drugs. The owners of the Van Zwanenberg slaughterhouse and meat factories were the first industrialists in the Netherlands to seek a close collaboration with the scientific community. They approached the famous pharmacologist Professor Laqueur, and the outcome was a company that was to grow into one of the country's first multinationals.

Organon was a vigorous participant in the rush to be the first to extract hormones. This was the time of the so-called hormone bubble; in labs all over the world scientists worked hard to isolate hormones and discover which bodily functions they influenced. Experimentation with medical compounds was not yet bound by government regulation, and the ethics of animal and human testing were left to the scientist and his own conscience. The tension between the interests of science and commerce was a crucial part of the equation.

I was curious to find out more about the men who'd committed themselves so fanatically to this cause. They were without a doubt ambitious and passionate, wanting to take humankind to the next level through their inventions and willing to sacrifice anything to be the best, to smash boundaries, to not be forgotten. How did their interests coincide and where did they collide?

I was granted permission to delve into the company archives of Organon, now part of the American company MSD but still headquartered in the town of Oss. After weeks of researching, reading, and speaking with the locals and the company's archivist, I had the germ of my novel.

To begin with, there was the matter of the brothers who were the directors of the slaughterhouse and meat factories. One of them, Saal van Zwanenberg, struck me as very ambitious. He was the one who looked for a scientist with whom he could start a hormone factory. He put his heart and soul into building that company, which became the first to produce hormone preparations on an industrial scale. At the time of the German occupation in 1940, he miraculously managed to flee the country, and to this day he is considered to be Organon's founding father, the simple boy with only three years of secondary schooling who became a captain of industry and a knight of the Order of Orange-Nassau, and was awarded an honorary doctorate.

The other brother appeared to be his opposite. It was he who was sentenced to two years in prison for the sexual abuse of several underage employees. I encountered the shocking court report, where his practices were recounted in detail, in the Brabant Historic Information Centre (BHIC). A year and a half after his release in 1940, he was killed in Auschwitz. The contrast between the two brothers, the exemplary one and the bad one, the successful one and the loser, couldn't possibly be any greater. Their story was so black and white that I began to question it. History is often reduced to simple truths, and in my opinion, this was a far too simple depiction of the truth, inspiring me to conjure up another version and give it a new dimension. This invented story, less black and white, is one in which good and evil are not so easy to distinguish from each other.

The once so inspiring collaboration between the businessman Van Zwanenberg and the scientist Laqueur had apparently degenerated over the years into a bitter fight. By the end, the two men wouldn't give each other the time of the day. Too many cooks spoil the broth, and after the war Van Zwanenberg cut Laqueur out of the company. That raises the question: How does a man justify to himself betraying the person to whom he owes his success when it becomes convenient? Another question is: Why are successful men often so incredibly careless when it comes to sex? Why are they prepared to risk their entire careers for a brief sexual encounter? Powerful men often grant themselves extraordinary privileges and do not consider nonconsensual sex as abuse or rape. They delude themselves into thinking that an ordinary girl should consider it an honor when a powerful man wants to sleep with her, whether willing or not.

In brief, the relatively factual history of the triumphant rise of a Dutch company that became a worldwide success combined with the imagined personal histories of the men who made that possible are the ingredients of *The Hormone Factory*, a fictional tale inspired by the history of the founding of Organon. The novel explores the mind-set of the men who contributed to progress and science, how they trod the thin line between humility and power, between scientific research and personal satisfaction, between the possibilities of progress and the limitations of the human mind. The form I selected is that of the protagonist lying on his deathbed looking back on his life, because that is the time of reckoning, the time to ask yourself the question: Have I been a decent human being, a mensch?

—Saskia Goldschmidt

1887 Van Zwanenberg Slaughterhouse and Factories is founded in Oss (provincial town in the south of Holland) by the twin brothers Van Zwanenberg.

1923 Saal van Zwanenberg establishes Organon to develop new medicine from meat waste.

1925 Chemists Ernst Laqueur and Jacques van Oss join Zwanenberg at Organon.

1930 Organon has a series of successful discoveries. They have international success applying hormones in medicine, leading to the birth of the contraceptive pill.

1938 One of the brothers is sentenced to prison for sexual abuse of one of the employees and will not survive deportation to Auschwitz.

1945 The other brother returns from England after World War II to continue his successes as businessman and benefactor.

2012 Saskia Goldschmidt was inspired by the story of the twin brothers to write the novel *The Hormone Factory*.

Saskia Goldschmidt was born in 1954 in the Netherlands and has been a drama teacher and children's theater director for twenty-five years. *The Hormone Factory* is her first novel. She lives in Amsterdam.

Hester Velmans is a novelist, editor, and translator of French and Dutch literary fiction. Her translation of Lulu Wang's *The Lily Theater* was a New York Times Notable Book of the Year, and she was awarded the Vondel Prize for Translation for her rendition of Renate Dorrestein's *A Heart of Stone*. She lives in Massachusetts.